The House on Valley Street

Siara Schwartzlow
Aug. 2018

SIARA SCHWARTZLOW

Copyright © 2017 Siara Schwartzlow
All rights reserved.
ISBN-10: 1543122558
ISBN-13: 978-1543122558

Special thanks to Mom for sharing her spooky stories. And thanks to T.W.R. Shelton, lifelong friend and consistent source of inspiration.

The House on Valley Street

The House on Valley Street

PROLOGUE

In 1978, at just eleven years old, Mom already knew.

She knew that there was evil in the world.

She knew that there was danger.

She knew that there was something in her house.

She knew that no one would believe her.

She peeled a heavy lavender afghan from her body and tiptoed from her bedroom to the kitchen for a glass of water as low snores seemed to echo from her mother's bedroom. The door was open just a sliver, and a small television hummed and cast a gray light on her mother's petite body, huddled on the edge of a king-sized bed and bundled like swaddled infant. Mom wondered why her mother – my grandmother – hadn't replaced her king-sized bed after my grandfather left, but she never had the courage to ask. No one mentioned him anymore.

The House on Valley Street

She padded lightly down the stairs, leaning close to the wall as though it provided some sort of safety net. When she reached the kitchen, she waited for the water to run cold and peered over her shoulder in constant surveillance of the shadows and black shapes that filled the space (the hat rack at the front door and the thick winter coat hanging from it; the wadded blanket covering a lace throw pillow on the sofa; the curtains that swayed ever so slightly when the furnace kicked on).

Drinking the water in the kitchen meant spending too much time in the dark.

Drinking the water in the kitchen meant standing still for too long.

Drinking the water in the kitchen meant it might come.

She moved quickly, the water sloshing back and forth in the glass as she padded up the stairs. Halfway up, she felt the sudden urge to run, to fumble up the stairs and away from an invisible force that surely meant to grab hold of one ankle and rip her down the stairs and into the darkness.

Each of her steps suddenly echoed as she ran, leaping wildly up the stairs.

THUD

Thud

THUD

Thud

THUD-THUD-THUD

The House on Valley Street

Thud-thud-thud

She stopped.

The echoes stopped.

And then they came again, fast and hard. *Thud-thud-thud-thud-thud-thud.* The steps careened toward her, racing like a freight train.

In one swift movement, she turned toward her bedroom and ran, her feet like weights that now only drug across the wooden floor. The thudding followed her, angry and panicked. Her heart pounded in her throat. Water trailed down the front of her nightgown.

She rounded the corner and leapt onto her bed, dropping her water glass to the floor, where it shattered and sent shards of glass sliding across the room.

The footsteps slowed, more deliberate and conscious now.

Thud…thud…thud.

She pulled her afghan to her chin and waited for some creature, some monster, some being to reach her bed, to drag her beneath it, to pull her into eternal blackness. She covered her face.

The thuds grew closer. They grew quieter. The hairs on her arms stood on end. Despite the blackness beneath the blanket, her eyes widened, nearly bursting from her skull when the end of her bed suddenly sank beneath an invisible weight that sat just inches from her feet.

"Karen?" Her mother called from down the hallway. "Karen? What was that noise?"

She couldn't answer. She couldn't bring herself to make a sound.

"Karen?" Her mother's bedroom door opened with a low squeak. Her slippers sounded scratchy against the floor.

The invisible weight lifted from the bed as quickly as it had come. Low, soft thuds seemed to move away from the bed. Suddenly, and with an unspeakable ferocity, the bedroom door swung shut, rattling its hinges.

"What in God's name?" Her mother jogged the rest of the way down the hall and nearly fell into the bedroom. "What is all this noise? It's 3 in the morning, Karen. What are you doing?" She flicked on the overhead light.

"I...I dropped my water glass," eleven-year-old Mom said, eyeing the puddles and imagining just for a moment that she would find giant, claw-bearing prints in them, but there was nothing.

"That doesn't explain why you slammed your door, young lady."

"It was the wind, I think," she mumbled. "I...I just closed my window. Sorry, Mom."

With a patient sigh, my grandmother said, "Go to sleep, Karen. We'll clean this up in the morning." And with that, Mom was alone again.

CHAPTER 1

I sat at my big-box store desk, my I-should-have-paid-the-extra-ten-dollars-for-the-better-one desk that wobbled when I pulled my hand-me-down rolling chair forward. The bottom drawer of the desk was missing its handle, and if I ran my palm along the underside of the middle drawer, I always came up with a splinter.

In the converted office of my two-bedroom apartment, I shivered against cold, plastic armrests, and my spine drug against the back of my chair when I slouched and sighed. On the other side of the window in front of me, the neighbor from upstairs dropped an apparently weighty black garbage bag into the trash can and slammed the lid shut while his pigtailed seven-year-old daughter, who had thrown quite the tantrum just that morning, stomping about on the floor above my bedroom, rode her bicycle in wild circles on the grass.

The tick-tock-tick of my keyboard filled the room, but the sound was at least partially absorbed by the stacks of loose papers, application packets, various pamphlets, and half-used notebooks that littered my workspace.

The screen in front of me read:

Why do you feel that you are qualified to work for and become a part of our growing company?

My cursor blinked.

With another deep, slow sigh, I tried to push my rolling chair away from the desk, but the desk wobbled too much, and my chair went nowhere. I kicked myself backward with a grunt, and the chair finally moved, but not before threatening to tip.

Dragging my bare feet, I meandered along the carpeted hallway and into the living room, where I opened the blinds to shed the stormy July afternoon's grayed light onto the secondhand, green couch and loveseat that crowded the small room.

I leaned against the glass and pressed my forehead to the window. It hadn't started to rain yet, but the weather man said to expect light drizzle late in the afternoon, transitioning to heavy storms that evening. I loved storms. The thunder and the lightening just reminded me of cozy nights on the couch, snuggled with a blanket and a bowl of popcorn, watching some awkwardly bad, low-budget horror flick. Then again, the neighbor girl – I think her name was Emma – would be forced inside for the night, undoubtedly to resume her stomping and squealing.

In my embarrassingly neglected kitchen, I found a frozen corndog in the freezer and placed it on a flimsy paper plate. I always avoided washing the dishes, and I regularly went to any lengths necessary to avoid accumulating dirty plates, smudged glasses, and crusted silverware. Paper plates were the way to go. I didn't care if it wasn't cost-effective to constantly buy disposable plates. It was sanity-effective.

While the corndog thawed in the microwave, the low hum filled the quiet, and I opened a can of soda, sipping while I paced the stained, linoleum tiles. Bubbles tickled my nose, and crumbs cracked under my feet.

What makes me special? I thought. I tucked a piece of my long, dark hair behind my ear. *Why would they want me?*

I reached beside the refrigerator for a first-apartment-grade, dollar-store broom and absently swept the floor while my hot dog rotated. I was briefly distracted by the thought of a hot dog spinning on those steel rolling bars in a convenience store for some twelve hours before a hungry high schooler peeled it from its perch after baseball practice. *Gross.*

The microwave sounded and filled the cramped kitchen with the scent of cornmeal. I curled the paper plate around the rolling corn dog and consequently coated it in the pile of ketchup I had carefully squeezed onto the plate beside it.

In the narrow hallway, I tripped over the tangled cord to the vacuum I'd wished were cordless and sailed into the wall. My shoulder knocked my university degree I'd just hung a day earlier from the wall. It clattered to the floor, crashing into the edge of a wine rack I'd been using as a movie shelf. I cursed. "Seriously?" I picked it up and reluctantly turned it over, hoping it was still intact. I'd just bought that frame, and if it was broken, I didn't really want to know about it. I painstakingly examined every inch of the glass. Not a scratch. I breathed a sigh of relief and tried to return it to its nail, balancing my plate with one hand. I imagine I looked like some sort of circus juggler, the kid who rides around on a unicycle or stands on a massive rubber ball, balancing some tall and awkward item in the palm of one hand.

When I hung the degree, I hadn't bothered to find a stud in the wall, so the nail slid in and out of the drywall easily. Every time I blindly aimed for the nail with the hook on the back of the frame, I merely pushed the nail further into the wall until it was eventually flush.

I gave up and left the frame on the television stand.

In my office, I shivered against the now-chilled seat and hunched over my plate, staring fixedly at my laptop's screen. It taunted me with the blink-blink-blink of the cursor.

> Why do you feel that you are qualified to work for and become a part of our growing company?

Determined to answer, I took a large bite of corndog and drew my laptop to the edge of the desk once more, placing my fingertips on home row, just as I was taught in middle school.

> I am a creative individu –

I deleted it.

> I can bring to you my ability to –

Garbage.

> All I want to do is write but I don't want to be a poor SOB for the rest of my life so I'm looking for a day job.

My fingers ticked wildly, but my pinky finger jackhammered the delete key immediately afterward. Again and again.

"I don't know," I said aloud. I tightened my ponytail. "I give up."

A low humming sounded from close by. It took me far too long to realize that it was my cell phone. Pearl Jam's "Jeremy" escaped from my pink and purple plaid, fleece pajama bottoms.

Incoming call from...
Dad

"Hello?" I answered, swallowing another bite of corndog.

"Sophie?" He paused.

"Hi, Dad." I said before I had fully processed his tone. He'd taken the day off from work to take Mom to the doctor for her headaches. My first thought was that they might want to get together for a proper lunch date following her appointment – something they rarely did anymore because of their hectic work schedules – and that he was calling to invite me, but that wasn't it; there was something else in the way that he said my name.

"I guess they found something." His tone was that of bullied teenage boy whose broken nose and black eye "weren't that bad." He feigned a casual demeanor, but his heavy exhales betrayed him.

"What do you mean?" My blood began to pound in my ears.

"In Mom's head." He seemed to have trouble forcing the words. "We're taking her in to Madison." He was shielded, guarded, unnaturally hopeful.

"When?"

He paused. "Today, I guess."

"So…" I dropped my corndog onto the plate and brushed my hand against my sweatshirt. My pulse was throbbing intensely throughout my body, but I steadied my voice enough to maintain the strength I thought he needed to hear. "What did they find?"

"An aneurysm."

CHAPTER 2

The hospital smelled bad. There was no other way to put it. It was too clean, too sterile-smelling, even though I knew it was anything but. My heart thumped in my chest, and my foot tapped seemingly on its own while my mind wandered. My dad sat beside me, hands clasped in his lap, baseball cap-topped head hung over his knees. My grandmother sat to my left and behaved overly confidently in the staff, honestly. She was too cheerful; she avoided the anxiety too much. It felt fake, forced.

We'd arrived very early that morning, around 4:30. I'd ridden with Dad, and I'd brought a pillow and a blanket for the hour-long ride – not that I slept. I couldn't sleep. The pillow was merely a symbol, I think, something to force a sense of calmness, regularity.

We'd been in the waiting room for about an hour. Very soon, someone was supposed to come and tell us that Mom was ready for her last visitors before the operation was to begin. Every person dressed in scrubs who passed through the airy waiting room sent a jolt of adrenaline shooting through my system. I hadn't spoken to my mom since the day before. They'd kept her in the hospital overnight for observation. Dad spent the night alone for the first time in thirty years. I tried to sleep. I really did. I'm sure he tried, too. "Tried" isn't the best word, truthfully. We didn't try. We went through the motions, but we didn't sleep – at least I didn't. I'd lain in the twin bed I had slept in as a child, now nestled in my college-grade apartment, and I thought. All night. I'd stared at the plaster on the ceiling and the walls. I'd counted the splotches of wall paint that had mistakenly been dabbed onto the ceiling. But I hadn't slept.

And now, my palms were sweating.

In the waiting room was a life-sized statue of a Holstein cow with a golden bell hanging from its neck. I couldn't fathom why anyone would care to stare at a cow while a loved one was cut open and prodded and sewn and stitched. The wall of local artists' work behind my seat, though, distracted me long enough to curb my nausea for at least a few moments of relief. The wall stretched at least fifty feet and curved away at both ends of the open space where an echoing hallway would lead visitors to curtained rooms and quick-stepping hospital employees to their lunch breaks.

I stood and shuffled along the display, absently picking at my nail polish. Chronic goose bumps covered my forearms in the sterility-inducing, chilled air. I admired the framed pieces along the wall and carefully read each nametag that accompanied the work, deciding whether I recognized surnames or whether I was familiar with the artists' hometowns. My shoes drug along the tiled hallway as I moved.

There were expertly proportioned landscapes dotted with distant silos and shaggy farm dogs. One canvas was decorated in my favorite genre: the abstract. There was something so appealing to me in the vivid colors and bold lines that communicated almost nothing but at the same time, a plethora of options. On an oversized canvas, a smear of red and orange spiraled from the lower corner of the foreground, fading and drifting softly into the background, its path darkened with hard, black lines. Yellow and green swirled along the path, spinning into elongated ovals. A midnight hue danced among the shapes and behind the angry path, almost directing its viewer to look beyond, to know that there is something on the other side of the immediate line of sight.

Hands in pockets more for comfort than anything else, I approached the coffee machine that sat in a nook with a built-in countertop interrupting the row of artwork. Regular or decaf were the only options. The faint smell of coffee escaping from the machine calmed me; it reminded me of the early mornings of my childhood.

For being in a hospital, the countertop was filthy. Dried coffee spills dotted the gray granite from the dispenser and drain to the cardboard boxes that were ripped open to reveal colored packets of sweeteners. White was for real sugar. Yellow and pink were for some chemically altered, artificial sweeteners. White outlines of spilled creamer decorated the area, too. It looked as if someone had tried halfheartedly to clean his mess, but only after it was almost dry. Several black, plastic stir sticks littered the counter. There was a perfect circle cut into the countertop, only about four inches in diameter. When I peered into the hole, I saw a mound of crumpled, brown-stained napkins and torn packets in white, yellow, and pink. I scoffed, louder than I intended. How could such a mess have accumulated without anyone feeling the need to, at the very least, empty the trash? I supposed, though, that everyone had more substantial concerns there than overflowing sugar packets.

Regular coffee, three creamers, and two packets of the artificial sweetener in yellow contented me enough that I was able to rejoin my family in the blue upholstered chairs of the seating area.

"Coffee sounds good," Dad said, standing. "Want any, Carla?" Grandma looked up from her magazine and shook her head with a slight smile. "No, thanks," she said before returning to her article on late-season gardening.

The receptionist seated behind the circular desk beside the cow in the middle of the open space clicked on her keyboard, her blond ponytail swinging each time the phone rang, drawing her attention from the screen. The ring was a shrill, obnoxious sound that echoed from the walls and the high ceiling. Panic was evident on every face in the waiting area with each ring that could have signaled that there were complications with this person's procedure, or Great Aunt Sunshine's procedure was taking longer than expected, or Uncle Freddie wasn't responding as intended.

Before Dad could fill his coffee, the rectangular buzzer he held began to vibrate and blink angry red lights. "It's buzzing," he said "They must be ready for us."

Together, my dad, my grandma, and I approached the receptionist, who said nothing but smiled and reached for the buzzer.

"They're ready in pre-op," she said after several strokes of her keyboard. Her pink lip gloss shimmered under the fluorescent lights when she said, "Room 2611. Follow me."

I guess I didn't need to worry about someone coming to escort us; the receptionist doubled as a tour guide. My family was silent as we marched behind the girl and into the elevator. She asked my dad to press 6 with a "please?" and a grin that was wholly inappropriate given our situation. I fought the immediate urge to scoff again. Her scrubs were decorated in rainbow hearts. What an obnoxiously cheery person. In that moment, I hated her.

No one spoke in the elevator. When it beeped, we simply followed her out and around the hallway, all eyes on the scuffed, white floor tiles. I didn't want to peer in at grieving families and worried parents and patients sleeping off anesthetics. Instead, I focused on the way the fluorescent lights hummed and ticked and reflected off the floor.

"Just at the end of the hall," the girl said before leaving us. Her perfectly white tennis shoes squeak-squeak-squeaked down the hall, and she disappeared.

Beeps and hums escaped from the doorway lit with an eerie glow. As though fearing what we may see through the doorway, each of us approached slowly. I led the way.

I don't know what I expected to see – a private room, at least. But this was a shared area. Violet curtains separated a row of beds that lined a whitewashed wall covered in wires and various machines. I scanned the wall of patients and immediately found my mom, sitting up against the wall and grimacing with obvious fear. Her eyes welled, and she reached for me with both arms.

"Hi, baby," she said through a strained voice. It killed me.

"Hi, Mom." I leaned over her, careful to not disturb the IV tube in the back of her hand or any of the sticky, white electrodes glued to her scalp. A sob began to work its way through my chest like lava building toward the peak of an ever-ready volcano, but I held it back. I wanted to pour out my emotions and be cradled against the bosom of the woman who raised me and kissed my boo-boos and tucked me into bed every night for twenty-five years, but I didn't. I needed to be strong. I needed to show her that I was confident that everything would be okay. I buried my tears.

"You'll be fine," I said almost sternly.

Mom didn't respond. She only stared fixedly into my eyes, the eyes of her only child, as nurses and assistants worked around us. It was as though only she and I existed in the moment. The rest of the world simply spun around us.

Dad stood across from me and rested his right hand on Mom's bare, freckled shoulder. His lower lip trembled, and he reached with his left hand to brush black baby hairs from her temple. For a moment, I was enraged at his willingness to be so emotional. I was angry with him for not remaining a strong force, for showing his fear, for giving me a reason to doubt the skill of the surgeons, and for giving Mom a reason to doubt that she would awaken sometime that evening with a titanium clamp having been masterfully placed inside her skull, feeling ready to conquer the rest of her life.

Grandma stood at the foot of the bed and said nothing; she only dabbed at sporadic tears with a crumpled tissue and sniffed every few seconds. She wore her glasses tucked into the neckline of her pink t-shirt. The nose rests of her glasses had left deep indents on each side of the bridge of her nose.

Nurses began to ask Mom questions and assure her that everything would be fine and that they would take the best care of her. I wondered how often they rattled that speech to terrified people every day of their careers. There was nothing anyone could say, though, to unfurrow Mom's brow.

"It's time to go." A nurse with very pale skin and many freckles patted Mom's foot and smiled. "It's time to say your 'see-you-laters.'"

Time sped. Tears poured down Mom's cheeks, and my heart thumped in my throat, but I tried my best to erase my fearful grimace whenever I realized it was showing. After hugs and kisses and exchanges of love and assurances of safety, my dad and grandma began to drift closer to the echoing hallway. Mom reached up once more to wrap her arms around my neck and shoulders, threatening to demolish the foundation of the fortress I had begun to build around me.

"I love you, honey," she whispered through heaves of sadness and fear. Her warm tears dampened my earlobe, and her sweet breath brushed the wisps of hair that had fallen out of my high ponytail and down my neck.

I hugged her as long as I could without falling to pieces in front of her. With a final heave of strength, I steadied my voice and said, "I love you, too. I'll see you in a few hours."

I turned away from her in such a way that still felt premature, but something deep within me took hold and helped me continue out of the room. Had I turned around and ran back to her bed the way a child runs to a parent after a weekend away, the four of us would have crumbled. She didn't need that. I resisted the urge to turn back to her helpless form, to run back to her side and curl myself into the crook of her neck the way I used to, but instead, I followed my father into the hallway in silence. There was nothing more to say for the moment. No one could force a statement of lighthearted confidence. No one could do more than stare at the floor. Meeting anyone's gaze would burst open a floodgate I wanted so badly to fortify – for Mom's sake and my own.

Hours passed slowly in the waiting room. The phone rang incessantly, sending a rush through my body with every shrill note. Buzzers sounded in the laps of hopeful family members. Nurses and surgeons padded through automatic doors and along the halls.

Grandma read her "Good Housekeeping" magazine, and Dad leaned his head against the popcorn-plastered pillar beside his seat. I sat frozen and gazed out the skylight high above my chair. Late morning crawled toward noon, and while food was neither tempting nor necessary, it provided a much-needed distraction.

"Anybody want to go to the cafeteria for a little bit?" I stood and wiped my palms across my jeans.

"I could use a bite to eat." Dad stood and rubbed his knuckles into his eyes. He seemed just as thankful for the distraction. With Mom out of view, Dad could, if only temporarily, look past the thought of scalpels and bone saws and forceps.

"Grandma?" I asked.

"I'm fine, dear." She didn't look up from the magazine.

We walked in an understood silence. When the elevator doors opened, a man in a wheelchair nodded toward us in a solemn greeting. An overweight, forty-something nurse stood behind his chair and smiled slightly. Her black hair was gelled and spiked straight into the air.

In the cafeteria, the basement of the hospital, we muttered bleak responses to the young men and women wearing clear plastic gloves and black hair nets behind glass cases of meats and cheeses and potatoes and rolls.

Each with a lunch tray filled with a foil-wrapped burrito and a bottle of soda, Dad and I sat at tall, black stools lined against a white, crumb-coated countertop. In front of our seats was a flat screen television playing a CNN morning newsreel. I was thankful for the opportunity to be reminded that a world still existed outside of my own mind.

As Dad and I ate, we forced a light conversation.

"It's supposed to cool down soon," he said between bites, his eyes half-heartedly on the television screen. "They say it's going to rain pretty good again tomorrow night."

His words seemed to drift past me. My focus was almost entirely consumed by the repeated alarms and pages sounding from the overhead speaker system. "I heard it was supposed to storm tonight, too," I managed.

"Dr. Reynolds to Emergency. Dr. Reynolds," a voice called.

Moments later: "Dr. Stanley to Trauma. Dr. Stanley." Each call began and ended with a stream of tones and sirens that sent a chill down my spine. My goose bumps had yet to subside.

"Hopefully we're done with the humidity for a while," Dad said between bites.

I pulled the foil wrapper closer to the bottom of my burrito and took a small bite. "That would be nice."

"Twelve have been confirmed dead in a tragic train accident in Pittsburgh. More on this story just after this break." A brunette news anchor smiled on the television, displaying her unnaturally white teeth set against the crimson gloss she wore on her lips.

"Did you hear about that accident?" Dad asked.

"No, I haven't. I've been pretty busy applying for jobs lately. I guess I haven't paid much attention to the news."

"Any luck yet?"

I shook my head. "But I'm working on applying for a copyediting job that seems pretty promising." Talking was making me feel better. I felt my shoulders begin to loosen and fall away from my ears.

A large man in bleach-stained, black sweatpants and an oversized, yellow polo shirt struggled with the door that led to the hallway just beyond where we sat. The man reached for the doorway and dropped the crutch that was supporting his right side. He stooped to retrieve the crutch and lost his balance, leaning hard into the doorframe.

Dad caught sight of the man and stood, briskly dabbing his hands on his jeans. "I'll get that," Dad said as he bent to retrieve the crutch. He leaned it on the wall beside him and gripped the man under the arm. "Here we go." He braced himself and heaved the man upward. The stranger's cheeks flushed, but he smiled, acknowledging that he did, indeed, need the help.

Ashamed that I hadn't offered my help sooner, I leapt to my feet and opened the door the man had been reaching for. He thanked us several times before carrying on through the cafeteria.

Dad and I smiled at each other and sat down at the stools again. Just as we exhaled and lifted what was left of our lunches, the PA system chimed again. "Dr. Fischer to Neurology. Dr. Fischer."

We froze.

I looked into his pink-rimmed eyes, and he stared into mine. Neither of us breathed for a moment.

The House on Valley Street

Through the panic, I said, "Mom would still be in an operating room. So that can't be for her because they would have paged someone to the O.R. instead."

My comment seemed to have made sense to him because his features relaxed from a look of panic to one of only concern. There was a substantial difference between the two.

Both of us had lost what little appetite we had at that point and resolved to give up on lunch. After our shaky hands returned our empty lunch trays, we silently made our way back to the waiting room, where Grandma was still seated, this time shuffling through her bag.

"Have you heard anything?" I asked. Though judging by her demeanor, I assumed that there couldn't have been any news.

"Nothing yet." Her light eyes were still rimmed with red from the morning's tears. Her nose was a bit red still, too.

A piercing ring cried out from the receptionist's desk. "Hello?" I heard her low voice, and her calm demeanor started to really irritate me. How could she sit there day in and day out, watching families tremble in fear, embrace for joy at the sound of good news, or crumble in pain at the sound of bad – and then just keep up her chipper 'hellos' like that? *Ugh.*

"For Karen?" she called out.

My heart leapt into my throat. Dad didn't hesitate whatsoever; without even glancing at me, he stood and walked to the counter, a forced smile on his face.

I stayed in my seat. I didn't want to hear clinical words or potentially bad news. Instead, I studied Dad's posture, noting his shoulders, his stance, the way he nodded his head. *Are they whispering? Why are they whispering?*

After too long, Dad turned around and faced us, a true, full smile on his face. His smile lifted a weight from my chest, and all I could do was sigh contentedly as he returned to his seat.

"What did they say?" Grandma asked.

"They're finishing up now. Everything went great." He was a new man. It was as though the color had returned to his face for the first time that day.

He reached his hand across my knee and squeezed it affectionately.

"The doctor will be down shortly to give us details on how things went," he continued. The air had lifted in the room. I felt as though we were close – not quite there, but almost in the clear. All I needed was to see her. I needed to talk to her. I needed to make sure.

Our conversations loosened, the room warmed, and our brows relaxed.

Moments later, a man who I recognized as Mom's surgeon strode through a set of double doors that led into the waiting room. He still wore dusty blue scrubs and a matching head wrap. Frameless glasses sat atop his head.

"For Karen?" he asked, smiling confidently.

"Yes." My dad stood, invigorated, and nodded toward me, as if to invite me into the conversation. Together, we marched behind the surgeon and followed him into a small office space that sat adjacent to the waiting area. He closed the door behind us.

"Have a seat," he said, kindly gesturing toward the two burgundy chairs that sat across from his small desk.

Quietly, we obeyed, as though he were our superior.

"Everything went perfectly as planned, and she's waking up now. She'll likely have a bit of tenderness for the next week or so." As he spoke, I studied the faux cactus that sat upon his desk, apparently having been there collecting dust for quite some time. There were no family photos on his desk or his walls. There was only a single, framed document, a medical license of some sort that hung on the wall above his black computer monitor.

"We started by opening up the skull."

The skull, not *her* skull. *Strange.*

Listening to the procedure was easier, though. Step-by-step sequences helped to remove emotion, fear, hesitance. It was impersonal. Clinical.

He continued, "We had no problem locating the aneurysm; there was no excessive bleeding, but I must tell you. We were almost too late. The original aneurysm, rather than bursting, had split into two individual bubbles. You're all very lucky. One more day, and we would have lost her," he said. Before waiting for that to sink in, he continued. "The clamp was attached to the bubbles to restrict blood flow and strengthen the weak spots. After, we closed the skull and stitched the scalp in a C-shape facing the left eye." He finished as though on a high note. In that moment, I could almost picture him rubbing his hands together as if to say that the deed was done; it was a piece of cake.

While the surgeon spoke, Dad nodded and asked the occasional question. The clinical aspect didn't seem to bother him. All he wanted to know was when she would be up and moving, back to her old self again. After assuring us that it wouldn't be more than a couple of days before she would begin to feel well again, he added, "And when you see her, don't be alarmed by her eyes. She will likely have blood pooled beneath her left eye, closest to the incision, resulting in what is essentially a black eye. This will pass over the next several days."

He asked us if we had any additional questions, and when we didn't, he stood and opened the door for us. "We'll call down and let you know when she's awake and ready for visitors. It won't be long," he said, walking us out of the office and back to our seats in the waiting room. A moment later, he disappeared behind the double doors.

"Alright, honey." Dad almost cheered as he squeezed my shoulder.

"What did he say?" Grandma asked. "How did it go?"

"Everything went fine, and she's waking up." Dad answered.

"Oh, thank God." Grandma said, smiling. Over the many years that my parents had been together, there had been numerous disagreements between my dad and my grandma, mostly surrounding money. But they ignored that then for Mom's sake.

Grandma tucked her magazine into her oversized bag and stood. "I'm going to go freshen up a little in the bathroom," she said, stretching. "Don't leave without me."

It felt like even more weight had lifted from the room. Mom was waking up. The surgeon said everything was fine. Dad was happy. Grandma was happy. I was happy. Mom was safe. We were relieved, but for only a moment longer.

The surgeon came bursting through the double doors once more. The expression on his face was *wrong*.

Something's wrong. What's wrong? What happened?

My adrenaline charged through my body, and my soul was torn into pieces when I saw my dad's expression shift from relief to terror in a moment.

The surgeon didn't wait for privacy. He panted, standing in front of our chairs. "She's not waking up as we had hoped. We believe there may be a blockage in her brain, and she's having a stroke. We need your permission to run an angiogram from her groin to her brain to loosen any blockages there may be."

My head swam. Dad continued the conversation, and all I could do was sit.

I looked to my right and saw Grandma emerge from the bathroom. Her expression transformed when she saw my face. Her eyes sunk. Her smile faded. Her brows arched. She understood.

Something had gone wrong.

No words were necessary. Grandma sat silently in the chair next to me, and tears dripped down her face. Every several seconds, she wiped them away with the same crumpled Kleenex she'd used that morning.

I couldn't think. I couldn't feel. All I could do was sit, close my eyes, and let everything fade to black.

CHAPTER 3

My knees trembled when we entered the darkened room where Mom was waking up. My lungs constricted as I focused for the first few moments on the geometric-patterned drapes closing out the late afternoon sun.

After a moment, I settled into the far corner of the room, near the foot of her bed. A large bandage covered her head, and the doctor was right – both of her closed eyes were black and blue. She lay on her back and leaned slightly to the left.

A piece of me withered away from deep in my core when I saw her hair. Around the bandage, her hair lay knotted and caked with leftover glue from the electrodes. A portion of hair in the shape of a large "C" had been shaved away to make room for the incision.

She was so helpless, so frail, so injured.

A young male nurse paged through a clipboard from his position beside her bed. He probably told us his name, but I wasn't listening. Brent? Brandon? It was irrelevant.

"How long will she be like this?" I blurted, almost without thought. I feared she would never wake up. I needed her to wake up. I needed to see her eyes open. I needed to feel like the worst was over; I wasn't yet convinced.

"We don't know." He said, almost absently, still perusing his paperwork. My cheeks flushed red with anger. "Sometimes patients don't wake up. This part is touch-and-go."

How could he say this to me? How could he say this to my dad? What a piece of shit. I hoped his family would go through the same thing. I doubted he'd want to hear a resident nurse tell him his mother may never wake up, never open her eyes again.

The rush of emotions careening toward me in that moment prevented me from holding onto my anger. I couldn't hold onto anything. So I focused on the machines. I studied Mom's pulse on the monitor.

78.

82.

80.

75.

Time passed in a fog. I stood. The nurse talked. He wrote. He moved about the room. I stayed.

Dad sat in a powder blue, leather chair against the far wall. He must have felt better having seen her. The air around him felt lighter. He breathed a little easier. His frown lifted but didn't disappear altogether.

Just seeing her wasn't enough for me.

The surgeon returned and spoke quietly with my dad. To be honest, I'm not entirely certain what their conversation held. I couldn't focus anymore. I merely caught bits and pieces.

"…may have trouble tying her shoes…"

"…walk again…"

"…still young…

Meanwhile, Brent-or-Brandon was still prodding. He reached below Mom's blanket and began pinching her leg, just as the surgeon was leaving.

He must have had a fleeting moment of selflessness after noticing the bewilderment my dad and I mirrored; apparently, he felt the need to explain. He said, "What I'm doing here is testing your wife's ability to move her legs. I'd like to get a reaction from her, and hopefully we can see her move both of them."

He pinched and pinched. "Karen?"

Nothing happened.

She merely lay there, eyes closed, breathing slowly and steadily. He pinched harder. "Karen?"

Nothing.

The House on Valley Street

A young male nurse paged through a clipboard from his position beside her bed. He probably told us his name, but I wasn't listening. Brent? Brandon? It was irrelevant.

"How long will she be like this?" I blurted, almost without thought. I feared she would never wake up. I needed her to wake up. I needed to see her eyes open. I needed to feel like the worst was over; I wasn't yet convinced.

"We don't know." He said, almost absently, still perusing his paperwork. My cheeks flushed red with anger. "Sometimes patients don't wake up. This part is touch-and-go."

How could he say this to me? How could he say this to my dad? What a piece of shit. I hoped his family would go through the same thing. I doubted he'd want to hear a resident nurse tell him his mother may never wake up, never open her eyes again.

The rush of emotions careening toward me in that moment prevented me from holding onto my anger. I couldn't hold onto anything. So I focused on the machines. I studied Mom's pulse on the monitor.

78.

82.

80.

75.

Time passed in a fog. I stood. The nurse talked. He wrote. He moved about the room. I stayed.

Dad sat in a powder blue, leather chair against the far wall. He must have felt better having seen her. The air around him felt lighter. He breathed a little easier. His frown lifted but didn't disappear altogether.

Just seeing her wasn't enough for me.

The surgeon returned and spoke quietly with my dad. To be honest, I'm not entirely certain what their conversation held. I couldn't focus anymore. I merely caught bits and pieces.

"…may have trouble tying her shoes…"

"…walk again…"

"…still young…

Meanwhile, Brent-or-Brandon was still prodding. He reached below Mom's blanket and began pinching her leg, just as the surgeon was leaving.

He must have had a fleeting moment of selflessness after noticing the bewilderment my dad and I mirrored; apparently, he felt the need to explain. He said, "What I'm doing here is testing your wife's ability to move her legs. I'd like to get a reaction from her, and hopefully we can see her move both of them."

He pinched and pinched. "Karen?"

Nothing happened.

She merely lay there, eyes closed, breathing slowly and steadily. He pinched harder. "Karen?"

Nothing.

He pinched harder yet.

"Ow!" Mom slurred the word, starting out quiet and booming toward the end. She felt it. But she didn't move. "Hurts!"

"Okay. Sorry, Karen." He glanced over his shoulder toward us. "That's what we're looking for." He removed his hand from below the white cotton blanket and patted her thigh. Something in his movement, patting her leg that way, told me he was arrogant, like he thought himself above her. Above us.

My soul cringed to see her that way, to hear her cry out that way, but a part of me leapt with joy when she spoke. At least she could do that.

"I'll check back on you in a little while." He spoke to her like she was a child who was hard of hearing. "I need you to try to keep those eyes open, okay?"

At his cue, I saw her struggle to open her eyes. One eye opened further than the other, though still only enough for her to get a blurred, fleeting glimpse of the nurse.

When he was gone, I moved to the head of the bed and clutched Mom's hand. "Hi, Mom." My throat was chalky, my mouth dry.

She grunted lightly and spoke what loosely sounded like, "Hi, baby."

I swallowed hard to refortify that wall. "How do you feel?"

"Tired. Leg hurts." The words were barely audible. Her eyes had fallen closed again.

"Your leg hurts?" I gently lifted the blanket away from her legs and looked where the nurse had been pinching. Large purple bruises riddled the inside of her thigh.

That bastard.

Dad noticed and grimaced but said nothing. He pulled his chair closer to the bed and began to caress Mom's right arm. She remained still.

The day continued that way into the night. Mom rested, Dad and I sat near her bed, and various staff members came and went, muttering things about procedure and "standard this" and "recovery that."

Late in the evening, a middle-aged, female nurse lifted Mom's blanket off of her to adjust a cord attached to one of her monitors, leaving her naked back end exposed. The indignity in that moment, those ten seconds of exposure, left a mark like a searing scar in my mind. I stood and tugged the blanket over her rear. The nurse merely continued with her work.

That night, Dad and I slept on a two-person chair in a small, nearby waiting room specifically designed for families of patients in the Intensive Care unit of the Neurology wing. A family slept across the room from us: a mother, an uncle, and two young boys who were only just old enough to grasp what was happening to their father. Beside us slept a middle-aged man who wore tattered sneakers and light-washed jeans from the early eighties. While he slept, he pulled his Chicago Bulls baseball cap over his eyes, crossed his hairy arms over his chest, and extended his feet in front of him.

I recoiled at the beeps and alarms sounding from various rooms along the hallway. They all felt like emergencies.

The night passed slowly. I turned left and right on the hard, wooden arm of the seat we shared, and my body was curled in as small of a ball as it could be. Sleeping in street clothes was uncomfortable, unusual. My jeans jabbed my stomach, and the hood of my sweatshirt cramped my neck. I was being suffocated. Dad was still, but I couldn't imagine that he would feel well-rested in the morning, either.

As soon as the sun began to show through the windows, we woke. The single man was gone, and the family was sorting through a bag of clean clothes for the children to change into. The boys' brown hair was disheveled. They stood quietly and waited for instruction while the mother dug for clean underwear.

I had no clothes to change into, but I did have a toothbrush. I was thankful for that.

I stretched, as though I'd had a restful night. "Do you want to find the bathrooms?" I rustled through my purse and dug out my toothbrush and a travel-size tube of toothpaste I'd packed the morning prior.

The House on Valley Street

The family restroom was large and cold. I examined the white toilet seat, as I always had. You never know what you'll find on the seats. It looked clean – none of the standard public-restroom hairs on the seat, no pee splatters.

After I'd used the toilet, splashed cold water on my face, and brushed my teeth, I found Dad studying a collage of hospital employees in the hallway.

"You ever thought about being a nurse?" he asked. "Or a doctor?"

I shook my head. "Too many germs. I couldn't handle it."

"Good." He took the toothpaste and went into the bathroom.

When he was finished, Dad and I made our way back to down the hallway toward the service desk. Overnight, the staff had moved Mom from a recovery room into a standard room in the same wing.

"Room 1231." The bright-eyed attendant said. "Go down the hall and take a right. It'll be the second door on the right side of the hall."

Dad smiled and nodded in appreciation. "What do you want to do for breakfast?" he asked me. Talking about anything that wasn't hospital-related felt like a relief.

I shrugged. "We could go down to the cafeteria or take a little road trip. It might be good to get out of here for a little bit," I said, keeping track of the room numbers we passed, each plaque divided by a bland, floral oil painting. I tried to avoid it, but I found myself looking into the open rooms we passed. I saw a man being helped into a sitting position on the bed. I saw cleaning people making empty beds. I hoped that the rooms were vacant because the patients had been dismissed to go home. I shuddered to think otherwise.

As we neared the end of the hallway, a gut-wrenching siren echoed from a nursing station to our left. The nurse stood and jogged past us, leaving in her wake the scent of fruity body spray.

When we passed through the doorway to Mom's room, her bed was empty. Bile rose in my throat, and my heart lurched. "Mom?!"

I moved about the room, searching behind doors and under the bed for any of her things. I moved the pile of blankets, knowing that her body didn't lie beneath it, but searching just the same.

"In here," she said, sounding almost like herself. Following her voice, I opened the door to her ensuite bathroom, and what I saw haunted me in that moment and forever since. Mom sat on the floor, propped against the wall, naked, weak, stranded, unable to move. Her arm hung limp at her side. One leg was bent at the knee; the other was extended straight in front of her.

"I had to pee." She smiled an unknowing smile, a naïve smile, a perfectly inappropriate, child-like smile, a sagging smile.

Not a moment later, a nurse came rushing in and gripped Mom by a wide cloth belt that had been wrapped around her waist. She expertly tugged her to her feet. "I'm just weak, I guess." She grinned, but only half of her face fully responded.

The nurse was a tall African American woman with a heavy Jamaican accent. She wore her hair very short, and her makeup was minimal. "We get you back in da bed, now," she said.

"I have to pee." Mom repeated and tugged lightly against the nurse's grip with her left arm.

The nurse followed Mom's lead into the bathroom and closed the door behind them. While they were occupied, I avoided Dad's face. I didn't want to see the look of despair I imagined it held. I didn't want to process what I had just seen. I didn't want to think about such a shift in my mom's mentality. I felt a temptation to shut down, to cry, to scream, but I didn't. I forced it away and prepared to rejoin Mom when she was finished. In fact, I blatantly ignored what I had just witnessed and sat in a chair pulled up to the edge of the inclined bed.

In desperation for normalcy, I reached for the television remote that was wired to the bed and clicked aimlessly through the channels, pausing briefly on any program I recognized. Spanish soap opera. News. The Family Feud. News. Televised church service. News. I continued clicking until Mom returned.

The expression on her face when she was being escorted didn't fit. She was too happy. She was beaming. As she hobbled to the bed, she stared at me and grinned. Looking into her face saddened me. One side of her smile didn't lift quite as high as the other. I couldn't tell if she was relieved that the surgery was over and that she was alive or if she was just happy to see me.

I scooted to the edge of the bed to make room for her, and she slid in next to me, not without struggle from both herself and the nurse. She tried to wrap her right arm around my shoulder, but when the arm didn't follow her brain's command, she quickly redirected her attention, almost as though she didn't recognize what had happened.

"How's my baby?" she said, nuzzling my shoulder.

"Good. How did you sleep?"

"Like shit." When I pulled away, I saw that there was saliva gathering at the corner of her mouth.

Dad chuckled and immediately stood from his seat at the end of the bed to wipe her face. "Are you hungry?" he asked.

"Yeah. The shit they gave me this morning wasn't enough. Just some toast, yogurt, grapes. I'm hungry. The assholes."

Dad and I smiled at each other. "Do you want us to grab you something for lunch?" Dad asked.

She thought for a moment. "Yeah, a giant beef-and-cheese sandwich with curly fries." She made drooling sounds in her best imitation of Homer Simpson. I couldn't help but smile.

Dad stooped to kiss her forehead and said, "We'll go get you some shortly."

"Get it now," she said, flirty and childlike. She batted her eyelashes as best she could.

Another nurse knocked on the door and took a few steps in. She introduced herself and explained that her shift was starting. She wheeled a blue cart to the bedside and strapped a blood pressure cuff around Mom's upper arm.

I sighed in relief, not because I was comfortable with Mom's condition or because I thought our struggles were over. I was relieved because Mom wasn't uncomfortable. She wasn't distraught. Her spirit wasn't destroyed. Her strength, whether it existed because she didn't know what had happened to her in that operating room or because she didn't realize the severity of the condition, lifted me.

Dad turned to me as the nurse worked. "Want to head out now?"

I nodded.

"We're going to go get lunch, honey," Dad called to Mom, who was talking to the nurse about the highlights in her hair. "Ready?" He asked me, adjusting his navy baseball cap and tucking wisps of gray hairs around his ears.

I went. I didn't want to leave Mom, but I needed to get out of the hospital for a while. Besides, the nurse was keeping her company for the time being, and that made me feel better.

I inhaled deeply when we stepped outside. The sun was bright, and the air smelled of mid-summer. Dad and I squinted and shielded our eyes like vampires stepping out into daylight for the first time in decades, though it had only been a day and a half.

On the way to the restaurant, we spoke little. I flipped through the channels on the radio. Country music: too woe-is-me. Oldies: not upbeat enough. I stopped on an alternative rock station and bobbed my head to the bass beat of a song that I recognized as a remake of some decades-old hit. It was perfect – not too peppy, not too slow and sappy – until I listened more closely to the lyrics.

Though Dad seemed not to notice, I shuddered when the word "paralyzed" rang out in the refrain.

I changed the channel to a talk show and left it. Paralysis was the last thing I wanted to hear about, let alone in song form.

The drive-thru was empty; it didn't take long to get our food. The smell of warm bread and French fries filled the car immediately, and the heat from the bottom of the bag felt nice on my legs as we rode back to the hospital, despite the warm weather.

The House on Valley Street

The hospital Mom was in was widely regarded as the most advanced hospital in the region, though it certainly was not located in a progressive neighborhood. In fact, the area was entirely run-down. There was graffiti sprayed in red and green on the sides of the single-story brick buildings that lined the street. Most of it was symbols, though there were a few words painted in Spanish.

One short, stout man with a goatee was walking very confidently along the sidewalk when he suddenly threw his arms to his sides and tilted them up and down while he trotted back and forth, as though he were a child pretending to be an airplane. Brown curls bounced at the nape of his neck. As we passed, I pretended to be interested in the buildings behind him.

When we'd returned to the parking garage, the spot we'd been in before we'd left was still empty, so we parked there again. Our footsteps echoed to the door. Dad and I were the only ones in the elevator. I was grateful for that.

Mom was incredibly eager to have her food when we made it back to her room. Her happiness and oblivion made me hopeful, but it scarred my soul at the same time. I was happy that she was happy. But I was crushed that she didn't seem to understand. She didn't know that she'd had a stroke, and it was as though something was missing from her.

As she ate, she said, "I had a dream while you guys were gone." She slurred a bit, and some of the liquid cheese from her sandwich dribbled at the corner of her mouth. She siphoned soda from her paper cup with a ferocity.

"Yeah?" Dad asked.

"I dreamed I was at the house on Valley Street." She had particular difficulty pronouncing the word "house." "You and I," she said and nodded toward Dad, "were back at the house in the living room watching TV in the dark, and there was a creature, a demon banging on the door. But the demon couldn't get to us because my BB was guarding the door." She smiled nostalgically at the thought of the dog she had adopted when she was eleven. He had, of course, passed away, but not until the two spent 16 "magical years together," as she often repeated. She reminisced about his life daily.

"A demon, huh?" I said. I had always been skeptical of the stories she had told regarding her childhood in that house, the house on Valley Street, but now wasn't the time to challenge her. I merely listened.

She nodded and struggled a bit to remove the plastic wrapper from the rest of her sandwich with the use of only one hand while the other lay limp across her stomach. She continued, "It had claws and its eyes were black holes that were pure evil. It wanted our souls."

Mom had always been what I would say is "in touch" with her spiritual side. Again, I struggled to view the world the way she did. If I didn't see anything, I didn't believe anything. Plus, believing in these spirits and a heaven meant believing in a higher god, and believing in a higher god meant believing in a being who would bring her to the brink of death, then tow her back, just to permanently injure her with a stroke. It didn't add up in my mind.

"Since you want to be a writer," Mom continued, rambling in such a lighthearted way that made me smile, "you should write my stories about that house. Maybe if you shared the story of the home, the spirits there would rest."

She had a point. Maybe I didn't believe the stuff about the spirits, but I always enjoyed a good horror story. My childhood friends and I used to gather around the television late at night and huddle in blankets and pillow forts while we watched R-rated movies.

"I think I will," I said. The house would give me plenty of material to write on. I needed to hurry up and get a first novel out there if I wanted to make a career of writing.

"Really?" She seemed shocked.

"Yeah. Maybe I'll stay in the house for a while and write about it. You said it's been vacant for a while, right?"

Her energy was quickly dwindling like a baby winding down for an afternoon nap. She slurped sloppily on her straw. "I think." She popped the rest of her sandwich into her mouth at once, a bite that was far too big. "But I don't want you living there. It's not safe." While she talked, she pushed the sandwich further into her mouth with her fingers and struggled to chew it.

"I'll be fine."

She shook her head and swallowed audibly. "I don't want you going there. Something could attach itself to you," she said, rubbing her still-purple eyes, one at a time, with her good hand.

"I'll be okay, Mom." I realized a moment after I'd spoken that I should have conceded; I should have nodded and told her that I wouldn't do it, at least for the time being. I should have given her peace of mind, but I didn't. My mind was made up.

"We'll talk about it later," she said with a yawn that stretched farther to the left than the right.

She crumpled her sandwich wrapper and placed it, along with her drink, on her bedside table, leaned back in the bed, and with astonishing immediacy, fell asleep.

CHAPTER 4

The wheels of my white G6 smashed over the gravel driveway, and I imagined the overgrown weeds springing from the center of the path and brushing the underside of the vehicle. The gray, two-story home seemed to loom over the unattended lot where shin-high blades of grass bowed to dying dandelions. As my headlights lit the door to the home's detached garage, I wondered how long it had been since the weathered overhead door had last been opened. I decided I'd leave my car outside for the first night; I wanted to search through the garage first.

The man I spoke to on the phone about renting – my new landlord, I suppose – said that the neighborhood was safe, but I still didn't relish the idea of leaving my car in the driveway overnight, either. Besides, it was my first night alone in quite some time. I'd spent the 34 days Mom was in the hospital, plus the week following her return home, with her and Dad. I'd gotten used to the company.

When I opened my car door, the late summer air hung like a security blanket around me. I took a deep breath, drawing in the smell of a nearby bonfire. Cicadas buzzed in a tall oak tree whose roots seemed to battle the driveway's gravel path for claim to the territory.

My sandals slapped my heels as I approached the front door by way of a cracked sidewalk path. I stomped up several carpeted steps and reached for the cast iron storm door. For only a moment, I hesitated before sliding the tarnished key into the deadbolt. While I didn't expect any ghouls or zombies to leap at me, I couldn't help but let my imagination run. When I gripped the handle, I imagined each of the hands that had eagerly reached for the same handle in the past 35 years: recently manicured hands donning brilliant red polish, tough hands whose crevices were permanently stained by years of oil changes, tired hands cut and callused by days of physical labor. How many families had entered this home, believing that this was the deal of a lifetime, that it was to be the location of future birthday parties, graduations, marriage proposals?

I also imagined them leaving. I saw them shuffling out the door, cardboard boxes teetering in their arms. In that moment, I contemplated what might have caused the previous tenants to leave so quickly. Surely it couldn't have been what the rumors claimed, what Mom's stories indicated.

The House on Valley Street

The door let out a low groan when it swung open, and I stepped into what appeared to be a living room. A floral couch lay to my right, decorated by dusty, pink throw pillows. A half-burned candle sat atop a doily in the middle of a wooden coffee table that lay between the couch and a large, cumbersome tube television set topped with a pair of rabbit-ear antennas.

In short, it was a fairly normal room.

In front of me was a narrow, waist-high table that rested against a wall, creating a barricade between the foyer and the staircase. I briefly swiped a hand across the table and cleared a small area of dust before I set my black overnight bag and purse on it.

The stairs seemed steep to me – a bit narrow, too. Before starting my climb, I briefly examined the bathroom on my left. A stand-alone bathtub stood along the far wall. I pulled aside a burgundy and pink floral shower curtain to reveal the rust-ringed interior of the tub. Several stray hairs lay at the bottom. The curling hairs mimicked the pattern of the vines that decorated the wallpaper on three of the room's walls. Behind a peach-colored toilet, wallpaper pulled away from the wall in what looked like the result of a years-old leak that was never fully repaired. I imagined my mother as a child, splashing in the tub during her nighttime bath and learning to use the big-girl potty, on the back of which now sat a half-used roll of toilet paper. Then, I pictured her toddling up to the sink and stepping up a small, rusted step stool to smile at her reflection and learn how to brush her baby teeth.

When the thoughts of my mom became more than I wanted to deal with, I made my way out of the bathroom and plodded up the stairs.

Upstairs were three bedrooms, one of which looked as if its previous inhabitants left half of their belongings and simply took off in the middle of a perfectly normal day. On the bed was a pile of strewn clothing, clothing that appeared to have belonged to a woman. On the dresser were several types of makeup: a mascara tube, a fluffy powder blush, and two shades of red lipstick. What caught my attention more than anything else in the room were two mannequin heads on the edge of the vanity. Both wore women's wigs, one brown with blunt bangs and the other black with wispy layers.

For the first time since arriving, I felt uncomfortable, almost as if I could feel tension in the room. It was tangible. The way that everything lay strewn about the room as if the items' owners could return any minute and pick up exactly where they left off was bothersome. I felt almost as if I were intruding on someone's life.

Beside the master was a tiny bedroom that resembled a broom closet more than anything else. The tiny room would be sufficient as a nursery, but not much else, and it was completely bare.

Across the hall was what appeared to have been a child's room. I investigated the closet space and the view from its second-story window – the typical things a person examines upon moving somewhere new.

As I peered at the faded pink and lavender zoo animals that bordered the tops of the walls, I thought again of my mother as a child. This must have been her room – it just felt like it. That wholesome thought suddenly drifted away when I again envisioned someone leaving, fleeing the property so as to leave the mess that lay in the master bedroom.

The only sign of recent inhabitants in this room was a lonely porcelain doll on a small bookshelf in the corner.

A thought struck me at that moment: the master bedroom set the perfect scene for the opening of my novel. I knew that the authentic, first-hand account of my rustling through drawers and trying on hats or pearl necklaces would certainly grip any reader. All I needed was my recorder.

I scrambled down the steps, my sandals flapping and flopping along the way. Just as I reached the bottom, my cell phone vibrated in the pocket of my skinny jeans. It was a text message from Lucee, my best friend since fifth grade.

How's the house? Are you possessed yet?

I chuckled a bit and replied:

Not yet! The house is nice, I guess. Mostly normal.

I tucked the phone away and unzipped my overnight bag. At the bottom, beneath clothes, toiletries, and several pairs of patent heels, I found my silver, handheld voice recorder. It felt good in my hand. It was comfortable, though I'd never used it before.

The recorder had been a graduation gift from my mom, along with a framed family photo taken when I was just a toddler. I placed the recorder on the table and pulled the photo from a zipped mesh compartment in my bag. The three of us – Mom, Dad, and I – were posed stiffly before a gray backdrop. Mom sat on a wooden chair. Her hair was huge, eighties-huge. Her perm stood, at minimum, five inches above her head. Her red, silky blouse was tucked into a high-waisted black, leather pencil skirt that she wore with black tights. Dad stood behind her, one hand placed on her shoulder. A tail of then-fashionable mullet trailed along the shoulder of his pine-colored, velvety dress shirt. I sat on Mom's knee in a baby pink, ruffled dress, white lacey socks, and black patent shoes. Mom's right hand was placed lightly on my lap, her red nails shining against the camera's flash.

I lightly brushed dust from the top of the frame and set it up on the table before returning to my recorder. Something excited me in being able to use it for the first time, like a brand-new notebook and a new pack of pens. It was enticing. I'd wanted to use it for quite some time, but I hadn't had a good enough reason. I pressed the red button, and when the bright light flashed, I spoke.

"The rumors floating through our world are sometimes just that – rumors, stories, fables, myths." I paced through the living room, fingering a dusty, crocheted afghan draped over the back of the couch. "Other times, those stories may hold some truth, even when there is very little, if anything, to hold as proof. It's for that reason that I bring to you my story, my family's story, that of the house on Valley Street."

I realized at that point that I had yet to see the kitchen, and I thought it best to record my immediate reaction as I did – authenticity and whatnot. I could go back and edit in the transitions when I needed to.

"The doorway leading from the semi-furnished living area into the kitchen is narrow. It appears as though there was once a door here." I ran my fingers along three screw holes that at one point held a door hinge in place. As I crossed the threshold, my sandal caught on an upturned corner of one of the kitchen's pale yellow, linoleum tiles.

"The kitchen is quaint and wholesome, though dated. Pale yellow floor tiles reflect little light, as years of children scurrying and parents pacing have scuffed their shine. The light plays against the neutral walls, creating just enough shadowy movement to leave a visitor feeling uncomfortable."

I drug a hand along the countertop. "The appliances have seen years of use – mothers baking cookies, fathers warming middle-of-the-night baby bottles, children searching the refrigerator for after-school snacks after dropping coats and shoes near the kitchen's back door. Now, in the near dark, nothing of note sits in the yard behind the home." I leaned against the screen door's glass and cupped one hand around my eye. I couldn't make out anything beyond a small, bare porch. "Except a storage shed," I added.

I turned back to the kitchen and drug my hand through a thin layer of dust on a small table nestled against the wall. I rubbed my index finger and thumb together like a judgmental mother-in-law assessing the cleaning prowess of her son's new wife. "The only seating in the room is –

I spun toward the sound of the knocking. The figure of an elderly man stood in the doorway I'd just been standing at. He smiled and waved, apologetic for having startled me.

"Hello," he said in a heavy southern accent when I opened the door. It reminded me of a cartoon chicken I used to like when I was small. "I'm sorry to have frightened you. I'm Gene. I'm your new neighbor." He reached his hand toward me.

"I'm Sophia Wesley." I took his hand and smiled, embarrassed. "No worries. I was just investigating the new territory." I gestured to the space around us.

"I do hope this doesn't sound strange, but my wife and I have developed a bit of a routine for introducing ourselves to new neighbors here." His dark eyes wrinkled into a half smile, and he lifted his navy-blue baseball cap, revealing a bald crown before immediately putting it back on, pushing what was left of his white hair down over his ears. "So many people have come and gone from this house that we have to joke about it. We always want to introduce ourselves the minute we notice someone new. If we don't, who knows if the people will still be here when we get around to stopping by?"

I laughed, probably more than was necessary, but the man looked uncomfortable and I wanted to put him at ease. "That's funny! I've heard that a lot of people have come and gone from here." A thought occurred to me then: Gene could be my first interviewee for my novel. "How long have you lived in the neighborhood? You might know my mom. She grew up here in the seventies."

"Darlin', I can hardly remember my name some days." His grin revealed teeth stained from years of morning coffee and tobacco. It wasn't until then that I realized that I had forced my first guest to have an entire conversation with me in a doorway. How foolish.

"Would you like to come in and sit?" I stepped aside and gestured to the two-person table behind me.

"No, darlin'. No, thank you." He tucked a hand into the pocket of his overall pants, well-worn and stained by years of hard work. "I'd track mud all through your new place." He lifted one foot to show me his boots. They were cowboy boots, worn in, aged, in a good way. They had spurs on the back and a pointed toe that only an old man like Gene could pull off. "And I don't mean to impose. I just thought I'd swing by and say 'hi.'"

"Well, that was very nice of you. Which house did you say was yours?"

"The one right across the yard here, darlin'." He had begun backing away from the door, onto the patio. "If you ever need anything, you just let us know."

"Thank you. It was nice meeting you!" I called. He nodded in agreement and continued walking out of the light and across the yard.

"One more thing," he called. "I'll take care of the yard work, if you don't mind. I've been doing it for years now. I've come to enjoy it. Keeps an old man busy."

He winked and tromped through the freshly trimmed grass of my new backyard.

Gene pulled himself up several steps with noticeable effort and tugged open a screen door that closed softly behind him.

His home was as aged as the one in which I stood, but its immaculate landscaping made up for its years. Roses and peonies skirted his home's foundation, punctuated by greens and yellows of decorative grasses that seemed to glow in the porch's light. White and gray river rocks filled in the spaces between.

The cement patio leading to his backdoor was well-manicured, its cracks free of weeds and grass. Several hanging plants dangled from the roof's overhang. Vines dotted with white and blue flowers twisted and overflowed from the baskets.

It was obvious that he would do a better job of caring for the yard than I would.

As I turned away, my phone vibrated again.

> Boring! Let me know when the ghoulies pop out. ;)

I laughed aloud and replied,

> You'll be the first to know!

Cell phone and recorder in hand, I made my way through the foyer and to the base of the stairs, looping my duffle bag over my shoulder along the way. My shadow danced eerily against the far wall of the bathroom, such that I did a double-take as I walked past -- not because I didn't think it was my own shadow. I did. Of course I did. Who else would it belong to?

In what was to be my bedroom, I tossed the duffle onto the bed and emptied its contents. I folded three sweaters and two pairs of jeans. It had seemed just yesterday that the weather was scorching hot, but at some point over the month that we'd spent at the hospital, the weather had shifted. It was as though that time represented a black hole in my life. Walking out on the last day, pushing Mom out of the hospital in a wheelchair, felt like waking up from a coma. It was as though someone had pressed the pause button for more than a month and then suddenly decided to resume watching.

The House on Valley Street

When I'd gotten that call from Dad, it was summer. When we brought Mom home, it was autumn.

When we went in, I was whole. When we came out, I was broken.

What happened in between is still largely a mystery to me, lost in some void.

When all my clothing was hung and folded, a short stack of bath towels now nestled on the dresser, I dialed home. Dad answered.

"How's Mom?" I asked.

"Okay. She's sleeping on the couch." He sounded tired, worn. "How's the house?"

"It's fine," I paced absently to the window as we talked, and I peered out at the rapidly darkening street. Two teenaged boys rode by lazily on low-riding bicycles. "It's pretty big for just me. The neighbor came over – old dude. He said he wants to mow the lawn."

"Sounds like a deal," he said.

We continued that way, speaking in brief snippets about our day, until Mom stirred in the background.

"Who's that?" she asked.

"It's Sophia. Do you want to talk to her?"

"Tell her I love her." Her voice was muffled, and her speech was still slowed, a bit slurred.

"Tell her I love her, too. I'll talk to you guys later."

After hanging up, I lay on the bed, remembering cable specials on the absolute filth found on comforters in hotel rooms that glowed under black lights. I tried to reason with myself since it was a home, not a hotel, but it certainly felt more like a hotel than anything else. After all, it was already furnished. The new landlord had told me that it would be, but it was still a bit shocking, a little uncomfortable.

I groaned aloud. I couldn't handle it. I stood and tore the comforter from the mattress. I pulled the sheets off, too, and piled them all on the floor.

I pulled my three towels from the dresser and placed two flat across the mattress and draped the other over the pillow so I could cover up with it later. I'd resolved to wash the bedding in the morning. Thankfully, I'd brought my own pillow from home. It was the same pillow I'd brought to the hospital. I never stayed overnight anywhere without it.

Both wigs still sat on the dresser in the room across the hall. Since I had always wondered what I'd look like with bangs, I made my way to that room. I reached for the shorter wig, hesitated, then pulled it from the mannequin head. The strands were dry and brittle, coated in a layer of dirt and grime. Despite the dirt, I placed the wig lightly on my ponytailed head and tucked baby hairs behind my ears. I studied my reflection.

"Ugh," I whispered to myself. "Way too dark." The dark wig stood in too strong a contrast to my pale skin.

The bangs of the wig fell into my eye lashes, and as I swept the strands away, the faint smell of cigars came to me. I tugged the wig off my head and sniffed at it. The smell was so overwhelming that it burned my nostrils. I was shocked that I hadn't noticed it before.

Pinching them between my index fingers and thumbs, I brought the wigs downstairs, opened the front door, and dropped them onto the front step. If there was one thing I hated, it was the smell of cigars. Mom had smoked them since I was small, and despite my repeated expression of disapproval, she had refused to quit.

Night had fallen, and the only light came from a streetlamp at the end of the block. A low hum grew as the same group of bicyclists sped past, pumping their pedals powerfully.

"Hurry up!" One of the boys said.

"Be quiet!" Another whispered loudly.

They burst into a devilish sort of laughter and disappeared around the corner.

I locked the door.

In the bathroom, I brushed my hair and my teeth and washed my faced, committing to a good night's rest. I planned to dive headfirst into my project in the morning. Early to bed, early to rise, as they say.

In my bedroom, I turned on the small television that sat atop a short bookshelf in the corner, tossed the remote onto the bed, and flipped the light switch in the doorway. I trotted back to the bed and climbed in quickly, admittedly uncomfortable in the dark room.

Though the television was on, I paid no attention to it. It served as background noise, mostly, and perhaps a nightlight.

Instead, I studied the cracks and water stains and spider webs along the ceiling until I fell asleep.

CHAPTER 5

Morning came quickly. When I opened my eyes, it took a moment to realize where I was. The cracked ceiling was unfamiliar. The golden curtains weren't what I remembered from my apartment. Was I still at Mom and Dad's house?

Slowly, sleep's fog faded, consciousness seeped in, and I remembered where I was. I propped myself against the headboard with my pillow at my lower back and looked about the room. There was always something so strange and different about seeing any house, any room early in the morning for the first time. It reminded me of sleepovers at friends' houses as a preteen.

Tossing my towel-blanket to the side, I swung my feet out of the bed and stood on the cold floor. The golden light streaming through the windows cast a new spotlight on all of the dust mites and crumbs beneath my feet. I suddenly felt like I was intruding. I felt like someone was about to return home to pick up where her life left off. I felt like I should leave the room.

It was as though I couldn't move my feet quickly enough. They needed to carry me from the room, yet they were too slow, too unresponsive to my commands. The hairs on my arms stood on end, and my legs were covered in goose bumps. Something told me that if I didn't move my feet, something would move them for me.

I moved quickly from the room and into the hallway, where I paused and childishly peered around the threshold back into the room. I don't know what I expected to see. I suppose there wasn't anything in particular. I just wanted to look, just to check. The room appeared as it had the day before. Nothing moved. No one was chasing me. There was no monster under the bed.

I padded across the hall and peered into the master bedroom. The lipsticks and blush brushes still lay strewn about the dark dresser. The morning glow made the room feel more eerie but homier at the same time. I half expected to smell bacon wafting up the stairs, but the lonely scent of must and dirt reminded me of why I was there. I needed a story. I needed motivation.

Feeling foolish, I pulled on a hooded sweatshirt and traipsed down the stairs to the bathroom, my bare feet slapping against the cold steps. The first thing I needed to do was clean up the master bedroom. I tapped my chin, wondering where I might be able to find a box large enough to hold all of the junk strewn about that room.

Hood up and drawstring tied, I opened the front door and jogged to the garage through a light rain, hoping to find a cardboard box or a storage bin or something out there that I could use. I reached for the brass handle on the side door and turned it, but nothing happened. As though the handle was not attached to any sort of mechanism, it spun to the right. I turned it left. It spun to the left. With both hands, I turned the handle again, but it kept spinning, too loose. It occurred to me then that the door must not be latched, so I raised one leg and gently nudged it open with my knee, both hands still on the handle. With little resistance, it squeaked open.

The light of the morning brightened the black space, which was almost completely empty. On the far wall was a tall shelving unit holding rusted paint cans decorated with drips and runs of dry paint in burnt orange and sea green. To my right was a workbench that I'm sure any handyman would have loved to use. Above the workbench was a white pegboard wall, empty, but waiting for tools and rope and tape and whatever else might be useful for a regular Mr. Fixit. Below the workbench was a repurposed metal cabinet, rusted and peeling. On its front was painted a child's colorful rocking horse, though most of it was peeling off.

I scanned the space from my right, to the far wall, and lastly to the overhead door. Just inside it was a pile of broken-down moving boxes, probably four or five all together. I took the top one, rather surprised that my search had been so successful so quickly.

Inside the master bedroom, I unfolded the box and tucked the flaps to secure its bottom. Then, tucking it under my arm, I swept the room.

It was strange touching someone else's things: makeup brushes, silk blouses, dirty socks. It was too intimate. But it needed to be done, so I worked quickly and thought minimally.

By the time I finished collecting all of the strewn belongings, I had filled two boxes. I briefly considered storing them in the closet, but then I realized that I didn't want to look at them every day. That would be just as uncomfortable as touching them.

"Ugh," I grunted when I lifted the box. The scent of a woman's spicy perfume wafted upward.

I was careful to lift with my legs, as Mom had always taught me. I never did master that, though, so I felt a light pull at the small of my back. I groaned again.

Wobbling left and right, I hauled the first box down the stairs. I huffed each time my sandals slapped onto a new step. When I thought I had reached the bottom, I gingerly reached out a toe as one would in testing bath water to be sure that there wasn't another step I wasn't prepared for. When my toe found no ledge, I trudged to the door, propped the box between my thigh and the wall, and reached for the handle.

A few kids were riding bikes in front of the house again. They squealed and yelled at each other. One kid pulling up the rear had old-school headphones on and belted some rap song I had never heard before. And he didn't leave out the swear words. He must have been only 12 or 13 years old, certainly the youngest of the group by several years.

In the garage, I plopped the box in the corner and went inside to do it all again. I stomped back up the stairs, lifted with my legs again, and hobbled down the stairs once more. When both boxes lay tidily in the corner of the garage, I had just one more task: I needed to park my car inside it. With f-bomb-dropping hoodlums biking around the neighborhood, I thought it a good idea. I imagined coming out to the car one morning and finding a slew of lovely pictures drawn on it in Sharpie marker. I frowned, opened the car door, and made a mental note to stop leaving the keys in the ignition.

*

Fresh mug of hot chocolate in hand, I sat at the kitchen table, watching the morning light dance off specks of dust gently floating downward from the ceiling. I leaned my head against the wall. *How could this house lead to a novel? It's so...normal,* I thought. *Sure, the home has what I'd call experience, since so many families had come and gone, but –*

That's when I heard it.

A creak.

A groan.

A steady rhythm gradually becoming louder.

And then I realized: the stairs.

A moment of stillness confirmed what I had feared. Someone else was in the house. And he was on the stairs. Dragging steps combined with scrapes and hard thuds that echoed through the foyer. I placed my mug onto the table as quietly as I could, and with some courage that I didn't know I had, I stood to tiptoe to the threshold and see whoever it was that had entered – surely one of the hoodlums.

Placing one foot steadily in front of the other, I pressed my back against the wall and shuffled toward the front of the house. Memories of Dad teaching me self-defense tips as a child flashed through my mind. I balled my fists, making sure that my thumb was not tucked inside – that was one of Dad's tips. *That's a good way to break your thumb,* he'd said. *That's right – give 'em a kidney shot,"* he'd said when we were play-fighting once.

The thuds and creaks continued, keeping a steady rhythm. I could almost see around the corner. The landing was just beyond my sight. Another step forward, and I would know. I would see. I would come face to face with someone.

But then what? I was unarmed. I should have grabbed a kitchen knife. But what would I do with that to a child? Nothing.

My line of vision extended from the front door to the light switch on the wall, then to the far corner of the room, then to the entrance to the bathroom, and finally to the base of the stairs. One step up, two steps up, three steps up, and then I saw it – the girl.

She was thin, too thin. Sick. She was just a child, a child whose body was torqued and twisted into an unnatural form. Her dark, stringy hair stuck to her wet chin in clumps.

My breath hitched in my throat, and I could do nothing but stare. The girl's flesh was pale with a sickly undertone. Yellow and green blotched her skin, and she wore nothing but a dark piece of cloth that hung around her hips. She must have been seven or eight years old.

Suddenly, I remembered a story Mom had told me of a girl who'd lived nearby. Mom had babysat her, but she was very ill and died when Mom was 16. There's no way --

At that moment, the girl's tilted head seemed to rotate on an unnatural axis over her left shoulder, and she met my gaze. Her mouth hung open, and more saliva pooled out from the large gaps in her soiled teeth and sickly red gums. Her gait picked up from a slow hobble to a trot, and finally to as close to a run as her body would allow.

The House on Valley Street

Almost falling down the stairs, legs hardly carrying her, she staggered. She moaned. She grunted. She growled. She screamed a guttural scream that grew from her bowels and reverberated off the ceiling.

For a moment, my legs were frozen. I didn't know what to do or where to go. And then I ran. I turned back into the kitchen, and in my panic, I ran directly into the table, toppling the mug of hot chocolate onto the floor. I slid through the puddle and lunged toward the screen door while the slapping sound of the girl's lopsided gate padded quickly behind me on the tiles. The growling and gurgling seemed to crawl up my spine, up the back of my head, and around to both of my ears where it sat and stewed. Just as a scream burst through my chest, I fell through the door and into the backyard.

I panted and choked on my way to the large elm tree some thirty yards from the door and waited, anticipating the sound of the door swinging open violently as the girl fell from the home. But there was nothing. I strained to hear, but still, there was nothing. My pulse gradually slowed, and I peered out from behind the tree, slowly stretching my neck toward the home. I knew I wasn't crazy. I wasn't going to be one of those girls who thinks she's losing her mind because of "stress" or "a new environment." I know what I saw.

"Everything alright over there, darlin'?"

I gasped when his voice ripped me back to a sense of reality.

The House on Valley Street

"Oh! Gene, you startled me." I felt like an utter idiot. Gene tipped his baseball cap and stood at his home's back porch with both hands on his hips.

"Apologies," he called with a smile. "Is something wrong, darlin'?"

I couldn't tell him what I thought I saw -- what I *know* I saw. "Oh, er, yes," I stammered unconvincingly. "There was a... spider. A huge, furry spider." I nodded convincingly and gave a shudder.

Even from across the yard, his expression was clearly one of disbelief, even though he feigned concern quite well. "Well, you just sit tight, and I'll come on over and take care of that for you." He brushed his hands together as if clearing them of dirt.

"Oh, you don't have to—"

But before I could finish, he had disappeared into his home, leaving the white screen door swinging behind him. A moment later, he reappeared with a rolled newspaper and an apparent resolve to annihilate a certain arachnid.

Gene opened my door first, and I trailed behind him as a small child passes behind her father in a haunted house on Halloween weekend.

"Be careful," I said. "I spilled a mug of hot chocolate on the floor." My voice trembled just enough to give me away.

"Where is that little monster?" Gene asked.

"What?" The girl's staggering, creaking body was tattooed at the front of my mind.

"Where did you see that spider, darlin'?"

"It was on the door of the fridge." I felt guilty lying to such a sweet man, but at least he was going with it. He didn't question a thing.

His worn cowboy boots clicked across the kitchen as he approached the fridge, scanning it from top to bottom and side to side. White hairs crawled up his neck from below the collar of his grungy white tee shirt. Several more stuck out from his ears. "Must have gotten spooked when you ran." He chuckled. "I don't see anything here."

"It probably scuttled under the fridge. It's no big deal. I overreacted." I motioned to the mess of hot chocolate on the floor. "But thank you for trying," I continued while I mopped up the mess with a wad of generic paper towels. "I feel stupid, really. Maybe I was seeing things. It could have been a ball of dust."

"Oh, I'm sure you weren't, darlin'. Lots of creepy crawly bugs 'round here."

"Where did you say you were from?" I asked.

"Well, I've lived here for most of my life," he said. "Came here when me and Estelle were married."

I brushed my hair from my face with the back of my hand. Careful to avoid turning my back to the front of the house, I dropped the dripping wad of paper towels into the garbage can. "Your accent is still so prominent for having lived here for so long. You know, they say that people who are new to an area tend to adopt the dialect of their new surroundings."

He chuckled and huffed. "I suppose mine is so deep in me that it'll stick around forever. Not going anywhere."

"Exceptions to every rule, right?" I rinsed the sticky chocolate from my hands, one at a time, still conscious of the threshold to the foyer behind me.

"That's right." He smiled. "Well, if there's nothing else, I better be gettin' out of your hair, darlin'."

My heart dropped at the thought of being alone in the house again, but I didn't want to let Gene in on my discomfort any more than he already was. "Alrighty. Thanks again for trying, though. I'll hopefully have my head on straighter next time -- I won't come flying out of the house like a maniac." I chuckled uncomfortably.

"Don't you worry about it." He made his way toward the door. Reaching toward the handle, he turned back toward me and asked, "Are you sure there's nothing else I can help you with?"

"I'm sure. Thanks, Gene."

"Well, then, you have yourself a good afternoon, darlin'." He tipped his baseball cap and left.

The house felt hollow, as though the sound of a pin dropping would echo from wall to wall. I strained, but I heard nothing from the second floor, and there was no longer any creaking and groaning coming from the steps.

Maybe I had imagined it after all. It had seemed so real, though. I didn't think a dream or hallucination or whatever it might have been would be so realistic, so detailed.

There's no way, I thought.

I forced my legs to carry me to the base of the stairs, where I stood and stared upward for minutes, trying to understand what had happened only minutes before. But there was no sign of the girl's presence whatsoever. There were no prints, no puddles of the saliva that had been dripping from her mouth. There was nothing.

Did I really see a ghost?

Was that the same girl Mom babysat?

What happened to her?

Why was she in this house?

I sat on the couch, defeated, and dialed Mom's number. It rang three times before I ended the call. I didn't want to frighten her. I didn't need to drag her into it. She had her own things to tend to. I just needed to get out of this house, to get my mind off the girl. So, like any good writer, I started with the research.

CHAPTER 6

A small, golden bell tinkled from the top of the bookstore's entrance when I walked in. I brushed my windblown hair from my face, tucked it behind both ears, and pulled my scarf from around my neck before slipping it into my canvas shoulder bag. The small shop felt warm and inviting; the light in the room had a warm glow, and the smell of freshly ground coffee wafted toward me. My cheeks felt like they were thawing. I moved silently across the entryway, carefully taking in my surroundings as the carpet beneath my feet absorbed any sounds of my movement.

"Welcome to Chapter One. Is there anything I can help you find?" A young man spoke from behind the service desk. His question startled me, and he noticed.

"I ..." I smiled apologetically. "I'm looking for some books."

The House on Valley Street

He nodded, eyebrows raised, and glanced over his shoulder toward the aisles of used books filling the store. "Is this the part where I tell you you've come to the right place?"

Feeling foolish, I replied, "Well, I'm looking for a specific type of book."

He waited politely.

With a wince and a shrug, I gave a 'what-the-hell' sigh and asked, "Got any séance books?"

"Séance books?" He repeated. His tanned forehead wrinkled with his response. "You're one of those sorority girls, huh? Weekend with the ladies? Going to get a little crazy tonight? Conjure up some dead people?" His smile was charming, and his dark eyes wrinkled at the corners while his dimples deepened. His teeth glowed against his skin.

I knew how my request must have appeared. I assumed that I was probably not the only person who had asked for those books that day. "No, but if you know of any good parties, let me know." I winked exaggeratedly.

He smiled a youthful grin. "This way," he said. He turned from me and emerged from behind the service desk. "Our paranormal section has been getting a lot of attention lately. Halloween's coming sooner than you'd think."

I smiled politely but didn't respond. As I followed, I studied the way his jeans hung around his hips and how they just barely reached the bottom of his boots. He wore a fitted, gray tee shirt beneath a red apron tied at the nape of his neck and at his lower back. I noticed that his dark hair wisped slightly over his ears. "Here we are." He nodded in the direction of the aisle. "Is there any specific type of séance book you're looking for? We have 'how-to' books, we have books written by people who claim to be mediums, and we have books that take a more historical approach." He made air quotes on "historical."

"Well," I started, eyeing the shelves. "I'm looking for…" I was distracted by the titles: *Losing Love: A Guide to Conducting a Séance; When They're Gone; Contacting the Dead; My Journey into the Underworld.* "I'm sorry." I turned back to him. "I suppose I need to brush up on my, er, communication skills."

"And the living just doesn't float your boat anymore?" He crossed his arms and leaned casually against the shelf to his right.

I briefly wondered if he was doing that move that high school football players do during their team photos; was he crossing his arms so that he could push his muscles out and try to look tougher than he really was? "No. I, uh…" I scrunched my nose and said, "I'm living in a home that I think might be –

"Let me guess. Haunted?"

"It's not like that." I realized how ridiculous I sounded. "I'm not a sorority girl. I'm not even in college anymore. I'm actually writing a novel."

"So it's a house that only exists in your imagination?" He grinned sideways.

"No. I'm living in my mom's childhood home, and I'm writing a novel about it. She always believed it was haunted. And some strange things have been happening." I emphasized "strange."

"Strange things that go bump in the night?"

"No." I frowned and grew frustrated with this stranger who appeared to believe himself quite qualified to judge me. "I'd just feel more comfortable if I investigated some things further."

He held his hands up in front of him and stepped backward, as if giving up a fight. "Fair enough. If there's anything else you need, Miss, or if you don't find what you're looking for, let me know. My name's Dylan."

He pivoted on his heels and sauntered off, whistling the tune from *Snow White.* I scoffed and pulled my bag off my shoulder and placed it on the blue-gray carpet at my feet before squatting and running my fingers along the colorful spines of the books on the lower shelves. A thin layer of dust lay on each shelf. There were books about contacting deceased pets, becoming a medium, and helping spirits cross over to "the other side."

I paused when I noticed a text called *The Cultural Afterlife.* What might make an afterlife particularly cultural? The cover of the red book was rough. It had been covered in a thinly stretched fabric. Beneath the title was an etching of a howling wolf.

When I opened the book, the smell was tart and heavy; I could taste its age. The yellowed, onion-skin pages were stiff in my fingers, and the binding cracked when I opened it fully.

A small child ran past me, apparently in the middle of a session of Hide-and-Seek with the other children who attended the store's story time events. I closed the book until they were out of sight. Something about them knowing what I was reading made me uncomfortable, self-conscious. When they were gone, I read,

> "The Egyptian peoples believed that the afterlife simply represented yet another opportunity; therefore, the ancient peoples were put to rest with supplies sufficient to sustain living once the soul regenerated. Ancient Egyptians looked forward to the opportunity to put these items to use in a journey to what they felt would be an eternal paradise."

I paged further into the book, opening to the middle. I read,

> "Traveling into the afterlife requires the soul to pass through a journey, one that puts the soul to rest. Individual members of the tribe sought preparation of the journey prior to death."

I moved to the back of the book, some twenty pages before the end. There, I read,

> "The soul splits into two segments: the depraved and the pure. The depraved soul is escorted into the Underworld by malevolent, terrible creatures, whose sole existence is misery, whereas the pure soul joins deceased loved ones who serve as escorts into a land of everlasting ecstasy."

I closed the book with a thump and tucked it into my bag, briefly hoping that there were no cameras watching me. All I wanted was to use my messenger bag as a sort of shopping cart, but I knew how suspicious it must have appeared to tuck things away as I did. Maybe I was jaded.

I smiled briefly at a white-haired woman who eyed me from the end of the aisle. She merely averted her eyes from behind bifocals that were tethered to her neck by a turquoise beaded chain.

Before I was fully satisfied with my selection, I pulled two more books from the shelves: one on the general steps in conducting a séance and one memoir from the perspective of a female medium who claimed to specialize in helping spirits "cross over." I added them to my messenger bag and paced along the aisle once more, my boots dragging quietly along the thin carpet.

Near the front of the aisle, the topics of the texts turned to organic eating, and at the end, propaganda techniques. As it turned out, the paranormal section was quite small, though well-used.

At the service desk, Dylan routinely entered the cost of each book into his computer. As he worked, I eyed the red and blue posters on the wall advertising a Dr. Seuss Celebration Night. A stack of white business cards that said "Chapter One Books" and below, "DYLAN SLOAN, OWNER," was neatly piled beside an upcycled soup can filled with faux-daisy-topped pens.

"Do you buy people's used books?" I asked casually.

"Not exactly. We work on a consignment system. Six fifty, please."

While I fished through my bag for the money, he continued, "People bring in lots of books each weekend. We only take in inventory on Saturdays. If the book sells, we split the income from the sale, fifty, fifty."

"That's smart. Did some voodoo-practicing lady with a purple beehive hair-do and pop-bottle glasses bring these in?" I nodded toward my books.

He opened his eyes wide as if to say, *You have no idea.*

"That bad, huh?" I passed my money to him. "I can't help but feel like you don't believe in any of this." The entry bell rang again, and a middle-aged woman in a lightweight, gray pea coat entered the store with two small children, a boy and a girl, at her heels. Dylan greeted them with a polite, "Good afternoon," when they passed behind me.

"You're right," he said. "I don't." He stacked the three books and wrapped his long fingers around them. He opened a plastic bag with his other hand.

Before he could place the books in the bag, I stopped him. "I don't need a bag," I said. "I'll just put them in here." I held open my messenger bag. "Why?" I carefully lowered the books into my bag.

"Why, what?"

"Why don't you believe in this stuff?"

"No particular reason, I guess. I just don't." He paused with a slight smile. "Have a nice day." He nodded and added, "And good luck."

His short answer felt almost offensive to me, but why should a complete stranger open up to me about his beliefs, anyway? I turned toward the door. "Thanks."

The air outside was crisp. The sun was warm, but the breeze was bitter, as it often is on early autumn days. My messenger bag kept beat with my steps, slapping against my hip. I slid my hands into the pockets of my jacket and wove through small crowds on the sidewalk. Two men wore gym shorts, and each pushed a stroller, speaking in brief spurts to one another. A woman wearing a taupe trench coat and clicking, high-heeled boots strolled past, talking authoritatively into a cell phone. Her long, blonde hair waved in the light wind. At the end of the block stood a small group of teenagers, all underdressed for the chill weather and holding Styrofoam cups of hot chocolate, chatting excitedly about a matinee film they had just seen in the nearby movie theater.

My shoes smashed crisp leaves. I envisioned the pages of the books in my bag waving back and forth with my steps. I wasn't exactly sure of what I was going to do with those books. Surely I wasn't actually considering carrying out a séance in that strange home by myself. *Is a solo séance even possible?*

To me, the books were more of a comfort. I wanted to learn about people's belief structures. Even if there truly was nothing supernatural happening in the home, and even if all of the things that happened there were in my imagination, I comforted myself in knowing the information in those books would nevertheless be useful for my novel.

CHAPTER 7

I sat at the kitchen table, laptop and books at the ready. The wooden chair was cold against my back, and I rubbed my hands together while my computer started up. I sipped fresh hot chocolate and crunched on several tiny marshmallows that floated in the mug.

I fluidly ticked at the keys, tapping my bare toes on the linoleum. I listened to the familiar voice that played out from my small recorder, and my fingers effortlessly kept pace. It took only minutes to transcribe the entire recording.

After reviewing the layout of the home, I thought it an appropriate time to dive into the books I'd purchased. I started with the medium's perspective in a text called *Dimensions Unseen*. What better place to start?

I nestled the book in front of me, pushed away the laptop, and tucked the rest of the books away to the other end of the small table. I positioned a brand new, crisp-paged notebook, one of my favorite things, beside me.

The woman on the cover was older, at least in her sixties. She wore her hair in a short, tight perm that was slightly reminiscent of a poodle I had seen on the way back from the bookstore. The woman's name was Claudette Paxton, and she wore a high-necked, glittering black sweater and very heavy eye shadow. I smiled. The book designers must have been going for the card-reading, fortune-telling, wide-eyed stereotype.

I flipped to the back cover. It read,

"Claudette Paxton is a renowned medium who has gifted the world with tales from the other side in three books: *Life Beyond Loss, The Wide Other Side,* and the newest installment, *Dimensions Unseen.* She currently resides in Baltimore, where she lives with her husband, two sons, and Golden Retriever, Ruger."

I paged through the book, skimming passages I thought might hold some meaning for the house. Each chapter read more like a fairytale, beginning with lines like, "There once was a young girl who…" and "This is the story of a young man who…" The fragmented retellings only gave me examples; they didn't tell me what any of them *meant*.

Toward the end of the book, there was one story Paxton titled "A Boy and his Gift," which caught my attention. Perhaps it was the photos that gripped me more. One was of a young boy kneeling on a baseball field, one hand holding a wooden bat that rested on his shoulder, the other hand draped casually over his knee. He wore pinstriped pants with knee-high, white socks and a firetruck-red jersey with a matching cap. His smile was slight, subdued, so as to maintain an air of athletic toughness, I assumed. But there was a smile in his slightly downturned eyes.

The other photo was nothing but a tree in someone's backyard.

The accompanying story read,

"The following story takes precedence in my mind above most other encounters I've experienced in my full, hectic career.
When I was in my early fifties, I came across a young man named Dennis Rodriguez, who, along with his entire family – mother, father, and teenaged sister -- had tragically passed away in a horrible motor vehicle accident on the way to one of his Little League baseball games."

I was intrigued. I continued.

"Dennis came to me by way of his baseball glove, which I had purchased at an early-summer rummage sale in a small Iowa town I was passing through on a book tour. Of course, I knew nothing of his story at the time, so I purchased the glove for my grandson to use during his summer visits to my home.

"After purchasing the glove, I placed it, along with several other small trinkets I had purchased, in a plastic crate in the backseat of my van and continued on my way. When I had driven no more than five miles down the highway, I heard a loud thud coming from somewhere behind my seat. I assumed a bird may have flown into the side of my van, or perhaps one of my tires had kicked up a stone that had hit the vehicle's undercarriage. I pulled over shortly thereafter to examine the vehicle, but there was no damage, no chips, nothing out of the ordinary. On a whim, I checked the backseat.

I discovered then that the baseball glove had exhumed itself from the crate while I was driving and had violently hurdled itself into the rear passenger window. I found it wedged between the door and the seat.

"Of course, in my line of work, this type of thing is perhaps interesting, curious even, but not out of the ordinary, not even jostling, generally. But when I lifted the glove, it tore from my hands and flew again toward the crate. It felt alive, aware. It moved when it wanted to. It seemed to me that the glove had some vendetta, some information to convey.

"That night, I established a communication line with Dennis, using his glove as a sort of harness for his energy. During our session, Dennis revealed to me that there was something he needed me to do. He requested -- quite politely, may I add -- that I return to his home and find the Father's Day gift he had hidden in the backyard. He asked that I bring it to his father's grave.

"The following weekend, I travelled to Dennis's home, located the large maple with a hanging branch, stood with my back facing the tree and my front facing the home, and sidestepped twice, just as Dennis had asked me to do. I turned around and found a small package tucked into a hidden nook of the tree.

"After hurrying from the yard in fear of needing to explain myself (which isn't easy in my line of work), I drove to the cemetery, found the family's headstones, and buried the small gift alongside his father's grave. I never found out what the gift was, but I must say, I am still terribly curious."

I frowned. I was baffled for a moment, and I didn't know whether I believed what I had read.

Why would a young child haunt his baseball glove, of all things? That didn't make any sense.

And weren't ghosts supposed to be people who were violently murdered and whose bodies were lying in unrest somewhere, awaiting a proper burial or justice or something?

And is a Father's Day gift really worth a soul's unrest?

It just didn't add up for me. But for whatever reason, I couldn't stop thinking about this woman and this boy's story.

For one thing, it made me miss my parents. This boy's concern for his father's happiness on Father's Day moved me. My eyes burned with unshed tears as I remembered watching a home video of myself as a small child giving my dad a handmade birthday card when he turned 32. I remembered my mom's voice behind the camera, telling me to hand the card to Daddy. And when I did, he knelt in front of me, read the card, and afterward, hugged me tightly and for a long time. I remember his eyes were red and wet when he pulled away.

But now wasn't the time for me to be emotional. I didn't need to start feeling sorry for myself. And so I resolved to finish my exploration of the home. There was only one place I hadn't yet ventured to: the basement.

There was something about basements that always made people fearful, especially the dark corners and cold, moist air. A basement felt like a void, like the "other" area of the house, so vastly different from the warm, lived-in main floor. People always talked about feeling the hair stand up on the backs of their necks when they walked up basement stairs, constantly fearing an echo to their footsteps, wondering what would happen if something followed them up the steps.

I stood from the kitchen table and closed Paxton's book. Assuming the basement would be chilled, I zipped my sweatshirt all the way to my chin and headed toward the basement door, which stood in the kitchen, opposite the screen door.

The basement door didn't close on its own and was held closed via a small hook that attached to the frame. I lifted the hook and gazed down into the darkness as the cool air washed over my feet.

One foot in front of the other, I padded down the steps, which were lit only minimally from the kitchen. The closest light was a bare lightbulb and pull string at the base of the stairs, which were warm, surprisingly, in comparison to the air. Each step creaked. A chill crawled up my spine each time that my heel touched a new step. I envisioned a hand reaching through the back of the stairwell and clasping its icy fingers around my ankle. I stepped quickly, just in case.

As my eyes adjusted to the darkness, I began to see clearly the cement floor and the lightbulb at the base of the stairs. A couple of boxes were stacked along a limestone wall that faced me. At the bottom of the steps, I reached up and gripped the chain that fell from the lightbulb and hesitated. I briefly considered whether the new light might show me something I didn't want to see. I imagined, too, something reaching for my back slowly, shakily, then limping away madly, fleeing from the light like a vampire from a crucifix.

What I didn't know couldn't hurt me, though.

I scoffed at myself and rolled my eyes exaggeratedly before tugging on the chain. The bulb ticked to life above my head and lit the small space with a dull glow. I ran my hand along the damp limestone wall, tracing the crevices between each rock with my index finger and thumb. To the right of the stairwell was an open storage space that curved back along the stairwell and extended beyond it. A dark doorway stood at the far end; beyond it was only blackness.

As my fear rose again, the backs of my knees trembled, and I felt the urge to leap up the stairs. But I waited. I listened. Only the dull hum of silence reached my ears.

Ignoring the image of the hobbling girl staggering down the stairs to me, I took a deep gulp of a breath and lowered my hand from the wall. I needed to check this area out. This was the whole reason I came down.

Research, I told myself. *This is research.*

I couldn't ignore the room that lay through the dark doorway. It looked as though the doorway was directly below the outside wall of the home. This extra room was more of a bunker than a basement space; it wasn't under the house. It was just under the ground.

I lightly fingered the few boxes that lay along the wall. In one was a stack of towels and oil-stained rags. In another were newspaper-wrapped dishes. And on top of the boxes was a pile of browning newspapers that crisped like onionskin at my touch. The only thing I found of remote interest was an old hat. It must have been an antique. It appeared to be made of a light rawhide. The brim spanned widely, and it curled up around the edges. Age had warped its shape. The cream color darkened to a golden brown on the inside, where years of dust and sweat had sunken in and dried.

The rest of the space was bare and cold and smelled of must. Despite the stereotype, though, it appeared quite clean. There were no cobwebs or thick layers of dust. The space was simply bare.

I drug my bare feet along the icy concrete and moved along the side of the stairwell toward the dark room.

There's got to be another light in there, I thought.

I could have gone upstairs to find a flashlight, but it was unlikely that I would have found the courage to return to the basement after obtaining one.

I hugged the wall and inched across the threshold. In the blackness, I caught sight of a shimmer, a light spot.

Another step forward.

It was white. Or was it silver?

Another step forward.

Was it moving?

Another step forward.

It was hovering two feet from the ceiling.

Another step forward.

I recognized it. It was only a small, silver ball tethered to the end of another lightbulb's pull string. I reached for it again slowly and drew it downward.

When I retracted my hand, it was covered in sticky, stringy webs that had been wrapped around the pull string.

By comparison, this room belonged in another house. It was filthy. The putrid odor of stagnant water and backed-up sewer filled my sinuses. Wiping my hand across my thigh, I spun in place and surveyed the area. Black mold clung to the corners. A thick layer of dust clung to the top of the lightbulb.

The walls seemed to seep acridity. Nothing lay in this room but an already-tripped mousetrap dotted with dried blood.

I frowned at the thought of a small, furry, terrified mouse writhing and spinning and struggling when the trap clamped down on its back, failing to snap its neck. I remembered the sound from my childhood home. In the early hours one morning, when the house was all but silent, a trap had suddenly snapped, and its wooden base dragged and clicked against the floor for seconds that felt like minutes. I lay in bed, tugged the blanket around my chin, and listened helplessly to the panicked shrieks that escaped the mouse.

I shivered.

Poor things, I thought. *Live traps aren't impossible—*

And then I heard it.

Behind me, a low, groaning creak sounded, not unlike the sound that the girl's footsteps had made on the stairs. Its pitch steadily climbed higher and higher before coming to a sudden stop. My body was covered in goose bumps. I pivoted with a painstaking slowness, my chin leading over my right shoulder.

Just beyond the doorway lay an open door that led to a storage area beneath the stairs, a cubby. The door was open wide. My feet cement blocks, I urged myself to move toward it. My fingertips had gone numb, while heat coursed through my face and neck.

I peered around the open door and into the cubby, which seemed to stretch forever, far beyond the far side of the stairwell. My knees twitched with the urge to turn and run back up the stairs and into the warm, well-lit kitchen, but my feet, seemingly bolted to the cold concrete, stayed planted.

Several feet inside the cubby was mounted yet another bare bulb. I stretched a trembling hand out in front of me, and just as my fingertips were reaching past the point of my sight and into the blackness, a rush of cold air blew through my fingers. I gasped and retracted my hand violently, happening to slap the lightbulb's pull string, sending it into a pendulum swing. The chain tapped the bare bulb with an echoing *tick, tick, tick.*

As the chain swung, it slowly came into focus, but only on its backswing. For a fraction of a second, I could see the rusted ball before it swung away from me again.

Lips slightly parted, eyes narrowed, I reached forward and waited, measuring the string's pattern:

to,

fro,

to,

fro.

I gripped the chain and tugged.

The bulb shed a glow on wet cement walls. They led some twenty feet along a narrow corridor that passed below and behind the staircase. It lit only half the distance.

The House on Valley Street

Though my scalp and ears tingled and sweat pooled in my palms, I inched my way into the cubby, the fingers of one wet hand wrapped around the doorframe, clinging to it like a life raft.

I don't know what I was looking for or what I expected to see. I don't know why I kept moving forward. But I did.

I let go of the doorframe.

The corridor was narrow enough that I could turn both hands away from my sides and drag my fingers along the damp stone walls. The ceiling lay just above my head such that an average-sized man would need to duck to move through. While my feet shuffled seemingly of their own accord, the edge of the darkness moved closer. It shuddered and bobbed in time with my pulse pounding in my throat.

My curiosity had gotten the better of me. I suddenly wanted to know what lay beyond the edge. What, if anything, dwelled in the blackness?

Time crawled while I moved along the narrow passageway. When I reached the edge of the light and lined my toes along the threshold as though it were a 50-meter start line, I stared further into the shadows. The shadow was a brick wall as dense as the concrete I stood on. The darkness was a poisonous gas that I couldn't touch. It was the lava of which children feign fright while hopping from couch to chair and couch again. It was danger.

The House on Valley Street

I gradually began to make out a shape against the back wall of the cubby. The bulk of its mass lay close to the ground, perhaps hip-high on me. Something tall and narrow extended straight above it along the wall. I blinked furiously and squinted, waiting for the image to take shape in front of me.

It came in pieces.

There was a rounded edge near the top of the mass, and the shape below widened, then narrowed again. But the shape was not solid. I could see bits of wall through gaps in the mass. The rounded edge gradually came into focus and then its neck and then its shoulders and then its arms shackled above it and its legs folded beneath it.

I turned and ran up the stairs, trusting that the echoing I heard was only a reverberation of sound, and not something following in my footsteps.

CHAPTER 8

"I need to talk to you," I said to the guy named Dylan at the service desk of his new and used bookstore.

"Find the ghoulies you were looking for?" he asked, not a bit thrown by my aggression. He grinned but didn't look away from the computer screen he was seated at.

"No. Maybe," I stuttered. "I don't know."

He raised an eyebrow and slowly leaned back in his chair. "Are you going to tell me you saw something spooky? And you need more books about the subject?"

I tucked my hair behind my ear and composed myself briefly with a deep breath and heavy exhale. "Actually," I nearly shouted, "I don't want more books *on the subject*. I'm wondering if you can tell me where I might find a public records building."

"And what exactly does that have to do with me?"

"You happen to be the only person in this town who I know -- sort of know." I tapped my fingers along the top of the desk near his stack of business cards. "And I thought you might be willing to help me."

A young father in a suit and tie and his two small boys dressed in pirate costumes stepped up to the desk, ready to check out. He smiled politely, and I stepped aside.

"Find everything you were looking for?" Dylan asked the man cheerfully. My heart lurched warmly at the sincerity in his friendliness. His smile shone through his dark eyes, which wrinkled slightly at the corners.

"We did. Thank you," the father answered.

"We found five!" The youngest boy placed three books on the desk.

Dylan chuckled at the child and tapped at the cash register. "Five? Well, that should keep you busy for a while."

Their loose conversation continued while I stood and waited, glancing from my feet to the various tables strategically placed about the store to the signs that hung from the ceiling above each aisle of books. I noticed a film section at the back of the store.

When the children's books were bagged and paid for, Dylan wished the family a good day and returned his attention to me. When the bell at the top of the door indicated that they had left, he said, "What do you need public records for?"

The House on Valley Street

"I was hoping to research the property I'm living in." I sighed. I knew this sounded incredibly cliché, but it was the truth.

"Well, it's a small town. I've lived here my whole life. I might know something."

"Really?" My eyes widened, and I subtly squared my shoulders.

"Yeah. But I'll need something from you." He lowered his voice and leaned further across the counter, wordlessly beckoning me to do the same.

I glanced around and leaned in. "What?"

"Your address." He sat still and smirked at me.

Wow.

I frowned and stood straighter still as something between a grown and a sigh escaped me. "Do you know where Valley Street is?" I asked, my cheeks burning.

"Sure do."

"It's the gray, two-story house."

"The one that's been empty for a while?"

"That's the one."

"Hmph." He curved a fist under his chin in animated thought. "I've heard some things," he said.

I waited.

When he didn't say anything, I asked, "And?"

"Well, I'd love to talk to you about it more, but you see, I'm a little preoccupied with work at the moment." He indicated the all-but-empty retail space. "But if you'd like, I can get ahold of you after work." In one fluid motion, he snatched a business card from the stack on top of the desk and slapped it and a pen on the counter in front of me. "Just leave me your phone number, and I'll get back to you."

I raised an eyebrow.

"I won't stalk you or anything. I'll call you after work." He smiled that sincere smile of his.

"What time is that?" I carefully took the pen and printed my phone number onto the card. I paid special attention to my handwriting. Handwriting told a lot about a girl, I'd always thought.

"I'm closing at 6 tonight. In the meantime, try doing some research online. You'll probably find some interesting stuff there. There must be some kind of public records available."

"Right." I tucked my hair behind my ear. "I probably should have tried that earlier." I dropped the pen onto the countertop and reached across to hand him the business card. When he reached for it, I couldn't help but hope that our hands would touch, that I could feel his warmth, but it was a fleeting hope.

A young couple, who I thought were the store's only remaining patrons at the time, were headed toward us, each towing a small stack of books, and I took that as my cue to leave. I thanked Dylan for his willingness to help and excused myself from the store.

The air was getting colder, colder than was typical for early autumn. The midafternoon sun shone through the trees that lined the street. I watched each line in the sidewalk pass beneath my feet, a child's rhyme repeating itself in my mind: *Step on a crack, break your mother's back. Step on a crack, break your mother's back.*

I knew the rhyme was nothing, but Mom had already been through so much that I thought it best to avoid the cracks anyway. Just to be safe.

I tightened the belt around my waist and tucked my hands into the pockets of my peacoat. I cursed the world every time my purse slid from the top of my shoulder and I had to take my hand out of my pocket again to resituate it.

Few people shared the sidewalk with me. None of the shops I passed seemed to be filled with customers, either. One shop called Midday Sun was full of what looked to be handmade décor. There were some moon paintings, some incense, lots of candles. It must have smelled great in there. But the only person inside was the owner, who was unloading boxes into a display at the window. She nodded at me and smiled as I walked by.

Since kids had gone back to school, I assumed it must have been a slow week in town altogether. Even the traffic was slow. It was peaceful, though. Birds tweeted. The sound of the wind passing through bunches of crisp leaves made me feel warm, despite the chill.

I remained securely in my own mind for the entirety of my walk back to the house. I thought about everything – Mom, the hospital, her recovery, Dylan, whether our meeting that night would be awkward, Lucee -- but I didn't think about the house at all until I saw it.

How could the outside world be so alive, so friendly, but the inside of my home, however temporary, was spiraling into a Stephen King novel? Maybe stress did have something to do with it – with me and the way I was *perceiving* things. Mom's stroke was a lot to take in. I *was* unemployed, though money wasn't keeping me awake at night; my savings account was all that I needed for a few months. To say that I was questioning my career choice was an understatement, but still, hallucinations?

Something drove me to look into each window facing the street as I approached the house, just to be sure that no drooling, double-jointed ghost-child peered back at me. Of course, I saw nothing. I knew I would see nothing – nothing but aged, lacey curtains. But I was dubious, nonetheless.

The door handle was warm in my chilled hands, and when I turned it, a welcoming rush of warmth poured from inside. The house felt clean. Safe. Maybe this was just your typical home, after all. Maybe all those tenants who fled had financial issues, or maybe they were criminals. Maybe they had family emergencies.

I checked the time. There were still two hours to fill before Dylan would be calling.

In the kitchen, I glanced at the floor where my puddle of hot chocolate had been after the incident on the stairs, and I shivered but quickly pushed it from mind. I couldn't focus on that if I wanted to write. I wouldn't be able to get anything on paper.

The chair at the kitchen table drug noisily against the floor, and it felt unwelcoming, rock-hard against my back, like it didn't *want* to be sat on. I opened my laptop and began my search with the county's public records website.

I perused the site, but most of what it offered were birth records, marriage and divorce records, and obituaries. I was expecting to sit in front of a screen and click through newspaper clippings like all the protagonists do in the scary movies, swiping across murder stories and missing children files and unexplained disappearances, but there was nothing like that available publicly. I suppose I could have gone into a newspaper archive, but online access cost money that I wasn't yet desperate enough to spend.

Just as I was about to forfeit, I found a search link on real estate transfers among click-bait ads for a dating website ("Hot singles in YOUR area!") and a (FREE) weight-loss consultation ("10 foods you should NEVER eat"). If I wasn't going to be able to dig into murder mysteries and the like, at least I could look into the very real world of property records. The search bar required only an address and a city.

My search returned only two results. *How could there be only two results if so many families had lived here over the years?* I thought, frowning.

The first was a deed transfer that occurred in 1966, when my grandmother purchased the home from a man named Donald Baker and his wife, Glenda. The second was in 1987, when my grandmother sold the home to a couple listed as Mr. and Mrs. E. Hexton. I clicked on the transaction, but there were little details available. It said that the transaction occurred on April 17, 1987, and that the cost of the home was below the national median value for home sales.

I chewed absently on the back of a ballpoint pen, considering the ways that this information could possibly be useful, but I couldn't come up with anything. I probably could have guessed that the home had sold for less than a fair price, and the names of the people who owned the home told me nothing. I guess I'm not sure what I was looking for. My expectations had been muddled by years of horror flicks.

I closed my laptop harder than was necessary and with a case of mental whiplash, started suddenly to think about Dylan. *He'll be here soon. I mean, he would call me soon. Then he'll be here. He* will *be here, right? Or are we meeting somewhere?*

In the bathroom, I smoothed my hair against my head and tugged my bangs to the side, so that they lay just so. *This is weird. Is this weird?* I'd just met him, and I was suddenly concerned about the way I looked. Admittedly, my hair was less than impressive, though he had already seen it at the bookstore that day. In a word, I looked ... lackluster.

Hairspray bottle in hand, I fluffed and sprayed a messy-on-purpose ponytail and pinned my bangs back from my face, which, now that I looked at it, could use a touch up, too. I darkened my liner, curled my lashes, added mascara, and dabbed some pink gloss onto my lips. I didn't want to look like I was trying. But I *was* trying -- at least a little.

I stood perpendicular to the mirror and turned my head every time I needed to see myself, examining the way my sweater clung to my midsection. I couldn't bring myself to look squarely into the mirror, anyway. I wouldn't turn my back on the rest of the house – on the stairs.

Every gust of autumn wind sent a creak passing through the house like a wave. The heat kicked on, and the low roar frightened me – not as though I wasn't expecting it; the roar felt like a growl, conjuring images in my mind that sent chills down my spine. It was as though the furnace was snarling at me, the walls working up to a guttural scream.

I jumped when my phone vibrated in the back pocket of my jeans. I took a deep breath, assuming that the caller ID number belonged to Dylan.

It was a text from Lucee.

> What are you doing tonight? You want to get dinner?

I replied,

> Sorry! I'm going out with –

No, that wasn't quite right. I deleted it, then tried again.

> I have plans –

Too curt.

> Sorry! I'm doing some research for my novel. ☹

Thank God for the frowny-face. What did we do before the frowny-face?

The phone vibrated again. I braced myself for Lucee's retort, but this time, it was Dylan calling.

"Hello?" I asked, a minor tremble in my voice. My heart was beating fast.

"Sophia? It's Dylan."

"Hi."

"Hi."

We paused and each waited for the other person to speak. Phone conversations are so awkward.

"So, do you want to meet somewhere to talk about your ghoulie house?" I could hear the smile in his tone, and it warmed me somewhere in my belly.

"Sure. I don't know many places around here, though. You might have to give me directions." I noticed a smudge of mascara under my eye and stepped to the mirror, wiping it away with my index finger until I suddenly realized that I'd turned my back to the doorway. I leapt backward and turned slightly, still rubbing below my eye.

He chuckled briefly and said, "There's a coffee place across the street from the bookstore. Does that sound okay?"

"Yeah. Er," I glanced around, though I don't know what I was looking for. My courage, maybe. "I can be there in 15 minutes. I'll walk."

"Are you sure? I can pick you up."

"I'm sure. I could use the exercise." *Stupid. Cliché. Why did I say that?*

"Alrighty then," he said. "I'll see you in about 15 minutes."

I tucked my phone into my pocket and swiftly grabbed my jacket off the console table along the stairs and tore out of the house, slamming the door behind me, glad to be rid of the burden the home seemed to carry if only for an hour or two more.

The air smelled of burned leaves, one of my favorite scents. It brought back memories of working in the yard with my dad. I smiled and kept a brisk pace toward the book store, thankful for social interaction and for an excuse to spend more time out of the house – not "out of the house" as in the common phrase, but out of *that* house.

CHAPTER 9

The walk took less time than I had anticipated, and about ten minutes after I had left home, I spotted the café. Its brick façade was well lit in the waning daytime. A wrought iron sign reading "Mocha Minute" perched above a maroon awning. I peered inside and spotted Dylan sitting at a table near the entrance. He still wore his fitted t-shirt and loose jeans, well-worn boots at the bottom. The only thing missing was his red apron.

When I walked in, a tall brunette girl called from behind the counter, "Welcome to Mocha Minute!" The warm smell of fresh coffee hung in the air.

I half-waved in her direction before heading toward Dylan, who smiled politely.

"How was your workout?" he asked.

"Workout?" He caught me off guard, and I tried to process his comment as I draped my jacket over the back of my chair. "Oh! My walk? You're a funny guy." I feigned comfort with him, mimicking his tone, even though I could feel the tension in my shoulders mounting.

"I'd like to think so."

I sat and suddenly became very interested in the silver aluminum stars mounted to the wall behind Dylan.

"So what would you like?" He nodded toward the wall-mounted, backlit menu behind me. It was full of handwritten specials in pink and green fluorescent markers.

"Did you order already?"

"No. I thought I'd wait for you. You know, to be polite."

I felt a warm sensation rise from my stomach and spread into my face. I smirked briefly, then bit my lower lip. "Um," I said, "I'll just have hot chocolate, I think. It's kind of my thing this time of year."

"Got it." I watched him walk to the brunette girl and order two hot chocolates with whipped cream. And I watched her grin at him, clearly taken by his charm. A moment later, he was headed back to the table, carefully balancing a too-full mug in each hand. She watched him the whole way.

"There ya be," he said, placing a mug in front of me and situating himself in his seat once again.

"Thank you. How much do I owe you?" I blushed, realizing that I should have sent money with him when he went to order. Better yet, I should have ordered for myself. He didn't need to do that.

"Nothing." He shook his head and sipped at his mug.

"No, really. How much? It's the least I could do since you agreed to meet with me."

"Nothing." His bright green eyes peered over his mug. "It was on the house."

"What do you mean?"

"I know the family who owns this place. I used to work here when I was in college."

"Oh, wow." My stubborn eyes darted to those silver stars again. "Well, thank you." I took a sip of the rich, thick liquid.

"Don't mention it." He handed me a drink napkin. "So. Your house."

I dabbed at my mouth. "I looked online, but there really wasn't much to look at."

"What did you find?"

"Next to nothing." I took another drink from my mug and winced when it burned the roof of my mouth. "I got the names of the past two owners and proof that it sold for less-than-market value. That's about it."

"Riveting information."

"I know. What do the people around here think about that house? I'm sure there have been loads of rumors flying around since no family ever seems to stay there for longer than a few months."

"Lots of rumors," he said, running a hand over his short, dark hair. "I've heard everything from alien invasions to sacred burial grounds."

"Is there any proof to any of those theories?"

"Nope."

I frowned and waited. *If he didn't know anything for sure, why did he offer to tell me what he knew?*

"But there is a common theme among the more reliable sources, I guess," he continued. "A lot of people seem to think that there used to be a cemetery where the house is now."

"Doesn't that happen more often than the public realizes? I mean, states exhume bodies and move cemeteries as necessary, right? Happens all the time."

He raised an eyebrow. "Uh, first of all, I don't know how it is where you're from, but I've never heard of anybody moving an entire cemetery. And the problem isn't that they moved the cemetery. It's that they moved the headstones but not the bodies."

"Like that movie from the eighties?"

"Which movie?"

"The one where the girl gets sucked into the TV."

"Poltergeist?"

"Yep. That's it. That was a pretty pertinent plot point in the story."

"Well, I don't know about that, but that's what a lot of people believe. And the house has been there longer than that movie's been around, you know."

"I can't use that, though. That would be plagiarism." I twirled the stir stick in my mug.

"Not if it's true. And you're trying to write a true story, right?"

"As true as I can."

"Why?"

That wasn't a question that I had really anticipated. Who asks a writer why she wants to write something? I've heard questions about inspiration and the like, but not such a blatant *Why?* like that.

"My mom grew up in that house, and she always told me stories. This summer, she had a stroke. And I guess I wanted to write to provide some legitimacy to her stories – and maybe occupy my mind a little."

Dylan sat listening to me politely, genuinely considering what I had said. "In that movie," he asked, "was there anything specific about the bodies?"

"I don't think so," I said.

"Well, the people around here think that the bodies all belonged to a single family, like a private cemetery."

"If it was private, how did the state get ahold of the rights to it?"

"I don't think they did. None of the stories make the people who moved the headstones seem very respectable -- not really the law-abiding types."

"How many?"

"How many what?"

"How many bodies?"

"I've heard people say there were around 10, and I've heard people say there were more like 40."

"Has anyone ever gone digging?"

"Like to dig up the bodies?" He chuckled.

"Yeah. Why not try to fix the problem?"

"I don't know. People don't usually do that kind of stuff. I guess it's just a story that kids tell each other while they sneak around the house on Halloween."

"Do you know how it started?"

"Are you sure you're not a reporter? You're good at the questioning thing." He watched me fiddle with my fingernails as I listened. I shrugged with a smile in response. "I guess there was a body found there years ago," he said. "A few decades after the house was built, the owners decided to do some landscaping and ended up finding a body – that's what the stories say. There was an investigation, but nothing really came of it. Everyone believed it was the body of a girl who had gone missing a few years earlier. Then the story sort of faded away."

The image of the girl on the stairs flashed in my memory so vividly that I jumped, splashing hot chocolate on the wooden tabletop.

"How do you know all of this?" I dabbed at the mess in front of me, suddenly hyper-aware of the brunette girl, who was cleaning tables nearby, and I leaned in closer to Dylan.

"My grandfather told me the stories. I lived with him."

"Is he close? Maybe I can talk to him, too."

"He died."

"I'm sorry." I sheepishly stared at the melting whipped cream swirling on the surface of what was left of my hot chocolate.

"It's okay. He's got to be happier now."

I waited for him to continue, but I wasn't going to ask. I didn't want to pry.

"He had cancer. We didn't find out until he died, though. We knew something was wrong. We knew he was sick, but he never got any help. He hated doctors."

"I know the feeling." I thought of how angry Mom was when she found out about her stroke. She blamed the doctor. She loathed him. *"Those fuckers did this to me!"* she'd said on one particularly rough morning after struggling to bathe herself.

The tone of our conversation had suddenly shifted, and it felt uncomfortable. I had just met Dylan, and I was already prying into his emotions.

"Do you know the name of the family?"

"What?"

"The name of the family who owned the cemetery?"

"No. But some people say they were all members of the Pakutset tribe. There are still a lot of members around here."

I pulled a pen from my purse and wrote the tribe's name on the back of my hand.

"I've never heard of that tribe. Then again, I guess my knowledge of early American history is lacking."

He smiled comfortingly and tipped his mug back, draining it. "A lot of people have never heard of us."

"Us?"

"My family is part of it. Distantly, but still a part. Grandma Iris makes sure we all know it."

"Very cool." *Cool? Come on, Sophia,* I thought. *You've got to do better than that.* But I didn't know anything about modern tribal practices or whether there even were any.

"No."

"No, what?" I asked.

He smirked. "I don't have a headdress or loin cloth or anything."

I paused only a moment to picture him in a loin cloth, then shook the thought away. "So what exactly does it mean to be a member of a Native American tribe? Are there certain ceremonies or anything that you take part in? Or is there an annual convention?" I chuckled to myself.

"Oh, you're funny," he said, glancing to the brunette girl who was now sweeping the floor behind the counter. "We mostly pass stories among ourselves. It's an identity, I guess, more than a club membership."

I tucked my pen back into my purse and followed Dylan's eyeline to the girl who was clearly beginning her end-of-the-night routine.

"What time does this place close?" I asked him.

He glanced at the clock on the wall. "Fifteen minutes ago."

"Shit. We should get out of here. I'm sure she wants to." I nodded toward the girl.

Dylan smirked again before gathering our mugs and bringing them to the counter for the girl. Back at the table, he shrugged his jacket over his shoulders and tucked his stool in.

"Thanks for meeting me here," I said, buttoning my jacket. I swung my purse over my shoulder.

He held the door open for me and waved back at the girl. "Thanks, Audree," he called. The door swung closed behind us, and the cold breeze hit my face sharply. "No problem," he said. "I'm glad I could help."

I shivered and lifted the collar of the jacket around my neck. *Audree, huh?*

"Do you want a ride home?" he asked, noticing my chill. He tapped a button, and the red coupe in front of us beeped.

In a second, I thought back to the advice given to me as a child about never getting into a car with a stranger. "No, thanks. It's not far." I smiled politely. "But I appreciate the offer."

"Suit yourself. Have a good night. You'll have to let me know where the research takes you." He saluted me and opened the driver door as I turned away.

Was that an invitation to sit down together again? No. He probably just meant that if I happen to run into him in the bookstore again, then he might be interested to know how the book is coming along. That's all.

"Sophia?"

I froze and wondered if this was a romantic comedy. All I was missing was the rain. *Is he going to ask me out on a real date?*

"I forgot to give you this," he called. When he reached me, he held out his hand and offered me a book. I'd be lying if I said my heart didn't sink at least a little. I don't know what I was hoping for, but yet again, movies skewed my perception of a realistic night if only for a moment at a time.

I accepted the book. "Thanks."

"It's a cleansing book." He held double quotes in the air.

In response to my expression, he continued. "You know. Blow some smoke around your house and tell the spirits to get lost." He winked. "I thought you'd like it." He zipped his leather jacket to his chin. "Let me know how it goes." He turned on his heel and headed back to the car, leaving me to page through the book on my chilled walk home, relying on sporadic bouts of light shining from streetlamps in order to see the words. But the task proved impossible, so I tucked it into my bag, buried my hands in my pockets, and doubled my pace.

Despite the chill in the air, a warmth rose from my belly and spread up my neck and across my jaw, sprawling like vines on an abandoned brick building. For the first time in a while, I wasn't worrying about something I couldn't control. I wasn't feeling anxious about how my decisions, my choices would affect the next step in my life. I wasn't butterfly-effecting my life in fast forward.

I knew that the way I was feeling was ridiculous and that Dylan was just trying to help me – platonic, that's all. Plus, I'd literally just met him. Maybe it was just the human contact I was infatuated with; no – that couldn't be it. Dylan was gorgeous. And polite. And funny.

Rather than becoming my usual self and thinking myself out of my happiness, I shrugged my shoulders in a *what-the-hell* sort of way, and I decided to go with it. Stop thinking. I was happy. I was giddy. *Don't think.*

I deeply inhaled the smell of burning leaves and exhaled with a soothing sigh. The dark was not frightening; it was calming, comfortable, even. The sound of my feet skipping and tapping along the sidewalk created a rhythm I almost swayed to. A few blocks away, a dog barked once or twice.

About a block ahead of me, someone was sharing the night, and she was walking my way. I briefly contemplated crossing the street and using the other sidewalk to give her space, but I knew that would make me look paranoid. I'd just have to avert my eyes to avoid the awkward eye contact that goes with things like this. Or maybe I could take the high road and give her a nod and smile like normal people did. I'd be prepared. *Smile. Eye contact,* I told myself, squaring my shoulders as I walked.

As she got closer, I noticed that her footsteps mirrored mine. I reveled in the volume increase on my personal beat. It wasn't often that I came across someone with the same or even a similar gait as myself. I was far too short compared to anyone else. My little legs had to move quicker.

She must have noticed me, too, because she stepped off the sidewalk and continued walking on the edge of the road. She passed just beyond the scope of the streetlights so that I could see only her shoes -- nothing else except her silhouette. She had good taste in shoes. She wore cognac riding boots very similar to mine.

I whistled to myself as I walked, keeping pace.

My ear suddenly started ringing. Mom always told me that meant someone was talking about me. I stopped whistling and rubbed it vigorously for a moment.

The House on Valley Street

When it stopped, I resumed my tune.

The ringing began again.

I tried again to clear my ear.

The hum stopped for a moment, then picked up again, louder this time.

Then I realized that it wasn't ringing. It was an echo. I must have had some water in my ear. My whistling was echoing.

The girl continued moving toward me, her right hand near her face.

I prepared to smile at her, ready for the challenge, but that annoying thing that usually happens when I'm in an uncomfortable situation happened again. I averted my eyes for a moment before she passed by, but at the last second, I found my courage and glanced at her with a smile in my eyes.

And in that moment, I looked into a face that was mine, eyes that were mine, hair and skin that was mine. But my awed expression wasn't returned. My lips parted in shock, but hers peeled back thin and taut to bare yellowed, twisted, cracked teeth. She snapped her jaw shut, and several crumbled bits of tooth tumbled down her chin – my chin.

I kept walking. She kept walking.

I felt my head turn before I made the decision to look back consciously. As my chin reached over my shoulder, her brisk footsteps were still clicking and dragging away from me. When I had turned all the way around, she was gone.

The House on Valley Street

I didn't know what else to do, so I ran. I was panting and the air was burning my throat but I couldn't stop. Although she had disappeared, I didn't know whether she would come back. What if she was watching me? The rules didn't apply. She could appear and disappear as she pleased.

When I could see the front door, I jammed my hand into my purse and fingered its contents, desperately searching for the key.

Chapstick.

Receipt.

Loose change.

Blood pounded in my ears, and my fingers searched wildly through my bag in the dark as I ran. Several coins hit the pavement and rolled to the curb.

The wind blew a low-hanging branch on a willow tree across the street. A shadow seemed to sway from behind the garage. Every sound, however hushed in the night, sent a surge of adrenaline coursing through my already-charged system.

My fingers finally curled around the cold key and seized it. My feet pounded up the driveway, and I leapt onto the front stoop. While my trembling hand searched for the keyhole, my head pivoted back and forth over my shoulders, swinging like a dashboard hula girl.

Suddenly, it was all gone. All of the nighttime sounds – the wind blowing, the bats flapping, the dog barking – had stopped. It was the calm before the inevitable storm. My scalp tingled at the sudden silence.

The key rumbled into the lock, and I threw the handle to the side before crashing through the door with all of my weight. I slammed it shut behind me and sat in the dark foyer, waiting, hoping she couldn't get in.

CHAPTER 10

"This is the dumbest shit we've ever done," Lucee said, paging through the book Dylan sent home with me the night before. She sat at the kitchen table.

"I know. But I hope it works." I kept replaying the night before in my mind. A ball of anger rose in my throat – anger at myself for having been so helpless, anger at myself for having sat frozen on the floor of the foyer until I fell asleep, anger at myself for letting my guard down. Despite my upset, I found myself glancing over my shoulder toward the front door much too often.

"Yeah. That's what all of the twenty-something single girls in the scary movies say before they play with a Ouija board and piss off whatever ghosties are hanging out in their house." She tucked her blonde hair behind her ear and reached for another book, oblivious to what had happened the night before.

"It's true." I chuckled and poured a glass of chocolate milk for each of us. The sound of Gene's lawn mower created a dull hum in the kitchen. I wondered why he pushed both lawns rather than using a riding mower. At his age, he must be exhausted after all of that. Then again, I supposed that doing things like that was what kept him in shape, if that's what he was.

"Chocolate milk?" Lucee smiled. "I haven't had this stuff in forever."

I smiled from behind my cup and held it up for cheers. "It's our thing. Later on, we can have cookie dough ice cream with bananas." Our glasses clanked.

After a moment, I said, "Ready for this?"

"Let's do it."

We sat at the table and again reviewed the instructions. "We need an item that belonged to the deceased."

"And do you have that?" Lucee asked.

"I think so."

She looked at me questioningly.

"There was so much stuff left here, and there have been so many families living here that I can't be sure what belonged to who. I just picked the oldest-looking thing I could find."

"Which is…?"

I reached below the table and lifted the hat from my side. Its age was evident through the musty smell that wafted from it. The smell was just as potent as it had been when I'd found it.

"Where did you find that?" Lucee asked, fanning the air in front of her nose. "It stinks."

"It was in the basement," I said, lightly fingering the stains along the brim. "I just brought it upstairs this morning." The anger I'd felt against myself fueled my determination to go downstairs and retrieve it – angry or not, I'd jogged up the stairs and closed the door with a punctuating thud when I'd made it back up.

"Dude! What the hell is up with all of these sorority girl scary movie clichés? Did you find a creepy doll down there, too? Something with eyes that open when you tilt it up? Cries and calls you its mama?"

"No dolls. No weird locks of hair. None of that." I laughed nervously and slid the fragile artifact between us.

"Alright," she said. "Dirty old hat. Check. What else do we need?"

I read, "Along with the artifact, the performer will require a bundle of lavender, a ceramic or glass bowl filled with water and a pinch of sugar, and a box or bin large enough to contain the chosen artifact."

"Check, check, check. But isn't it usually sage that all of those hex-givers use?"

"Not this time, I guess." There was an asterisk on the page beside the word "lavender," with instructions to "READ MORE IN APPENDIX." I flipped to the back of the book and trailed a finger down the page. "Like sage, lavender is a popular tool for ridding homes of spirits," I read. "While sage is said to rid the area of negative energy, lavender merely calms the spirits, facilitating possible communication if the homeowner wishes to pursue it."

"So you don't want to get rid of it? You just want to give it some happy pills?"

"Er...I guess." I flipped back to the instruction page. "I would like to – you know – communicate if the opportunity arises. I think that would be good for my book." I shrugged nonchalantly, though a chill ran up my spine at the memory of a girl in my own image waltzing past me the night before.

"Alrighty then," Lucee said. "Smelly hat, check. Lavender, check. Water bowl, check. Big-ass box, check. Are you ready for this?"

"Are you?"

"If you ask me again, I might say no." She frowned and wrung her hands on the table in front of her. "This house is freaky enough without us trying to conjure its spirits." She made air quotes at the end of her sentence.

"That's not what we're doing. We're trying to cleanse the house. That's it. It's like giving it a bath." I sounded far more confident than I felt. My fingers trembled around the thin pages of the book.

I tucked the hat into a plastic tote bin and lit the bundle of lavender with a match, as per instructions. It smoked heavily. "It says here that we need to take the bin into each room and put it on the floor in the middle. Then we have to," I paused and skimmed down the page, skipping to the necessary bits, "hold the bowl of water up to the corners of each room and wave the lit lavender over it, 'ushering the smoke to the edges of the room.'"

"Start in here?" Lucee asked.

"Let's do it." I handed the lit lavender to Lucee before sliding the plastic tub and the hat across the floor. I stood beside it, spinning to ensure that I was indeed in the center of the room. Then I carefully lifted the bowl of water from the table and retrieved the smoking lavender.

"Is there some chant or spell or something I'm supposed to say?" I asked Lucee while I balanced the water bowl in the corner near the stove.

She dragged a finger down the page. "Uh," she said, turning the page. "Jesus."

"What?"

"Well, at least it's not in Latin or something."

"What am I supposed to say?" The water bowl was getting heavy, and the smoke was starting to slow from the lavender.

The House on Valley Street

"It says you should call out to the home: 'Feel the clean; feel the calm.' You should repeat that into every corner."

I sighed, feeling every bit a nutcase. "Okay," I hissed. "Feel the clean. Feel the calm." I whisked the smoldering lavender over the top of the bowl, pushing the light smoke into the corner.

"Feel the clean. Feel the calm," I chanted into another corner, then another. When I finished the fourth corner of the room, I rolled my eyes and sunk.

"Now what?" Lucee asked.

I shrugged. What exactly was I expecting? Did I think that the cabinet doors would all swing open and slam closed in tandem? Did I expect all the dishes to come crashing to the floor at once?

"I guess we move on to the next room."

"Do you think it worked?" Lucee asked, dragging the tote toward the living room.

"We'll see."

I continued the chant into the four corners of the living room, then the bathroom.

"What do you think we should do about the stairs?"

"What about them?" Lucee asked, leaning against the rail post and watching me move out of the bathroom.

"There aren't any corners."

"They're also not a room." She raised one eyebrow.

"Touché." I never did tell her about the girl careening down the steps.

We tromped up the stairs and performed the cleanse in each of the bedrooms.

By the time we were done, the lavender bunch was a sooty, sagging mess, and the water in the bowl was contaminated with ashes. I briefly considered the symbolism in that as we made our way silently, feeling foolish, back to the kitchen. *Did the water absorb the filth from the home? Did it sacrifice its purity for the sake of the cleanse?*

Ugh.

Too much literary analysis in my background. I overthought things far too often, and that never got me anywhere.

"Do you feel as stupid as I do?" Lucee asked.

"Without a doubt." I poured the water down the sink and drenched what was left of the lavender before throwing it in the garbage can.

"Do you think it did anything?"

"I doubt it."

"Well, then. That was fun, but I've got to get going." Lucee swung her studded, leather bag over her shoulder.

"Already?"

"Sorry, dude. I have to work in a couple of hours," she said. "I need to get ready."

The House on Valley Street

"Aren't you ready enough to pour some drinks for sweaty old guys?" I teased.

"Ha-ha. Very funny." She swirled what was left of her milk to kick up the chocolate that had settled on the bottom of the glass before tipping it back and draining it. "Do I have a milk mustache?" she asked.

My back was turned to her as I stacked Dylan's book on top of the others and wiped dribbles of lavender water from the table. "Yep," I answered without looking back.

"We should hang out next Saturday night." She stood from the table. "I have the night off for once."

"Really? A night off on a Saturday? Isn't that when bartenders *want* to work? You know, make the most tips?"

"Yeah, but sometimes it's worth it to have a night to myself." She zipped up her slim-fitting jacket and pulled a rhinestone keychain from her back pocket.

I walked her to the front door. "I'll text you Saturday." I said, giving her a quick hug. "Thanks for trying all of this." I waved a hand around to indicate the corners of the room. I didn't quite know what to call "this," so gesturing was my best option.

"Not a problem. Let me know if all the paint peels off of the walls or something later today. You know, retaliation. House is pissed." She winked.

"Nice. Thanks for that." I looked over my shoulder to the kitchen and mocked fear, though part of it was genuine.

"Have fun with that. See you Saturday." Lucee pushed the door open. Just as she stepped onto the stoop, the wind ripped the door away from her and slammed it into the siding. "Shit! Sorry, Soph!"

"No big deal," I called. "Drive safely!" Lucee hurried to her car while I stood admiring the dark clouds blowing across the sky. A low rumble of thunder sounded in the distance. Just as Lucee's headlights ticked on, I shut the door.

With a sigh, I returned to the kitchen to finish cleaning up. I broke down the box and washed the bowl the water had been in. I tucked my laptop up against the wall on the table and stacked the books on top. The only thing left was the hat. It needed to go into the garage with the rest of the things I'd packed away. I tucked it under my arm and headed outside.

I heard the rain before I opened the door. It was pounding the roof, and droplets were hitting the sidewalk with so much force that they seemed to be bouncing. The trees in the front yard were bending so far in the wind that I thought their branches were likely to snap at any minute. I closed the door.

"Nope. Not tonight," I said aloud. The hat would need to wait. I took it back into the kitchen and planned to leave it there overnight.

In the bathroom, I tied my hair back and dabbed my face with a warm wash cloth. I couldn't help but feel my skin crawl while my back was turned to the bathroom door. I didn't like feeling like the entire house was at my back, as though it were alive and spying on me, watching me move about from room to room. It was as though the home was reaching for me.

The storm was still strong, pounding against the siding. The wind drug branches across the roof, and I could hear them scratching along. Had I not realized that it was the storm, I would have been terrified of the sound. It screeched and whipped. But it came and went.

By the time I finished brushing my teeth, the wind had picked up considerably. Strong gusts were blowing back and forth, throwing branches all about. With a sudden, powerful gust, I heard glass break from across the house.

"Shit." I wiped my mouth and left the bathroom, padding softly toward the noise. *I don't want to have to call Gene about a broken window this late,* I thought. But there was no one else to call.

I kept my eyes to the floor, on the alert for shards since I was barefoot. But none came. Everything was as it had been minutes before in the foyer. The same in the kitchen. I looked out the screen door into the backyard. I don't know what exactly it was that I was looking for, but there was nothing out there that could have made that noise. The trash can had tipped over in the wind, but there was no glass in it. And even if there were, it wouldn't have been that loud from inside the house.

With a shrug, I turned on the kitchen faucet and ran it cold. The gusts were frantically whipping branches across the house, back and forth, *swish, swish, swish, swish*. It was a loud, reverberating sound. When I opened the cabinet door to retrieve a cup, I jumped. My breath hitched when I saw the ceramic shards strewn across the shelf. It was the bowl that had held the lavender water.

Swish, swish, swish.

The sound had moved into the house, behind my head. *Back and forth, swish, swoosh, swish.*

I slowly turned away from the cabinet, my heart throbbing in my throat. Behind me, the wet, burned lavender was being whipped back and forth at eye level. It tore to the left, then to the right, violently throwing droplets of water across the floor and the countertops.

I couldn't move. My back was to the countertop. The lavender's path had created a wall, trapping me where I stood.

Swish, swish, swish.

I couldn't take the sound. I panicked. I ran through its path. I ran right into it. It was cold, but I kept moving. The lavender crashed to the floor and lay unmoving. I slammed the bathroom door closed behind me and strained to hear anything following me from the kitchen, but all I heard was the swish, swish, swish of branches clawing against the house.

CHAPTER 11

"Hello?"

"Dylan?" I breathed too heavily into the phone.

"Sophia? What's wrong?"

"Nothing. I'm sorry." I fingered the shower curtain.

"For what?"

"For calling like this. I just got a little freaked out and you're the only person I know around here and I thought I might feel better if I got to talk to someone." I imagined him standing from his desk at the store and moving to the office space to speak with me in private. It was almost six o'clock. He'd be closing soon.

"What scared you?"

"Nothing in particular," I lied. I didn't want him to think I needed to be institutionalized. "I think I'm getting inside my own head too much. This house is starting to ... to mess with me."

"I'll come over. I'll be there soon." And with that, he hung up.

I stared at my phone, almost in disbelief. It was the evening, and a man, a gorgeous, strong, smart man, was headed to my home for nothing more than to help me feel better.

What if he thinks I'm crazy?

What if he's actually a creep who's trying to take advantage of me? I don't know him that *well.*

I pushed my mother's excessive worry gene out of my body for the time being so that I could revel in the fact that Dylan was coming over and that we would be alone. Together.

For the next ten minutes, I touched up my makeup in the smallest, most well-lit room of the house: the bathroom. All the while, my ears were perked like a white tail deer listening for a hunter on opening day. The storm was beginning to subside, and the swishing of the branches outside had slowed.

I sat on the edge of the tub, leaning forward over my knees, imagining -- though trying not to -- someone or something suddenly appearing in the tub behind me and ripping me from my perch. I sat in a chronic state of feeling chilled and being coated in goose bumps. The hairs on my arms reminded me of science experiments involving middle school students, balloons, hair, a lesson on friction.

The doorbell sounded.

I stood faster than I had expected my body could manage and nearly trotted to the door. When I pulled it open, Dylan almost fell into the house.

"You okay?" He asked when he saw my face. He reached both hands to my shoulders.

"Yeah." I closed the door behind him after he entered. I wrung my hands in front of me. "Just a little freaked out."

He raised an eyebrow and waited for me to continue. He tucked his hands into the pockets of his leather jacket, though they moved back and forth inside. It was as though the jacket were their restraint.

"Lucee and I tried to use that book you gave me the other night." Heat spread from my ears.

"You guys did a cleanse?"

"You got it." I sighed and glanced into the corners of the room as I led Dylan to the sofa. As soon as we sat, the hairs on the back of my neck stood on end again, but I didn't know whether it was the house causing it or my proximity to Dylan.

"And what happened?"

"Well, it didn't work, if that's what you mean." I tucked loose baby hairs behind my ears. "You could go look in the cabinet if you'd like."

He ignored the invitation. "Do you still think this place is haunted?" He unzipped his jacket and pulled it off his shoulders, revealing a gray button-down shirt and maroon tie.

Suddenly distracted, I asked, "Do you have plans tonight?" I nodded toward his shirt. "You look fancy."

"This? No. Well, yes. Nothing special, though. There's a book signing at the store tonight. I want to make a good impression. If I can get some more authors in, I might be able to grow the store."

"Who is it?"

"Who is who?"

"The author. Who's coming?"

"Some guy who grew up here. Zachary Peterson. He writes post-apocalyptic fiction."

"Zombie warfare?" I managed a smile through my tension.

"Something like that." He paused. The only sound was the tick-tock of the seconds passing on the dollar-store wall clock. "Are you going to tell me what happened?"

I rubbed my palms against my thighs. How could I explain it? If he wasn't there, he wouldn't understand. "It was pretty rough. I mean, the house all but exploded."

He frowned.

"It's hard to explain. If you didn't see it yourself, I wouldn't really expect you to believe me. *I* wouldn't believe me."

He said nothing, but indicated that he wanted me to continue. He leaned forward, elbows on his knees. His hands were clasped in his lap. Our knees were touching.

"We were in the kitchen at the table when we started," I said shakily. I shook my head, not at the memory, but at my childish reaction to Dylan. With a deep breath, I continued. "The book said that we needed to take the bowl into each room of the house and spread lavender smoke into the corners. The kitchen was fine. Nothing happened in there. This room was decent. It felt weird, but nothing really happened. We made it through each of the rooms just fine. But then things got weird after Lucee left."

"Who's Lucee?"

"A friend of mine." I continued, "When I was in the kitchen, I could have sworn that something was standing behind me. I didn't see it, but I *felt* it. I felt the whoosh of someone passing by, the waft of cold air." I left out the part about the dancing sprigs of lavender. I was realizing then how ridiculous I sounded. A gush of air? How terrifying. "I know it sounds stupid, but it's just nice to have someone else here with me for now."

"Where did your friend go?"

"To work."

"Why?"

I frowned at him as if to say, *Why do you think?*

"She just ditched you?"

"Well," I began. I didn't want to throw her under the bus like that. *I'd probably leave, too, if I didn't live here.* "She stayed for a little bit after we were finished, but she needed to go to work. I don't blame her. Besides, everything seemed fine while she was here."

A robotic voice chanted, "It-is-now-six-o'clock."

"I've got to get going," Dylan said, pulling his cell phone out of his pocket to mute the alarm. "The signing starts at seven, and I have to set up drinks and cookies and get everything ready."

"Yeah, of course. I hope it's fun." I felt like an idiot. He must be so uncomfortable. What did I expect him to do? Console me? Wrap me in his strong arms and rock me until I felt safe again?

"Do you want to come with?"

What?

"Really?"

"It'd be better than staying here all night. How boring. And I won't ditch you like your friend did." He chuckled a moment and then said, "I mean, if you don't want to, that's fine. I just thought you might want to get out of here for a little while."

For a moment, I was intrigued by his sudden vulnerability. Was he flustered? "I'd love to go. But I'm not dressed for the occasion." I tugged at my pink, fleece zip-up sweatshirt.

"You don't have to dress up. I'm just wearing this because I represent the store. You know, networking and such. You can wear whatever you want."

"I represent the town. I don't want this guy thinking we're all homeless." I laughed, feeling relieved at the thought of having a reason to leave the house if only for a few hours.

"He's from here, remember?"

"Still." I waved a hand toward Dylan's clothes and brought it back to mine. "I have something to live up to. I can meet you there. I'll be five minutes behind you. I just want to change into a dress."

"Don't you have to walk?"

"No. I have a car."

"Listen, Sophia. If we're going to make this a proper date, we should probably at least ride together."

My heart quickened, and my spine straightened. "A -- a date?"

"Well, yeah. It *is* a seven o'clock event on a Saturday night. We might as well call it a date, as lame as it might be." He smirked, all his confidence seemingly having returned. "I'll wait for you."

"Are you sure? I don't want you to be late to your own party."

"I'm sure." He crossed his arms and leaned back casually into the couch.

"Five minutes." I stood from the sofa and ran up the steps, pushing the thought of the drooling girl from my mind when I grasped the railing between strides.

"Five minutes," he called back.

Fifteen minutes later, I was dressed in a burgundy sweater dress and heeled boots with a wide knit scarf around my neck. My hair fell straight around my shoulders. I clicked down the stairs, calling over the railing, "I'm sorry I took so long. I couldn't find my boots. One was hiding under the bed."

He turned to face me as he stood and swung his leather jacket over his broad shoulders. "You look great."

I beamed. "Thanks."

"Shall we?" He opened the door and ushered me outside, where his car was already running, waiting for us along the curb. He saw my raised eyebrow and said, "Remote start."

The car seats felt warm against my legs. Dylan closed my door and walked around the front. As I watched him, I marveled at how free I felt with him, how comfortable I was already. Just knowing that he was downstairs kept my fear at bay while I was getting ready. I'd paused a fraction of a second before reaching under the bed for my boots, but other than that, I was fine. And now, from inside his car, the house didn't feel so ominous, so looming. It really was just a house – or at least it looked that way.

"Let's do this," he said, turning down the radio when he started the car. Apparently, he had been listening to something quite loudly before he'd arrived.

The neighborhood really was pretty. Many of the homes had high peaks, wrap-around porches, well-groomed shrubs and flowering plants lining walkways. This house just didn't seem to belong. It hadn't been cared for, loved, the way the others had. Frankly, it stuck out like a sore thumb – a sore, two-story thumb.

I always felt that a person's driving style revealed a lot about his or her personality. Reckless drivers lived recklessly. Careful drivers lived life carefully. Dylan's driving was... *gentle.* He pulled away from the curb smoothly and drove cautiously through the twilight, aware, at least seemingly, that kids or pets may be out and about. I liked that about him. I appreciated it.

We turned the corner at the end of the block, where Gene was carrying a black trash bag to the curb. He smiled softly and raised a hand in a salute of a wave. I smiled and waved back animatedly, telling Dylan, "That's Gene. He's a really nice guy."

Dylan peered through his lashes at the old man but said nothing. He only turned his eyes back to the road.

"What?" I asked. "Do you know him?"

"I know of him," he said.

"And you don't like him?"

He shrugged. "You know how rumors are." He looked again at the clock. "Shit. I only have twenty minutes to set everything up. The guy's going to show up soon."

I decided then not to press the issue about Gene, at least not with Dylan. I would try some investigation when I got home after our "date."

At the store, there was a line extending from the front door, but it only consisted of a handful of people: a few teenage girls, an elderly man and what appeared to be his grandson, and a trio of middle-aged women, all clutching gently used, post-apocalyptic Zachary Peterson novels to their chests or at their sides. Dylan pulled around to the back of the store.

We walked to the door in a comfortable silence. He expertly slid a key into the deadbolt and opened the employee entrance. He wedged his foot at the base of the door so as to hold it open for me and straightened his tie. I walked in but halted a few feet inside, waiting for direction.

Dylan slid past me in the hallway and said, "I just have to grab the food from my office." I waited outside the doorway to his office and watched him rummage through a coat closet behind his desk. There were no photos on his desk, no real personalization. There really was nothing but paperwork and various books lying about. A generic calendar was hung on the wall to the left. A blue inked X marked each day leading to today's date, which was circled and labeled with, "First signing!!!"

With a large Tupperware container of chocolate chip cookies and two bags of pretzels in hand, Dylan asked, "Would you mind carrying these out front? Just follow the hall. Lights will be on your left. I have to get the drink dispenser and the cold stuff from the break room."

"There's a break room?" I asked. "I'm impressed." I took the food from him and winked.

"I'm full of surprises." He smiled and ushered me toward the front of the store before disappearing into another room.

I switched the light on and marveled at how dense the space felt. It was warm and solid. The books seemed to absorb any noise or potential disturbance, though there was nothing but silence at the time. I admired several colorful posters showing penguins and white tigers tacked to a large bulletin board in the children's section as I walked through.

In the center of the store was a long folding table and a single chair. Assuming that was to be Mr. Peterson's presentation table, I thought it best not to place the food there. Instead, I found a small, blue children's table and dragged it several paces behind the signing area with one hand before setting down the snacks.

Moments later, Dylan appeared carrying a large drink dispenser under his arm, and his hands were full with a vegetable tray that he balanced on his palm and a plastic grocery bag full of serving bowls, paper plates, napkins, and silverware that hung from his pinky finger. In the crook of his other arm was a canister of lemonade drink mix. He smiled thankfully when I took the vegetable tray from him.

"I hope this is okay," I said, nodding toward the children's table. "I figured that big table would be where the action's going to go down."

"You got it."

Dylan mixed the lemonade while I emptied and arranged the contents of his grocery bag.

The clock on the wall read 6:55.

"Shouldn't he be here by now?" I asked.

"He said he would be here at 7, so I guess he has a couple of minutes." He wadded up the empty pretzel bags and tucked them into the grocery bag. "He's going to be coming to the back door, too. Can you put this under the register? I'm going to head back there in case he does come a little early. The door won't open without a key."

I hurried to the register and tucked the bag into a lower shelf. The area was remarkably neat. Not a thing seemed out of place. Papers were neatly stacked, as were his excess business cards. Every pen and pencil was nestled in a soup can that appeared to have been painted by a small child. It was covered in wobbly flowers and a bright orange sun.

Someone knocked on the front door, and I turned to see the small boy who had been waiting with his grandfather. I smiled apologetically and held up one finger to him to let him know that it wouldn't be much longer. The crowd outside seemed to have grown by at least a few people. It was no mob, but there was a decent turnout.

Sympathizing with the group of people waiting in the cold, I turned away and moved toward the back of the building, where Dylan was still waiting for Mr. Peterson to arrive. I found him leaning casually against the wall, arms crossed over his chest, peering out into the dark parking lot.

"Nothing yet?" I asked.

"An SUV just pulled in. I think that's him," he said, placing his hand on the door, ready to push it open. "He said he drove a silver hybrid."

A moment later, I spotted a thirty-something man with the collar of his tan trench coat pulled high around his face. He shuffled his feet donned in shining black shoes against the pavement and hurried to the door.

"Mr. Peterson," Dylan said congenially, holding the door open wide. "Welcome."

"Thank you." He entered with a shiver, quickly unbuttoning his jacket. "So sorry I'm running behind. I hope your customers haven't begun a mosh pit." He chuckled nervously. His British accent caught me by surprise. *I thought Dylan said he grew up here,* I thought.

"Not quite," Dylan replied politely.

Mr. Peterson rubbed his feet on the entry rug while shrugging off his jacket. "Wonderful. Pleased to meet you. Are you Dylan's girlfriend?" he asked me with a cheerful grin.

"I—," I began, struck.

"This is Sophia," Dylan saved me. "She's new to the area."

"Forgive me. How foolish." Mr. Peterson was quick to move from the subject. He clapped his hands once. "Right then. Shall we?"

Dylan led the way, and I played caboose through the hall and into the main lobby. Dylan directed Mr. Peterson to the table where he would be greeting and signing, and as Mr. Peterson was chattering away, Dylan pointed to the door and signaled for me to open it while he continued to nod and smile.

I didn't know what to do. *Should I say something before I let the people in? Are there instructions?*

It's time, I rehearsed in my head. *No, that sounds like a signal for a pregnant woman to start pushing.*

Welcome, I tried again. *Mr. Peterson awaits.*

What am I, a butler?

The small boy who had been waiting with his grandfather had pressed his forehead to the door in anticipation. I smiled at him and waved as I approached. When I opened it, a cool rush greeted my face, and when my breath had returned to me, I said, "Welcome. Come on in."

There. That was basic enough, right?

I held the door open and let the line funnel in.

Mr. Peterson addressed the crowd for a few minutes and answered a couple of questions before a giddy chatter slowly filled the space as people gathered in yet another line to await the opportunity to speak one-on-one with him.

Dylan sauntered over to where I stood at his desk and leaned back without speaking. His shoulder brushed mine.

"Not a bad turnout, huh?" I asked him after a few moments.

"Not bad," he agreed.

"I like him -- Mr. Peterson."

"I do, too. He's polite."

"I think the accent makes him seem extra polite," I chuckled. "Speaking of which, I thought you said he was from here."

"He is, but not originally. He was born in England and moved here as a foreign exchange student in high school. When the exchange program ended, he decided to stay here in the States for college. And he never left."

I nodded, watching how animatedly Mr. Peterson spoke with his fans. It was heartwarming to see, especially the middle-aged ladies who swooned over him. Each beamed when he asked how to spell her name.

It was almost 9 o'clock, and for the first time since I left the house, I thought about how daunting it would be to return. I didn't want to go back there. Not alone.

"Someday this could be you," Dylan said with a grin. "Except this place will be packed."

"If I'm lucky."

Dylan looked so handsome. His smile revealed shallow dimples in his cheeks. I briefly imagined what he would look like when the event was over. Would he loosen his tie? Unbutton the top few buttons of his shirt? Roll up his sleeves? The idea of him undressing captivated me.

The line was soon dwindling, and the store was clearing out. Happy customers left clinging to their newly-autographed books. When he and his grandfather were making their way out, the boy turned to me and waved excitedly. His red jacket was unzipped and sagging off one shoulder.

Just one customer was left, and he was speaking with Mr. Peterson.

Dylan asked, "Do you want to help me clean up after this?"

I nodded, "Of course."

"Because you don't have to stay after if you don't want to. I can run you home."

"I thought you had a car." I winked at him exaggeratedly.

"Funny." He moved to the back of the store and began to clear the snack table.

Minutes later, the store was empty save for the two of us and Mr. Peterson.

"What do you think, Sir Dylan?" Mr. Peterson asked from his signing table, gently pushing in the chair.

"I'm pleased with the turnout." His tone shifted – so businesslike.

"As am I, as am I." He shrugged his trench coat over his shoulders.

"Sophia would like to do what you do someday. She's an aspiring novelist."

"Are you now?" He regarded me with friendly interest.

I stuttered, "I am, but I'm only beginning. I have a lot to learn still."

"On the contrary, you've nothing to learn. You've something to *tell.*" Mr. Peterson wiggled a finger in my direction. He reached into the breast pocket of his jacket and withdrew a business card. "If you'd like some writerly advice, contact me. Publishers can be real arses." He winked at me and called to Dylan, "Is that it, then?"

Dylan brushed his hands together to rid them of the cookie crumbs he'd swept off the snack table. "I'll walk you out."

"Nonsense." Mr. Peterson shook his head. "I'll see my way out. Have a pleasant evening, you two." Something in his tone made me blush.

"I'll forward you the paperwork," Dylan said, taking several paces beside Mr. Peterson. He mentioned something about accounting and receipts before they shook hands and parted.

Mr. Peterson moseyed out of the building and left me and Dylan to finish the clean-up, though not much was left to be tidied, save for the stack of unsold books left on the signing table.

"Where should I put these?" I called to Dylan, who was dragging the snack table back into the children's section.

"You can just leave them there. I'll use that as a sale table this week -- try to get rid of the extras. Could you lock the front door?"

I nodded and turned the lock. When I turned around, Dylan was headed toward me, surveying the aisles, double checking that everything was in its place.

"Alright. Let's get out of here." He rested his fist on his hip and extended his elbow so that I could loop my hand through.

At the back of the store, he flipped the light switch, and the store went black. We paced silently through the back corridor and out the employee entrance, which Dylan locked, checked, and rechecked.

Outside, I admired the bright, clear sky full of shining stars. It was beautiful.

I shivered against the seat in Dylan's car. Watching, and no doubt listening to, my teeth chatter, he asked, "Cold?" and turned up the heat, which unfortunately, was blowing only luke-warm air. "It'll warm up in just a minute," he said.

I smiled gratefully, though I'm sure he didn't see me in the dark car. A mid-nineties rock song played quietly on the radio, and I found myself absentmindedly mouthing the words.

"You like Pearl Jam, huh?" He smirked, and his white teeth glowed in the blackness.

"I guess I do." My thoughts flowed to days standing on Dad's feet and dancing with him to Days of the New and Stone Temple Pilots when I was little.

Dylan reached up and loosened his tie. I glanced once but quickly averted my eyes.

All too soon, we pulled into the driveway of my temporary home. He switched off the ignition.

Should I invite him in?

I studied his body language. He sat casually back in the seat while his keys swung back and forth in the ignition. He sat that way for only a moment before unbuckling his seatbelt and reaching for the door.

"I'll just walk you to the door," he said, seemingly having read my thoughts.

Hiding my disappointment – or at least attempting to -- I led Dylan across the yard and to the house, where he stood back and watched me unlock the door. When I opened it, he said, "Maybe I'll talk to you tomorrow?"

I nodded.

He stood at the end of the sidewalk while I fumbled with the key, replaying my panic from the night before. When the key finally slid into the lock and the door swung open, he said, "Goodnight," and he left.

The House on Valley Street

CHAPTER 12

After lying in bed awake, imagining where my relationship with Dylan may lead, I'd finally fallen asleep sometime around midnight. Morning came quickly.

Hair astray and donning an oversized t-shirt and sweatpants, I nestled myself behind my laptop at the kitchen table again, running through all that had happened in the past several days: the things I'd seen, the people I'd met, the remedies I'd tried. Among all of that, though, one thing stuck out to me in particular. Why did Dylan react so strangely to Gene?

I sipped absently at a mug of coffee.

In the short time I'd known Dylan, he had never *not* smiled at someone. He was always friendly, or at the very least, cordial. But he seemed to regard Gene with a certain indifference. It was so uncharacteristic, even though I hadn't known Dylan very long. Maybe I was reading into it too far. I had a tendency to do that.

With a shrug, I returned to my laptop and began keying my account of the past several nights, beginning with the girl on the street. I wrote page after page of memories that weren't distant enough to numb my fear. Recalling the details of the girl's yellowed grin and the smell of the lavender whipping in front of my face had a physiological effect. My palms dampened. My heartrate quickened. I nervously tucked my hair behind my ear again and again.

I never thought about how difficult writing my story could be. Reliving the events through my memory and crafting them into my story made them that much more real. It had all happened, and I couldn't treat the occurrences like dreams – I couldn't walk away and never look back. I *had* to look back. I had to stare in the face of all the details of each encounter. I had to crawl through the memories and regurgitate them with some sort of eloquence, something beyond panic.

Even more difficult than transcribing each experience was trying to piece each together into some cohesive whole. The events didn't make *sense*.

Angry girl on the stairs. A girl who resembled quite closely someone Mom used to babysit.

Shackled skeleton in the basement.

A mirror image of myself, only evil.

Lavender whipping back and forth in front of my eyes. I couldn't make the events line up. I couldn't find a reason. There was no cohesion to my story. Thus far, things had just gone bump in the night – nothing more.

I pushed through each event, racking my memories for details for what seemed like hours before I became conscious of my horrible posture and my heavy eyelids. I felt warm and stiff. Rubbing my eyes, I contemplated what to do with my afternoon. It was barely lunch time; I had the entire day to fill, and I certainly didn't want to fill it sitting at the table and typing. I needed air.

After a quick shower and a dab of makeup, I was ready to go. In my car, I turned the windows down and the radio up. The afternoon's warmth was tickled by a cool breeze. This was what I needed. The drive to my parents' house would be an hour of silence, an hour of wind whipping my hair, an hour of distance between me and that house.

I flipped radio stations compulsively. Today's pop hits weren't my thing. I generally preferred talk radio, but today, I went with the alternative rock station. Nothing like a little grunge to get the kinks out.

Time ticked by, and before I knew it, I was turning onto the street I grew up on. A neighbor's familiar fish mailbox gaped at me as I drove past, its door flapping in the rush of air my car sent rolling against it.

The House on Valley Street

As soon as I pulled into the driveway, my parents' two Labradors began barking wildly. I slowed to a near crawl, in case they darted across the winding, tree-lined driveway. The sound of the gravel under my tires reminded me of late summer nights, when Dad and I would haul garbage cans to the end of the long driveway, which only grew longer in the dark. I was reminded of the putrid smell of those cans, too. I gulped audibly, suppressing sudden nausea at the thought of the maggots I'd once found crawling and squirming about in the bottom of one of the green cans.

The house gradually came into view. The garage door was open. Dad's late-nineties Saturn was parked inside -- a good sign that they were home. I hadn't called before I'd left Valley Street.

I parked the car and gently fought back against the two Labs, who were still barking and jumping excitedly. Marley's entire back-end wriggled, and Ziggy nearly knocked me over when she leaned against my leg, hoping for a rub. "Let's go!" I ushered them into the garage and up the steps. The various tags hanging from their collars jingled as they trotted alongside me. I let myself inside the house.

The smell of burning paper wafted from the small home's limestone fireplace, where an envelope of junk mail still glowed orange around its edges. "You're prequalified!" was still legible on its front in bold, black letters.

The House on Valley Street

The home's high ceiling was deceptive. The space should have felt large, open, and airy, but it didn't; it was dark, pressing. The ceiling was made of cedar planks, as were the walls. Everything was coated in brown.

The dogs bounded inside and around the corner, into the living room. The house was quiet. All of the shades were drawn closed, and no lights were turned on. A man's voice on a documentary of some kind purred softly from the television. Dad peeked his head around the corner from the chocolate-colored, suede couch.

"Sophie!" He swung his bare feet to the parquet floor and sat up excitedly.

"Hello," I smiled. The smell of instant coffee mingled with the smoke from the fireplace.

Mom was sleeping on the couch. She lay on her "good side," as she called it, and her affected arm was tucked into the crook of the other. Her palsied fingers were hooked onto the bicep of her left arm. She stirred. "Hi," she whispered, surprised. She didn't sit up. She didn't even open her eyes.

I sat in an antique rocker across the room.

"What are you up to?" Dad asked. "What are you doing all the way up here?"

"Her missed her momma," Mom had mastered her baby voice, even through sleep's fog.

"I just thought I'd come by and visit. I didn't have anything else going on." The truth was that I missed them both, and I was becoming too consumed in that house. I'd needed to get away.

Mom struggled to sit up.

"How are you feeling?" I asked her.

She grunted. "Head hurts." She leaned forward and cradled her head with her good hand.

I waited, avoiding making eye contact with Dad.

"I'm not using the wheelchair anymore," Mom said. "I was reading in my magazine that the best healing comes in the first six months after a stroke. So I have to keep working at it." She leaned over her knees and tugged one of her tennis shoes over her heel. She'd reached the point in her recovery in which she could walk, but not with bare feet or even socked feet; that posed too high a slip-risk. She needed shoes at all times. She reached her left hand toward her cane, but knocked it down. It slammed to the floor with a tinny clatter. I winced, not from the sound, but from the pain. My forty-five-year-old mother was damaged: physically, emotionally, wholly.

"Pick up your knee," Dad barked at her as she walked. His tone was stern and guarded. I could tell it hurt him, too, but he didn't want to show it. He focused on the recovery, the hopeful future, rather than the damaged present.

The tension was rising like mercury in the house already, and I had been seated for all of two minutes.

"I know, *Stanley*." She growled back.

Well, at least she is feisty with him still, I thought with a sigh.

"My ankle is supinating. It's hard. Don't you understand that?!" She had clearly been reading a lot about strokes. She was becoming a walking dictionary for medical jargon.

"Sup-in-at-ing?" I pronounced the word syllable-by-syllable.

"My foot keeps turning in. See? My mind's sharp still." She sat hard – almost fell -- on the cement ledge in front of the limestone fireplace and stuck a cigar between her lips before lighting it like a seasoned professional with a quick flick of her "good hand."

"You're really still smoking?" That struck a nerve with me. "Really?" I said.

She sucked hard on the cigar – so hard that her cheeks sunk into her face, much like someone making a fish face. I wouldn't have been surprised if she'd made herself lightheaded. "Those fuckers already took my quality of life. I'm not going to quit smoking and turn into a fat pig." She leaned into the fireplace and blew the smoke upward. She knew how I'd hated the smell all my life. But as much as she said she didn't want me around it, and as much as she'd chastised anyone who'd smoked around me as a child, she wouldn't quit.

The House on Valley Street

"Quitting won't make you fat," I said almost instinctually. We'd had this argument countless times before. It played out like a script every time.

"Bullshit."

I took a deep breath. *This isn't what I came here for.*

There were times when the house felt like a maze of daggers and eggshells, bleeding hearts and noise, silent screams and even quieter sobs – especially since the stroke.

I changed the subject. "So I got a few chapters done."

"Mmhmm." She puffed on the cigar again and blew it up the chimney. "Did you see the scratch on Marley's nose? He caught a groundhog yesterday. You should have heard him crying."

I was hurt. I was shocked – or maybe I wasn't. She didn't seem to even register what I had said. *Why isn't she asking me about what I've been doing? Doesn't she care about what I do?*

Dad noticed.

"How's all that coming?" he asked. "You rich and famous yet?"

I hesitated a moment. "No, not yet. But it's coming along. Dylan helped me get some books that I've been reading."

"Who's Dylan? Do I need to get my shotgun out?" he feigned lightheartedness through the heavy atmosphere of the room. He sat bolt upright on the couch and grinned.

I smiled. "No, Dad. No shotgun." Then, a thought occurred to me. "What did you say was the name of that little girl you used to babysit? The one who died a few houses down from the house on Valley Street?" I asked Mom.

"Her name was Molly Danielson." She seemed proud of herself for having recalled the girl's name. "One time, I was changing her diaper, and she bit me." And suddenly Mom was back in the conversation. Before long, she was recounting all the stories of Valley Street that she had already told me before.

She smashed her cigar into the ashtray, then spit on it to be sure it was out.

"Did you just spit on your cigar butt?" I asked, lip curled in disgust.

"Sure did."

"Why would you do that?" I asked.

"I'm not going to have it catch on fire and kill my dogs."

Another deep breath. The stroke clearly hadn't improved her compulsive behavior. She'd always struggled, but her condition had worsened in the weeks following her hospital stay.

"Anyways," I began. I didn't want to argue about how ridiculous that was. There was no sense in trying to explain it. I looked at Dad, but he only shrugged. "I asked because I wanted to research her. Maybe use her as a character in the book." The real reason was that I wanted to look up her obituary. Maybe I could find an old photo. See if that was the girl I had seen on the stairs. But something had told me that it was. I knew somewhere within me.

"Anything happen to you yet in the house?" Mom wore a sort of smirk, as though expecting that my experiences would prove that she wasn't crazy all those years, like my experiences could validate hers. After all, I had always been skeptical. I'd told her she was nuts. And I had thoroughly believed that.

"The house is creepy in itself," I said. "There have been a couple of freaky things, but nothing major." I downplayed it all. While I knew that telling her would make her feel better about her own experiences, I also knew that telling her would mean she wouldn't want me to go back. She would worry more. "I do think it's getting to me a little, though." Finally, the real reason I came. I wanted advice. "Maybe my mind is starting to play tricks on me."

She saw through it. "You saw something, didn't you?" She smiled again – grinned really, in an I-told-you-so kind of way.

Fine.

"A couple of things, but I don't know. Maybe I was just tired or—"

I wasn't tired.

"Did you see Molly?"

I sighed. "I *thought* I saw a girl on the stairs. She... she drooled a lot. And she couldn't walk well. But maybe it was just my imagination." I knew how crazy I sounded, and I didn't want that.

"I told you she had some kind of palsy. Molly couldn't walk much at all," Mom said. "I changed her diapers until she was ten."

"What happened to her?" I asked.

"Disappeared." Mom let her weight fall into the couch again and pulled off her shoes. "They never found her body, but they had a funeral for her. They figured she must have frozen to death one winter after she wandered out of the house."

"Why would they just give up looking?" A sick feeling settled in the pit of my stomach as I pictured a scared, lost child freezing in below-zero, Midwest temperatures.

Again, I think Dad sensed how I was feeling. "Maybe you just need to get out a little more," he interjected.

Mom merely continued to smile and nod, still satisfied at having heard a validation of activity in the house.

"Probably. I should see if Lucee wants to do something tonight."

"How is she?" Mom asked, lying down and pulling her affected hand over her head with her other hand to stretch the palsied muscles.

We talked idly about Lucee and the neighborhood and the dogs for the next hour or so, never mentioning the house again, as though seeing dead girls descending stairs was as common as having a picnic in the park on a breezy summer afternoon.

Mom yawned. "I have to nap. It's time for me to take my medicine." She opened several prescription bottles and made a pile of afternoon pills. Some were for depression. Some were for pain. Some were for muscle spasticity. It was no wonder she was so tired.

"I'm going to get going," I said, standing and stretching.

"Drive safely," Dad said when I hugged him. He gave me a little extra squeeze at the end. His smell reminded me of my grandpa.

I bent over Mom and hugged her, too. She was only able to reciprocate with one arm, and for a brief moment, I wondered if I'd ever feel her full embrace again. But I stuffed that away. What good does it to do sulk? "Give Lucee a hug from us," she said, already drowsy.

After patting and blowing kisses to each of the dogs and again telling my parents that I loved them, I left. Before I got out of the garage, I already felt weight lifting from my shoulders. I loved my parents, but being in their home drained me.

The drive home – or I should say the drive *back* – was therapeutic. I was able to cleanse my psyche of the rollercoaster trip home. This time, I settled on talk radio. The host was interviewing a superintendent about an upcoming referendum vote. I listened rather numbly to talk of budget cuts, program restrictions, and what I thought were empty threats to cancel extra-curricular activities, including sports. What American high school is going to cancel its athletic program? That's all my high school seemed to care about.

By the time the superintendent ended his discussion on taxes and mill rates and my brain slowly began to melt, I was again pulling into my new neighborhood. I met the home with mixed feelings. Part of me was glad to be back where I could relax and focus on my writing, but another part of me was wondering how I could possibly relax in that house. From the street, the house was ominous again, looming over me, taunting me as if threatening me to enter at my own risk.

I parked in the garage and closed the overhead door. Pausing at the front door, I frowned at the handle, remembering all the stories Mom had told me. The house really did look ordinary: ordinary windows, ordinary walls, ordinary doors. But I knew it was something more. Maybe I didn't believe in all of the supernatural stories I'd heard, but I knew what I'd seen inside.

With a swing and low creak of the heavy door, I went in.

Everything was as I had left it. I don't know why I was expecting any different, but a part of me was. A pale pink afghan still sat on the back of the sofa. My morning mug of coffee, now ice-cold, still sat on the kitchen table. A tiny dribble of coffee had dried on the tabletop beside the mug. I was suddenly conscious of the sound of a lawn mower rumbling in the backyard. Gene was pushing and pulling the mower expertly around the trees that flanked the small shed in the corner of the property.

I nearly threw myself into the wooden chair behind my laptop.

M-o-l-l-y D-a-n-i-e-l-s-o-n d-e-a-t-h

I keyed the words into the search engine and paused briefly before clicking the search button. Questions and possibilities tore through my mind in that split second: Did I really want to know if the girl I'd seen was the same girl Mom had babysat in her youth? What if it was? I knew that some level of comfort would come with the validation of my experience, but I also knew that if I saw the same young, thin face staring back at me from the laptop screen, I wouldn't feel any safer.

I pressed Enter.

The search returned 35,000 results. Jeez. My heart pounded in anticipation of what I might find.

I added "Williams County, IL" to my search and tried again.

There it was.

Molly June Danielson, age 10, tragically disappeared Sunday, Aug. 6, 1982. Molly's parents would like to thank the nurses and caregivers who helped treat her at home through her short but happy life.

I skimmed the rest of the entry, which listed those who preceded Molly in death – only a great-grandfather – and the names of her parents: Carolyn and Edward Danielson.

At the bottom of the page was her photo. As I scrolled, the photo became whole. Molly's hair was long and blonde, and she had bright, round eyes. She was a very dainty, pretty little girl.

But behind her grin was a trace, an inkling of the girl on the stairs. Behind her sparkling eyes was an image of the gurgling, the growling, the clambering girl.

A shiver ran down my spine. It was her.

I closed my laptop, pulled out my cell phone, and called Lucee.

CHAPTER 13

There was no answer. I sent a text instead.

I need a night out...Drinks tonight?

My heart was still pounding from my internet search as I waited for a reply. I needed out. Out of the house. Lucee never turned down an opportunity to go out; I was sure she would come with. But rather than wait for her reply, I did the only thing I could think of in that moment that would get me closer to another human being: I went to the backyard.

Gene waved cordially as he continued his path across the back of the property. Each of his passes had come together to leave a plaid pattern in the grass. He paused only a moment and tugged a thin handkerchief from his back pocket, brushed it across his brow, and shoved it away again.

"Looks great!" I shouted.

He cupped his hand over his ear, signaling that he hadn't heard me.

I pointed to the lawn and held a thumb in the air.

He tipped his hat and continued.

Inhaling deeply through my nose and exhaling through my mouth to bring my heartrate back to normal, I sat in a woven lawn chair and watched him make his final passes across the yard.

When he'd finished, he rolled the lawn mower into the shed and snapped the padlock on the door. Breathing heavily, he pulled the handkerchief from his pocket again and dabbed around his neck while he walked to me.

"And how are you this fine day, darlin'?" he asked.

"Pretty good," I lied. "How are you doing? It looks like you've been busy."

"Nothing but a little mowin'." He spun to survey his work.

"Thank you, again, for doing all of the yard work. I really do appreciate it." Talking to him – to anyone – was helping me to feel better. My fingers had stopped trembling, and my breathing had slowed.

"My pleasure." He sat beside me with a heave. "How are you liking the house?" he asked cheerfully.

"It's very nice," I lied again. I felt like insulting the home was somehow insulting Gene. He seemed to admire it. "A little drafty, though." I remembered the lavender whipping in front of me.

"She's an old house," Gene said. "Leaky windows, I'd bet. I'd be happy to take a look, help you get some plastic up before the first freeze."

"Thank you, Gene." A squirrel trotted by at the edge of the patio. "But I'd hate to trouble you. I'll see what I can do for now. Maybe I'll grab a roll at the hardware store and tape around the upstairs windows tonight. See if that helps." I'd dug myself a shallow hole that would only deepen if I offered to let Gene inside.

"Suit yourself," he said, standing. "I ought to have myself a shower." He tucked his handkerchief away again. "If there's anything you need, you just holler."

"Thanks, Gene."

He turned to leave.

"There is one thing," I said before processing the thought. "Do you remember a girl named Molly Danielson? She lived here in the eighties. She went missing and was never found."

He nodded. "I do," he said. "The searchers found a hole in the ice on the lake, not two miles from here. Said she drowned but never found a body, just her teddy bear." He paused. "Why do you ask?"

Good question. "My mom used to babysit for the Danielsons," I said. "Mom told me the story of Molly's disappearance, and I guess I was just wondering if you knew her."

"I did," he said. "Curious little girl, she was. Sad story. The whole neighborhood joined in the search, but nobody found anything 'cept that hole."

"What about her parents?"

"Don't know. They moved away about six months after the funeral."

"I would, too," I said. "I couldn't imagine going through that."

We stood in silence for a moment before I spoke again. "I didn't mean to keep you. I'll call you if I need any help with the windows."

"Not a problem, darlin.' Have yourself a good evening." He turned on his heels and shuffled through the grass. I stayed in my seat until he had made it inside his house. My phone still showed no reply from Lucee, so I took a deep breath, went inside, and jogged up the stairs. The fewer seconds I spent on them, the better.

The late-afternoon sun shone through the dusty window of the master bedroom. The day held a hint of summer's remnant. There was a glowing warmth in the air. I opened the window and breathed deeply. The smell of the freshly cut grass still clung to the breeze.

The breeze blew gently across the room while I fished through my clothes for something reasonable, though appropriate, for a girls' night out. Red batwing blouse? Too heavy. Distressed skinny jeans? Too student-y. I didn't want to look like a sophomore posing with a fake ID. I wanted a sexy, confident night out with my friend.

I. Had. Nothing.

I sent another text to Lucee:

> And can you bring an outfit for me? Something sassy. But not slutty. ☺ Thanks, doll!

It was uncharacteristic for Lucee to not have replied by then, but I didn't dwell on it. She probably had to work late the night before and was napping. I'd like a nap or two if I had to serve booze to handsy old men until 2 in the morning every day.

While I was getting ready, every creak and groan the house made forced me to think of Molly, to look over my shoulder, to expect a strange girl to come crashing up the stairs and into the bedroom. I tried not to look in the mirror for long; I couldn't help envisioning something standing behind me in it.

I began peeling through the items in the closet again. Since I still hadn't heard from Lucee, I settled on a black lace dress. It flared out nicely at the waist, but it was short enough that it didn't look like a child's dress. I tugged it off the hanger, scooped up a pair of pumps, and headed to the bathroom. For whatever reason, I felt more comfortable getting ready there.

Nearly an hour had passed, and when my hair was pinned and sprayed and my lashes curled and plumped, I checked my phone again. Still no response.

It was dinnertime, or past dinnertime, really, and I was all dressed up with nowhere to go. *Maybe Lucee's working an early shift*, I thought.

I sat at the edge of the bathtub and clutched my phone with both hands, staring at his name in my contacts. Did I dare?

I pressed the call button.

"What's up, Sophie?" he answered.

"Er, not a whole lot." I wasn't sure how to lead into these things properly, so I just went for it. "Are you doing anything tonight?" But I got tongue-tied, and it came out more like, "Roo-do-een-thing tonight?"

"What?"

I tried again.

"Do you have any plans for tonight?"

He paused for a moment, and when he spoke, there was a smile in his voice. "I'm just getting ready to leave the store right now. I don't have anything else planned, though."

"Do you want to get dinner?" I tugged lightly on my earring.

"Yeah," he said, surprised. "Absolutely."

"Great!" I stood and roused like someone who's been told she's being promoted. "I'll meet you at the store in twenty minutes."

"I'm on my way out right now. I'll just come pick you up," he said.

"Oh." *Why not?* "Okay. See you soon."

I ended the call and grinned, quite pleased with myself. Who says guys have to be the ones to initiate dates?

I threw all my makeup into the small basket I kept it in and wrapped the cord around my now-cool curling iron. Catching a glimpse of myself in the mirror, I realized that I would certainly look overdone. He'd think I'd been primping all day, just working up the courage to call him. I'd have to explain the situation with Lucee to him before he got any ideas.

Minutes later, Dylan's headlights passed across the front picture window. When I reached for the door, bag over my shoulder, I took a deep breath, tugged lightly at my dress, and smoothed the fabric around my waist. Before I closed the door behind me, I took one look up the stairwell and shivered.

"Wow," Dylan said from his driver's seat. He eyed my patent pumps. "You look great."

I grinned. "Thank you." I buckled myself in. "I had planned on going out with Lucee, who I guess must be working. But I didn't know that when I was getting ready. That's why I'm so … dressed up." I was speaking faster than

I should have been, and despite the evening chill moving in, my face was hot.

"I see how it is. I'm the backup." He winked in the twilight.

"That's not what I meant." I sighed contentedly.

"Where are we going?" he asked.

"My parents told me about this place. It's probably twenty minutes away. It's called Rose's. Good Italian food, I guess."

He nodded, "I've been there a few times."

"All it's cracked up to be?"

"Killer pizza."

I laughed and felt myself melt into the passenger seat. Dylan had a way of sloughing all of my stress and tension away. He made me feel so comfortable, so at ease.

"Pizza it is."

The drive passed quickly, and before long, we were seated at a corner booth in a newly renovated Italian restaurant decorated with wrought iron wine art and grape vines.

"So what's your type?" Dylan asked while he perused the menu. He peered over the top of it and smirked.

I nearly choked on my water. "My type?"

He closed his menu and leaned forward on his elbows. "Of pizza."

"Oh, I'm not picky." I chuckled lightly and took another sip of water. Unfortunately, I pulled the glass away too quickly and dribbled icy water down my chin. With a grin, Dylan handed me a napkin from the table's centerpiece.

A waiter stepped up to the table and asked whether we'd had enough time with the menus.

Dylan ordered. "We'll have a medium taco pizza," he said, "with everything on it."

I raised an eyebrow and admired our situation while the waiter gathered our menus and walked off. I was certainly overdressed. Most of the restaurant's customers were dressed in jeans and hooded sweatshirts, the occasional high-heel here or there. But there I sat, in full glam, next to a denim-clad twenty-something shop owner sipping on soda. It was perfect.

"How was business today?" I asked. "Downtown has been looking pretty empty lately."

"The morning was slow," he said. "But we had story time for little kids in the afternoon. That always brings a decent crowd."

My heart swelled. "Do you do that every week?"

"That I do."

"What does story time involve?"

"Well," he said before taking a sip of soda and peering over the cup at me. He crunched lightly on a piece of ice. "Each story time is a little different, but it always starts with a theme. And then a story. And then we do some activities based on the story."

"What was today's theme?"

"Autumn."

The restaurant door swung open and four young people burst in, staggering and laughing wildly. The group was made up of two couples – two men and two women. Each man had his arm draped around a woman's shoulder, and each woman walked like a newborn giraffe in too-high stilettos. One woman was laughing so hard that tears were streaming down her face, smearing black mascara and eyeliner down her cheek. The four of them slid noisily into a booth across the room from us. As one of the men slid into the booth, the leather seat caught on his leather jacket, making a loud rumbling sound, at which the four of them burst into laughter once more.

"Someone's having a good night," Dylan said, eyeing the foursome. The girls struggled to maintain their modesty while crossing their legs under the table, but their skirts didn't cooperate.

A waitress brought a pitcher of water to the table, and the bigger of the two men – a twenty-something with a blond crew cut and 5 o'clock shadow, lunged for the pitcher and began pouring the water but misjudged the distance between the pitcher and second cup and sent ice water surging across the table top. One of the girls plucked an ice cube out of the puddle and tossed it at the other girl's cleavage.

"It looks that way, doesn't it?" I said. "That poor waitress."

"Here we are," our waiter said soon after, lowering a pizza onto the center of our table. "One taco pizza. Is there anything else I can get for you right away?"

"No, thank you. This is perfect," I said, reaching for a plate.

"Actually," Dylan said, reaching into his pocket. "Just one quick thing." He withdrew a maple leaf cut out of orange construction paper. In a child's writing was scribbled, "You're awesome!" "Can you give this to that waitress over there?" He pointed to the girl at the lively booth; she was mopping at the spilled water with a wad of white bar rags.

"Of course," the waiter said, gently taking the leaf. "Anything else?"

"No, thank you."

My mouth hung open as I watched our waiter step to the girl, whisper in her ear politely, and point at our table. She unfolded the leaf, read it, and beamed. She waved, dropping several ice chips out of her rags and to the floor.

I wasn't sure what to say.

"One of the kids gave that to me after story time today," he said. "I figured it might make her feel a little better."

"I think it worked," I said, admiring the warmth rising from my belly. "That was amazing."

"Psh." He waved a hand in the air and pointed at this pizza. "*This* is amazing. Dig in."

Dylan was right – the pizza was good. We ate sloppily, laughed, and talked for what felt like hours. The customers were fading away, table by table, until the room was occupied by only us and one other couple. *Is that what we are: a couple?*

And suddenly, I began to feel very overwhelmed. My time was so blissful with Dylan, but so miserable in that house, where all I could do was fear for my safety or dwell on my mom's spiraling health. After a moment, tears welled in my eyes.

"What's wrong?" Dylan asked. His brow was furrowed. He leaned forward onto his elbows.

And that was all it took. Before I knew what had happened, I spilled my guts. I told him everything: the girl, the skeleton, the cleanse. When I had finished, I felt like a new person.

"That's – a lot," was his response.

"I'm sorry."

"Don't be. There's crazy stuff out there. Trust me." He slurped at what remained of his soda.

"What?"

"Hm?"

"Have you seen things like this before?"

"You mean someone as dressed up as you sobbing over a taco pizza? No. I can't say that I have."

I giggled and stretched. The clock above the bar said 11:06. "Holy balls! It's already after 11?"

"Do you want to go?" he asked after I had dried my tears and dabbed at my running makeup.

I nodded and smiled sheepishly. "I'm sorry."

"Don't be."

He left a stack of cash on the table and stood beside me. He held my jacket and waited for me to stand, too. "Oh, I can help pay. Let me get some money out of my purse." I bent to retrieve my bag, but Dylan scooped it up first.

"Not a chance," he said. He helped me into my jacket and passed me my bag. "Ready?"

I nodded.

It felt late. There were few cars on the street, and the day's warmth had given way to a black chill. We walked to his car side-by-side, not two inches apart. He smelled so fresh, so clean, so strong. My skin was searing, begging for him to rub against me, but we didn't touch.

The ride back took much longer, not because of traffic or detours, but because we took a longer route, a scenic route through country roads. "Where are we going?" I asked when Dylan turned off the main road.

"Just taking the long way," he said. "I thought you might need it."

I waited for an explanation.

"When I was younger and my grandma knew I was upset about something, she would take me for walks around our neighborhood until I talked enough that I felt better. I stuck to myself as a kid, so I didn't get very many opportunities to vent."

He waited. I waited. We rode in silence for several minutes.

"I'm sorry. Everything was going so well at dinner. I shouldn't have said anything."

"I had a great time. I'm still having a great time." He reached his hand across the center console and held it open. Without hesitation, I laced my fingers with his and smiled. I said nothing. I simply smiled a smile that I hadn't worn in too long.

"So this house," he said after a moment. "Why stay there? I mean, I know that you wanted to get some validation for your mom, but you have that now, don't you? Can't you leave it now?"

The thought had occurred to me before, but I had already signed the lease. "I will at the end of next month. I paid for all of September and October. The guy was nice enough to let me move in early and stay rent-free for the last week of August. I don't want to back out on him. Besides, how will I explain myself? Tell him I want to leave because of the literal skeletons in his closet?"

Dylan chuckled. "Who's the landlord?"

"I never met the guy. He's old. Said he was sick. Lives down south. Couldn't travel. So we did the paperwork via mail, and he shipped me a key."

"You know, you paid the money. It shouldn't matter whether you live there or not."

"I guess so. But I already subleased my apartment. And the alternative is living with my parents, and *that's* not happening."

He raised his eyebrows and waited. Even in the dark, I could read his expression.

"I love my parents dearly, but their house is one big bundle of stress. I can't handle it."

"I understand," he said, but he didn't probe.

"You do?"

"I do enough. What are you going to do at the end of the month if you already got rid of your apartment?"

"To be honest, I have no idea." He gently ran his thumb across my knuckles. "I wasn't expecting to want to leave so soon. I guess I'll see when I get there."

Our conversation drifted into a more casual tone. Our topics ranged from the bookstore to kids going back to school. Before long, we were pulling into my driveway, and I was forced to let go of his hand.

Dylan got out of the car and opened my door. But when I stood, he didn't back up to make space for me. Something was happening. I inhaled his scent, his warm, inherently male scent, and admired the width of his shoulders and chest inches from my face. I smiled, ready for whatever he sent my way, and looked up into his dark, searing eyes. He gently brought one hand to my face and tucked the other behind my lower back. "What kind of gentleman do you think I am?" he whispered. A moment later, I was lost in his kiss, lost in his smell, his taste, the touch of his skin. It lasted only a moment, but it was so powerful. His kiss held so much safety, comfort, and passion. When he pulled away, I still felt him on my lips and my tongue. I grinned and looked up at him through my lashes, speechless. "Should I walk you to the door now?"

Almost ashamed of how badly I wanted him to come in, I led Dylan through the grass and to the door. And true to his word, he gave me another kiss on my cheek and said, "Goodnight. And call me if anything else happens," before he turned to walk away.

"Wait." I called.

What the hell has gotten into me?

"Can you stay?" I didn't know what I was thinking, really, or even whether I *was* thinking. I just didn't want him to leave. Part of me wanted him, and badly, but another part of me just didn't want to be alone in the house.

He looked surprised, even restrained. "I don't know if –"

"Please? I just don't want to be alone."

He turned back to his car, which was still running, and said, "Okay. Just let me get my keys."

My heart was pounding in my ears.

Dylan was going to come in.

He was going to stay the night.

What is happening?

CHAPTER 14

I awoke the next morning to a light tap on the bedroom door. Dylan was standing in the entryway, politely shielding his eyes, just in case. "Sophia?" He called quietly.

"Hi." I pulled the comforter up to my chin, though I was wearing the same t-shirt and yoga pants he'd seen me in the night before. Inside, I beamed at his gentlemanly nature. I wondered whether all men were that way. Surely not. Something deep within me wanted so badly to usher him into my bed with me, just as I'd wanted the night before. I didn't know what had gotten into me.

"I've got to head to the store." He said, still not looking directly at me. "Are you decent?" I saw the hint of a tiny smile creep across his lips.

"You're funny." I rolled my eyes. "Of course, I am." I tossed the blanket off. "You can come in."

He stood where he was. "I've really got to go. I'm running late." He ran a hand through his thick, black hair.

"Did you sleep okay on the couch?" We had stayed up too late, talking, watching movies, and eating popcorn. I remembered nestling my face into his neck when he carried me up to my room after I'd fallen asleep downstairs. I also remembered a pang of disappointment when he walked out of the room after gently placing me on the bed.

He shrugged. "Did you get a good night's sleep?"

Surprisingly, I'd slept quite perfectly. Just knowing that he was in the house somewhere was enough to keep me comfortable through the night. No creaking floorboards, no stomping up the stairwell. "I did. Thank you for staying. I really appreciate it."

"Not a problem." He waved and padded down the stairs after promising to call when he was through at the store. When the front door closed behind him and his engine revved in the driveway, I tugged the comforter over my mouth and squealed with joy. This man made me feel so wonderful, so alive, so free, so comfortable. I beamed.

I was pulled from my ecstasy when my cell phone rang. I scrambled out of the bed and stumbled to the dresser, where my phone was vibrating.

"Hello?" I couldn't hide the smile from my voice.

"Soph? Hey! Sorry I didn't get back to you yesterday. I had to work really late. I was there until bar time. You should have seen this creep. Grabbed my ass. Troy threw him out before he knew what was coming. It. Was. Awesome. Did you end up doing anything? I hope you didn't stay bound up in that house all night."

I waited for her to take a breath. That girl could talk. "I figured that was what you were doing. Don't you have your phone on you at the bar, though?"

"Usually, but the manager was all over the place last night because some bus boy got caught stealing twenties out of the drawer."

"Oh. Well, no, I didn't stay 'bound up in the house all night.'"

I waited, unsure of how to proceed.

She waited, too.

Then, "Well, are you going to tell me what happened? You sound different."

"I went out with Dylan," I twirled my hair around my finger like a school girl.

"Oooh, how was that?!"

"Great. We went out to a place called Rose's and had pizza. He just left."

"He what?!"

"He just left."

"Sophia Marie! He stayed the night?!"

I laughed. "He did. Nothing happened, though. I mean, he kissed me, but that was it."

"Explain." Lucee never had an issue talking about guys, not since middle school.

"I just asked him to stay. For the company."

"Where did he sleep?"

"On the couch."

"You didn't even let him cop a feel?"

"Oh my God, Lucee. You're terrible. And for the record, I think I would have let him." I blushed. "He *chose* to stay on the couch. Pretty sure there was a spot ready for him in my bed."

"You little slut. I love you!" She whispered heavily into the phone. "I've got to see this guy. Send me a picture."

"I don't have one," I said. "But he is gorgeous. He has dark hair, and he's tall. He's got these shoulders that are strong and wide, and he dresses so well. You should see his jeans. And the way he *wears* his jeans."

"You so want him."

"I do." I flopped down onto the bed and stared at the ceiling.

"I'm coming over. I'll see you soon." And she hung up.

I didn't look in the mirror, I didn't go into the kitchen, and I didn't spend long on the stairs. I showered and came out of the bathroom just as Lucee was coming in the front door.

"Hello?! I hope you're decent because I'm coming in," she said.

The House on Valley Street

I met her in the entryway. Wrapped in her bear hug, I said, "What is that?" She carried a shallow cardboard box.

"It's a Ouija board." She gave me a cheesy grin that didn't reach her eyes. "Oh, come on. It was supposed to be funny."

"Aren't you the one who was making fun of me for fulfilling all the horror movie clichés in this house?"

"Yep. So what's one more?" She dropped her purse on the back of the couch and walked into the kitchen with the box. She sat. "So tell me more about this Dylan guy."

I paused at the entryway of the kitchen. I hadn't spent much time in there since the lavender sprig incident. With a deep breath, I crossed the threshold, some invisible barrier I convinced myself was protection.

"He's fantastic. I feel so good with him," I said. "He's funny, and he seems to genuinely care about what I have to say. And when he's nervous, he has this smile – oh, God, he's gorgeous."

Lucee's laugh escaped from low in her belly. I almost expected her to wipe tears from her eyes. "You're so cute."

I shook my head good-naturedly. "Don't laugh at me. I really like this guy."

"I can tell you do. Explain to me again why you didn't make a move last night."

"I don't think I'm really the 'make-the-first-move' type, Lucee."

"Okay, then. Why didn't *he* make a move last night?"

"Because he's a gentleman." I watched a bright red cardinal hop across the windowsill above the sink. "I asked him to stay to keep me company, and we watched movies and just spent time together all night. I fell asleep, he carried me to my bed, and he went back downstairs to sleep."

Lucee cradled her chin in both her palms and rested her elbows on the table, eager to hear more of my story. "Then what?" she asked. "Did he come back upstairs at all?"

"Just this morning," I said, "to say 'good-bye' before he went to work."

"And where did you say he works?"

"He owns a bookstore."

"Wow. A businessman."

"You'll have to meet him soon."

"That I will." She slipped the lid off the Ouija board box. "Oh! I almost forgot," she said, reaching into her bag. "I brought you this, too. I thought we could use it to write down whatever we get with this thing. Record our findings." She put on a Sherlock Holmes accent and produced a small green chalkboard and a box of white chalk. "Now we're ready." She propped the chalkboard against the wall and lay the game board across the table, placing the planchette in its center.

I frowned. "I don't think we should play around with this." Memories of my mom warning me against Ouija boards resurfaced. The word "portal" came to mind. I could hear Mom's voice in my head saying, "You'll open the door to evil." She was the reason I never played along at slumber parties when I was younger. To everyone else, it was only a toy, but to me, since my mom believed it to be, I thought it could be something more. I was afraid.

"Oh, come on." She pouted. "It's just a toy."

There it was. *Just a toy. Ugh.*

"Fine." I rubbed my brow. "Are we supposed to light candles or something? Dim the lights?" My sarcasm was palpable.

"Oh, shut up and hold my hands." She closed her eyes.

"Aren't we supposed to hold this thing?" I pointed to the planchette and gulped. I hoped she didn't hear the fear in my voice. It seemed foolish to be afraid of a toy, but that toy felt dangerous just the same.

"Good point." She placed her fingertips along the planchette, and I followed suit. She closed her eyes again. "Are there any spirits present now?" She called.

We waited.

Nothing.

"If there is a spirit present, make yourself known," she said again.

Nothing.

The only sound was the tick-tock-tick of the black and white, plastic clock that hung from the wall above the table.

"Molly? Are you here?" I asked.

The planchette twitched. Or was that me?

"Who's Molly?" Lucee said, removing her hands from the planchette.

"Dead neighbor girl."

"Fair enough. Molly, are you here?" Lucee asked after assuming the proper position again.

Still nothing.

"This is pointless, Lucee."

"Just give it a second," she opened one eye to address me, then closed it promptly.

We waited.

Knock, knock, knock.

We both sprang from the table, then smirked at each other and scoffed in harmony.

Gene stood outside the screen door. He raised his shoulders and frowned, apologetic for having startled us.

"Hi, Gene." I said, opening the door to invite him in.

"Hello, darlin'." He stood where he was. He held a chainsaw. "I'm sorry to bother you ladies. Didn't mean to frighten y'all."

Lucee waved to him.

"I was just doing a little bit of yard work, and I saw you had a dead limb in the back here. Just wanted to know if you'd like me to take care of that now. The chainsaw makes an awful racket, so I thought I'd ask."

The House on Valley Street

"Oh, Gene. That'd be great. Thanks so much." I looked past him and saw a large limb dangling from the oak beside the shed.

"They call that there a 'widow-maker,'" he said, following my eyeline. "It's awfully dangerous. I'll have it down shortly." He turned to leave.

"Gene, would you like some lemonade or anything? It's the least I could do."

"No, thank you, darlin'. I've got some iced tea waiting for me at home."

I smiled and nodded as he made his way to the back of the property, where he already had a ladder waiting.

"Well, that was nice of him," Lucee said. "What a sweet old guy."

"He really is. Chased away a spider for me once." I winked at her. "Nice try with the Ouija board, but I don't think it's going to happen."

"Guess not." She flicked the planchette with her index finger. "Maybe it's broken."

My pocket began to vibrate.

"Is that him?" Lucee asked.

I nodded, eyes wide.

"Answer it, you weirdo."

"Hello?"

"Are you having a good morning?" Dylan asked.

"I am. How has yours been?"

"Slow."

Lucee watched me expectantly.

"You know, I had a lot of fun with you yesterday," he added.

"I did, too." I said, beaming again.

"And I wanted to know if you'd like to go out with me tomorrow night. Like a real date. I'll dress up, too, this time."

I nodded animatedly for several seconds before I remembered that he couldn't see me. "That sounds great."

He told me that he would pick me up after he closed the store, and he hung up.

"Are you going to see him again?" Lucee asked.

I nodded. "Tomorrow night."

"Show me what you're going to wear. I might have to hook you up with something."

"You probably will," I said, leading her from the kitchen. "I wore my only decent outfit when I went out with him last night."

I grabbed hold of the banister and started up the steps, which creaked piercingly. *Is the banister loose?* I tried to wiggle it, but it stayed put. The creaking continued. Except it was less of a creaking and more of a squeaking. Lucee's expression told me that she heard it, too.

I bounced lightly on the step. Maybe it was a loose floor board.

Nothing.

And then I realized where it was coming from: the kitchen.

Lucee backed away from the steps and kept moving backward until she touched the wall. I edged past her and moved slowly, deliberately, one foot in front of the other.

The planchette was dragging across the board in swift bursts.

I stood frozen in the entryway to the kitchen, watching the planchette swing back and forth.

Lucee's footsteps steadily ticked behind me. Her steps took her to me and past me steadily. She stood at the edge of the kitchen table.

Her lips moved, but I heard nothing except the planchette whipping, scraping the table like a cat clawing at a closed door.

Thirty seconds passed like an hour. When the planchette suddenly came to a halt, I stood mute while Lucee pivoted on her heels and said, "R-e-l-e-a-s-e. It spelled 'release.'"

CHAPTER 15

The drive to the university was long. But that also meant that I had over two hours to think, uninterrupted. Even though I had been alone in the house for nearly the entirety of the past two weeks, with the exception of some time with Lucee and some with Dylan, the time I spent alone in the car cleared my mind enough for me to at least try to make sense of all that had happened around me.

Time to think also meant time to feel sorry for myself. I thought about Mom and Dad. I thought about how their relationship seemed to have grown stronger as they leaned on each other more and more. And I thought about how I felt that I was drifting farther from them, becoming less of a necessity, less of the main event in the attraction that was their lives. And I thought about how selfish I would seem had I ever told anyone that.

The weather was beginning to cool. Curled leaves of red and gold littered the dried grass along the highways and country roads I chose to travel.

The word "release" was spinning through my mind, replaying like credits on a white screen. Lucee and I had toyed with the letters, double-checking to be certain that "release" was the intended message. In the end, we were certain. We'd spent hours discussing everything I'd seen in the house, everything I'd researched, everything Dylan had told me about the rumors surrounding the house. We even talked about Molly. The only avenue I could think of to explore further was the history of the tribe Dylan belonged to. At the coffee shop, he had told me that some people believed there were bodies buried on the property and that those bodies belonged to members of the Pakutset tribe. The only person I knew of who was versed in Native American culture was a professor I'd had in my third year.

I brushed my hair from my face and switched the radio station.

"What's your annual income, Daniel?"

"Somewhere between ninety and a hundred thousand." The caller's voice sounded farther away, hollow.

I'd stumbled on a financial advisory broadcast.

"Daniel, your problem is that you have a non-matching IRA. You have to choose your program wisely."

The financial guru and the caller continued their conversation for several miles, and I became rather absorbed. I liked listening to the clinical, mathematical conversation.

It wasn't long before I made it to the campus, littered with students billowing in and out of dormitories, sweeping down the sidewalks on skateboards, huddled at crosswalks, impatiently waiting their turn, all nose-down in their cell phones and iPads.

I pulled up to the English building. Not long ago, I was spending the bulk of my time in that building, reading, discussing, and reading some more. As I inhaled the early autumn air, I was struck by a brief pang of disappointment at not being enrolled anymore. The beginning of a new school year, even in college, had always been so refreshing. New notebooks made my day. Or semester.

The inside of the building was dull, as it had always been. Gray, dried footprints muddled the still gray linoleum tiles lining the stairs. A corkboard perched against the white brick wall at the second-floor landing. A few fliers for new clubs and Friday night performances were pinned to it. But I kept hiking up flights of stairs instead of pausing to read. I needed the fourth floor.

When I had made it to the top, my breathing heavy, I dodged a pair of students chatting over a mutual hatred of a professor ("...and she gave me a C on my final last semester for no good reason *at all*...") and heaved open the door to the professors' wing. The hall split. To the left were the offices of foreign language professors. To the right were the English and literature professors. Tall, overflowing bookshelves lined the English hall. I stepped over a copy of Joseph Conrad's *Heart of Darkness*.

The last office on the right was Professor Tochek's. The door was open.

"Sophia, welcome," she said when I peeked around the doorway. "Come in."

Professor Tochek wore her hair short, close to her head on the sides and spiked on the top. She wore no makeup, though her alabaster skin was smooth and even. Her olive-green tee was baggy and draped around her hips. Her lips were chapped.

"What are you doing around here?" she asked, leaning back casually in her chair and crossing one leg over her knee. White socks showed above her flat dress shoes. She laced her fingers behind her head.

"Well," I said, sitting across the cluttered desk from her. "I know your area of focus has been Native American literature, and I was wondering if you could tell me anything about the Pakutset tribe."

"The Pakutset?"

"Yes. As far as I know, they're centralized in the Midwest, not far from here, actually."

"I've heard of them, but I can't say that I know much."

I glanced off to a photo of Professor Tocheck and her Yorkie.

"I know that they're a small group," she continued. "Historically, the tribe migrated less than most, partially because of its size. Fewer people to feed, fewer people to clothe, fewer reasons to leave."

"Do you know anything about their death practices?"

She raised an eyebrow.

"Anthropologically speaking, I mean."

"Well," she hesitated. "They share a lot of similarities with many of the other tribes that originated in this area." She rubbed her eyes like only a sleepless professor can. "They had a slightly different method of laying souls to rest, though. When a member of the tribe died, tribal leaders believed that they could stave off death for the rest of the members of the tribe if they burned the possessions of the deceased – a sort of hazmat process. Of course, they couldn't rely on science to explain germs and diseases."

I nodded as she continued.

"That's how it began. As time went on, the tribe adopted this practice as a sort of laying-to-rest. Gradually, they learned that burning everything someone owned didn't keep other people from dying. The process morphed into a ceremonial burning."

She absently picked up a pencil and tapped its eraser against her desk.

"Eventually, the Pakutset developed a fairly simply system. Whenever a member of the tribe died, one of the deceased's possessions was to be burned, and its ashes were to be placed in the mouth of the body."

I frowned. "They filled a dead person's mouth with ashes?"

She nodded. "When the possessions were burned, they were symbolically stripped of the ills of life: disease, hatred, war. But the ashes were returned to the body because whatever was burned was presumably something that the deceased enjoyed during life and would take with him into the afterlife."

"But why the mouth?"

"The Pakutset likened it to consumption. The item would almost become part of the deceased so that the two would be inseparable in the afterlife. No Bad-Ones, evil spirits, could steal the treasures."

"Bad-Ones?"

"That's just the tribe's term for a monster. Every tribe had its own creature to fear."

I was trying to process everything that Professor Tochek had said, but thoughts of Dylan's family kept surfacing. I was so intrigued by the thought of his ancestors moving through these rituals.

I wondered briefly if Dylan knew about these things. People often lose much of their heritage, especially ritual practices.

"What happened if nobody burned anything? What if the souls were never put to rest?" I pushed back the cuticles on my nails, but focused across the desk.

"Just that," she said. "The souls would never rest."

Our conversation gradually drifted away from the Pakutset and toward more surface-level topics. We discussed my moving and searching for a job, unsuccessfully. I briefly mentioned Mom's stroke, but when the topic came up, my breath hitched in my throat, and my eyes burned. I still couldn't talk about it.

After a short while, Professor Tochek said, "Well, it was great catching up with you, Sophia. I'd love to have you stay, but I have a student coming in shortly." She smiled broadly and ran her hand over her spikey hair.

"It was nice to talk to you, too." I stood and swung my bag over my shoulder. "Thanks for all your help."

The halls were far less crowded than they had been when I came in. Classes were going on, so I supposed everyone had somewhere to be. Only the occasional person bent over a drinking fountain or sat on the floor, cell phone in-hand, apparently waiting for something or someone.

I kept my eyes to the floor as I walked, mulling over all the information Professor Tochek had given me. Small puddles collected on a few of the steps. At the second-floor landing, a wet floor sign leaned against the bare wall. I pulled it out to the middle of the landing and continued on my way.

I didn't realize how warm it was in the building until I got outside. Despite the chill air, the smell of charcoal wafted from a nearby fraternity house. I unbuttoned my jacket and let some of the cool air hit my neck.

My phone vibrated in my jacket pocket, and my heart lurched when I saw it was Dylan. Why did he have this effect on me?

"Hello?" I gulped back my anxiety.

"Sophia, hi. How are you?" He was cool and confident, as always.

"I'm good. I'm actually on a bit of a roadtrip."

"A roadtrip?"

"A short one," I said, stepping around a mysterious, green puddle in the sidewalk. "I'm on a research mission at the university."

"How short?" he asked. "When will you be home?"

I glanced at my wrist before remembering that I wasn't wearing a watch. I never wore watches. "I'll be home in just a couple of hours."

"Good. Are we still on for dinner tonight?" There was a smile buried in his question. "Are you working up an appetite with all of that researching?"

"Definitely." My ears burned slightly, and I felt a warmth rising from my belly. And just like that, I stopped thinking about Professor Tochek's information download, about ashy dead people, about releasing anything.

"Perfect. I'll pick you up at 7."

The House on Valley Street

CHAPTER 16

"Burgers or tacos?" Dylan asked when I got into his car that evening. "I know a place for each."

The car smelled like him. It was clean. Masculine. I inhaled deeply.

"Burgers," I said, half a second later than I wanted to. "If that's okay with you."

He smiled, and his perfect teeth nearly glowed in the night. "Got it."

I admired less than subtly the way his t-shirt fit over his broad shoulders. There was always something about a man's shoulders that caught my attention. And his forearms. And his wrists. And his powerful hands ending in fingertips groomed enough to show that he takes care of himself but not so much that he would take longer to get ready than I would.

"What?" he asked.

Shit.

"I'm sorry. I was just," I stammered, "I was looking at your hands."

"My hands, huh?" He played into my weakness and gripped the steering wheel in a way that made my breath catch in my throat. His muscles tightened, and his knuckles turned white. His grip on the wheel had a grip on me.

And he knew it.

"It's nothing, really. I was just thinking."

He smiled and nodded, feigning belief in my reply before he relaxed his arms and changed the subject. "So what kind of burgers are we talking, here? Do you want the drippy, artery-clogging goodness, or do you want a veggie burger place?"

I raised an eyebrow and waited. When he glanced away from the road, I whispered, "Guess."

"Fair enough," he answered, clearly having understood my lack of a response. "Greasy goodness, it is."

I turned my head toward my window and watched my breath cause a growing and shrinking orb of condensation on the glass. Beyond it was a blur of passing cars, smudged by sparse sprinkles that had begun to coat the car. At least it was a warm rain. Cold rains gave me headaches.

I wanted to change the radio station, but I hesitated, wondering if it was "too soon" in our relationship to control his radio. Is that what we had? A relationship? Or were we just friends who happened to kiss once? I didn't want to be his friend, at least not *only* his friend.

We passed the rest of the drive in silence, which was strange, not because it was uncomfortable, but because it was perfectly fine. There was nothing remotely awkward about the silence. It was comfortable. It was safe. It was understood.

The restaurant was busy. Girls in t-shirts and jeans swayed this way and that way, their ponytails swishing side to side. A few guys were mixed in, but the service was definitely primarily composed of females. I noticed that the majority of the men were the ones carrying the bus tubs and almost violently clearing dishes from empty, crumb-covered booths, apparently not concerned with breaking the beer glasses and ceramic soup bowls.

"How many?" One girl asked when she met us at the front door. She wore heavy black eye makeup and false fingernails coated in honeybee yellow polish. One of her eyebrows was pierced twice.

Dylan held up two fingers and smiled politely to the girl, who bouncily led us to a booth in the far corner of the restaurant.

"Have you been here before?" Dylan asked me after the girl had left with our drink orders.

I shook my head. "Nope, but it's impressive. Check out Mickey." Above our booth, a four-foot tall, antique Mickey Mouse statue hung from the ceiling.

"Not bad."

"What's good here?" I paged through the brightly colored menu.

"This is my favorite." He reached across the table, flipped the page in my menu, and pointed to a photo of a massive burger.

I briefly read the description. Avocados. Bacon. Swiss cheese. Onion straws. "Deal. I'll get that."

"A girl after my own heart." He closed his menu and stacked it on top of mine. "How's the house been?" he asked.

I grunted.

"That awesome?"

I grunted again. "It's uncomfortable. And Lucee brought a Ouija board into the mix. I just don't like it there. But I feel like I have to stay, at least until I finish my book."

"Why?"

"For Mom."

The waitress arrived with our drinks and took our order. "Two Battle Burgers," Dylan said. "Please."

"Anything else?" she asked.

We shook our heads, and I handed the girl our menus.

"How is she?" Dylan sipped at his soda. "Your mom."

"Good, I think. I called her a couple times, but it's hard to tell over the phone. I can hear it in her speech still. But her mood seems okay most of the time…" I trailed off, stabbing my straw at the ice cubes at the bottom of my water glass. I didn't want to go down this road. I wanted a happy dinner. I changed the subject. "Hear any follow-ups from Mr. Peterson?"

"Not a thing. Guy's pretty standoffish, at least in a business sense. He's pretty fun to go out with, but he doesn't reach out for business often. It's a wonder he ever got published."

"You've been out with him?"

"Once."

"That's awesome! What did you guys do?" Somewhere across the restaurant, a plate toppled and clattered to the floor, where it shattered. We both flinched. The restaurant went silent and froze for a moment before all of the hustle and bustle and chatter resumed.

"We went out for a few drinks the night before the signing."

"Ah, a wasted Mr. Peterson. What's he like when he drinks?"

"I wouldn't say we were wasted." He laughed lightly, watching a small girl walk past holding a balloon in one hand and her dad's index and middle fingers in the other. "We only had a couple each. But to answer your question, he's about the same as he is sober." He took a drink. "Just a little louder."

Our conversation continued this way until the waitress delivered our meals.

"Are you ready to have your mind blown?" Dylan asked before we took our first bites.

"Let's do this." I pushed up my sleeves and rubbed my palms together over my plate.

He was right. It was mind-blowing. We laughed between drippy bites.

When our meals were finished and the bill paid, we made our way to the exit, dodging pulled-out chairs and small children moving about their tables while their parents finished eating. Dylan held the door for me.

"Thank you, sir," I said. I had eaten too much, but I was oh-so-satisfied. And conscious of my bloated stomach.

"What did you think?" he asked, walking close, but unfortunately, not close enough to touch me.

"That was fantastic. Massive, but fantastic." I shivered and pulled my shoulders to my ears.

Dylan opened the car door for me. When he made his way around and into the driver's seat, he said, "I've been coming here since it opened when I was little. My brothers and I used to come for our birthdays."

"You have brothers?"

"Two."

"What are their names?"

"Elliot and Jack. Elliot's older. He's my mom's from another marriage. Jackie's my little brother."

"Do you get along with them?"

He glanced sideways at me before pulling out of the parking lot.

"I mean, I don't have any siblings, but with the stories my parents have told about theirs, I figured maybe all siblings hated each other to some degree."

"Neither of them live here, so that helps." He smirked, and his smile flashed in the car each time we passed a streetlight.

"Far?"

"One's about an hour away. The other's about four hours away. I haven't seen either of them for a few years." He turned the heat up. "Are you warm enough yet?"

"I'm good." I nodded. "That's a long time to go without seeing your family. What are your parents like?"

"Curious, aren't you?"

"I am. Writers are made that way."

He sighed and glanced in the rearview mirror, though no one was following us. "My mom divorced her first husband a year before I was born, and she met and married my dad within just a couple of months. Turns out she was pregnant with me when they got married. They were together for a few years with Elliot and I. When she got pregnant again, things started changing. He wanted her to spend more time away from home, out on the road with him. He was a truck driver. After Jack was born, she basically decided to take off with her husband. She left us with our grandparents one day and never came back. Then, when I was 12, we got a letter saying that they'd both died. They overdosed together in a truck-stop bathroom."

My heart sank. This gorgeous young man has managed to do so well for himself in spite of having been dealt such a shitty hand.

"I'm sorry."

He was quiet for a moment. Then, "It was a long time ago. Besides, Grandma Iris has been good for us."

"Why did you stay?"

"What do you mean?"

"Your brothers moved away. Why did you stay here?"

He pulled into the driveway, turned the key to *Off* and turned in his seat to face me. "I like it here. Not all of us live in haunted houses." He nodded toward the house with a smile that told me he still didn't quite believe in everything I said happened.

I suddenly didn't want to go in. I found myself staring into each window, waiting for something – I didn't know what – to show itself, to glare from behind a dusty curtain. I shivered.

And then I spoke before I thought. "Will you come in?" I froze. "I mean, do you want to come in?" In that moment, I was thankful for the dark.

What must he think of me?

Dylan paused.

I stared at my shoes in the dark of the car. Even in the shadows, I felt him looking at me, gauging me.

"Are you okay?" he asked through a small smile.

"I'm sorry."

"For…?"

"I'm not a floozy." I forced a chuckle but continued to wring my hands in my lap. "I just thought it might be nice to have some company. I didn't mean that I wanted to… you know. Not that I don't. I mean, you're gorgeous –

Dammit.

"Oh my god. I'm so –

But Dylan's door was open, and he was walking around the car to my side. He opened my door and smiled warmly. "Thank you," he said.

"For what?"

"The compliment. You said I'm gorgeous." He grinned and blinked off into the middle-distance exaggeratedly like some daytime soap opera still-frame.

Dylan had such a way of lightening my mood. Even in the short time that I had known him, I recognized how different he could make me feel and how easily he did it.

"I'm going to stop talking now." I said, swinging my bag over my shoulder as we walked to the door. I became hyperaware of his hand so softly grazing the small of my back as he guided me to the house.

My hands trembled slightly as I fumbled with the key. I was sure he noticed. When I finally managed to open the door, I nearly fell into the house. Dylan stood back and watched me make a fool of myself.

What am I getting myself into? I thought. *I have no idea what I'm doing.*

"Are you sure you want me to come in?" he asked, peeking his head around the door that I had accidently let swing shut in front of his face.

I mumbled an apology and tugged the door open. "Yes."

There comes a time in a young person's life when she must throw caution to the wind, stop asking herself, "What if?" New things are scary, but they're exciting. And one cannot reach happiness and comfort without facing her fears.

At least that's what I told myself.

I dropped my bag onto the entry table and spun slowly to face Dylan again.

He stood with his hands casually tucked into the pockets of his jeans, a sheepish smile on his face. He opened his mouth to speak but couldn't find the words.

His gaze met mine, and before I knew what was happening, my body was carrying me toward him. One trembling foot in front of the other, I approached, watching him blush sweetly. Even in the dark, his cheeks shone pink.

We stood toe-to-toe, and I slowly raised my arms and laced my fingers behind his neck.

The House on Valley Street

As his lips parted to meet mine, he let a sweet, shaky breath escape.

For only a moment, the world stood still. My pulse throbbed in my ears. My senses heightened. I heard everything around me. I felt every inch of my body. I tasted breath that wasn't mine.

My fingers splayed across broad shoulders, and I reached up the back of Dylan's head, tugging lightly at his hair. His hands trailed down my back and rested on my hips, pulling me close so that our bodies were flush.

My body was acting of its own accord, moving when and how it wished.

His fingertips slid beneath the hem of my top, and he paused, pulling away from me and gazing down at my fervent eyes, as though asking my permission.

Words weren't necessary. I fumbled over the buttons on his shirt, starting at his neck and working downward, my lips eagerly reaching for his.

I felt him smile against my kiss.

CHAPTER 17

I stretched my arm across Dylan's chest and nuzzled his shoulder. He was warm and smooth, and he smelled so good. He stirred slightly, breathing through barely parted lips. With his eyes closed, his eyelashes fanned out over his cheeks. His chest lay exposed, and the comforter covered him only from the waist down. In my sleepy fog, I strained to remember whether he put his pants back on before he fell asleep. I considered lifting the comforter to check, but I thought it would be in bad taste. What if he woke up and caught me looking at him? I stowed my curiosity and figured I would find out soon enough.

I dragged my foot higher and searched below the comforter for his leg. The sound of my foot sliding along the sheets was loud and harsh in the quiet morning. The sun hadn't come up yet, and everything in the house was still and silent.

Except that sound.

I dragged my foot back toward me, trying to duplicate the noise I'd heard.

The scraping sound kept time with my foot's movement. Back and forth. Scratch and scrape.

I stopped moving.

Then I heard it again.

A blood curdling, slow scraping noise sounded near us.

I froze and turned my eyes toward the ceiling, but I was afraid to look behind me. I imagined Molly standing beside my bed, hovering, saliva dangling from her parted lips, inches from my head.

It was late – or early. It must have been 3 a.m.; maybe I was overly tired. Maybe I was hearing things.

Another low, slow drag echoed through the room. It seemed to reverberate off the ceiling and the walls, disorienting me so that I couldn't tell which direction it came from.

I tapped Dylan's shoulder. "Dylan?" I whispered.

His eyes fluttered, and he tugged the comforter closer to his chin.

"Dylan?" I nudged him again.

He opened his eyes sleepily and smiled broadly. "Hi."

"Did you hear anything?"

"No." He frowned. "Why? Did you hear something?" His eyes were drifting closed again, heavy with the promise of more rest.

I feared that Dylan would think I was insane. I let him fall back to sleep, and I mustered all the courage I had burrowed away in the deepest corners of my being and tossed the comforter aside before swinging my legs out of the bed.

Dropping my feet off the side of the mattress created a sensation similar to that which one might feel when blindly descending stairs and wondering whether there were additional steps or not. My toes sought the floor.

The shock of the cold sent a bolt up my toes, through my shins, and up to my knees. With a deep breath, and trying not to imagine someone – or something – staring at my Achilles tendons from beneath my bed, I stood.

A sudden snore from Dylan sent my heart lurching.

A low hum sounded just outside the room, soft and steady.

The furnace?

A vent?

A draft?

I continued, one foot in the front of the other, hyperaware of my shoulders and the back of my neck, half expecting warm breath to touch my skin.

"Hmmmmmmmmm."

The noise was quiet, but clear.

The doorway was within an arm's length when I heard it again, more distinctly, and realized that it wasn't just a sound. It was a voice.

"Hmmmmmmmmm."

Goose bumps covered my arms and legs at the sound of the pained groan, and chills ran along my spine. My fingers curled around the doorframe.

"Hmmmmmmmmm."

I peered around the corner and gasped. My breath hitched, and I struggled to remain standing on weakened knees.

A small girl, not more than eight years old, lay in a fetal position at the end of the hallway, her bare back to me, her face to the wall. She rocked slightly and moaned, clutching her middle. Straight, black hair fanned around her head, and she wore little clothing. An animal hide was draped over her legs, but she shivered nonetheless.

"Hmmmmmmmmm."

Part of me wanted to turn and run back to bed, lie beside Dylan, cover my head with the blanket, and remain there, motionless, until morning.

But another part of me wanted so badly to help the girl. She looked sick. Or hurt. She needed me.

Before I knew what was happening, I rounded the corner into the hallway, my eyes never leaving the girl's trembling body, her dark skin unblemished. I slid along the wall toward her, making as little noise as possible. I hadn't yet figured out what I would do when I reached her, but I wanted to be closer.

My body shook with a strength I hadn't felt before, and my breath came in ragged heaves.

"Hmmmmmmmmm."

My outstretched hand and splayed fingers reached inches behind the girl's shoulder. I don't know what I was expecting; I don't think I was expecting anything.

Less than six inches.

"Hmmmmmmmmm."

Just a little farther.

"Hmmmmmmmmm."

I felt the cold radiating from her skin.

"Hmmmmmmmmm."

A screeching cackle sounded behind me.

I wheeled around and caught sight of Molly, the girl who'd lived next door thirty years ago, standing crookedly in the doorway to the bedroom. Her jaw hung open, and a large string of saliva hung from her chin.

She grinned, and her uneven gate carried her into the bedroom and out of my sight.

I spun again, but the moaning girl had vanished.

Without thinking, I called, "Dylan!" and ran down the hall to the bedroom door. At full speed, I turned into the room and ran into the darkness. Just as I crossed the threshold, I saw her standing, waiting for me. Her shoulders were square to the

The House on Valley Street

doorway, and her head lay against her shoulder, cocked to one side. She grinned.

I couldn't slow down. I couldn't stop. I ran through her. *Through* her.

Cold surged through my body. I thought I might faint.

"Sophie?" Dylan sat upright in bed, holding his cell phone for light. He shone it in my direction, but it wasn't bright enough to reach me.

"There's something in here," I said, my voice barely audible.

"What?"

"There's something in here. I heard something. And then I saw something." I stood frozen to the floor. My ears tingled, anticipating any crashes, giggles, or breaths I may be able to pick out of the deafening silence.

"It's late. Maybe you dreamed it." He tapped the mattress beside him. "Come lie down."

I knew I wasn't dreaming. I knew what I saw. But what was I going to say? Our relationship was just beginning; I couldn't scare him away from me. I padded across the room as quickly as I could without jogging and wrapped myself in the comforter. I tucked my body as closely to his as I could.

I didn't dream it.

I saw them.

Two girls.

I saw them.

The House on Valley Street

I didn't dream it.

My eyes gradually began to fall, and sleep threatened the clarity of my mind. Maybe I had been imagining things. Maybe I had been sleepwalking. Was it all a dream? Had I even left the bed?

Dylan snored lightly beside me. I began to drift into an uneasy sleep, but I wouldn't let go completely. I dangled in the middle ground, not awake, but not asleep, for minutes, maybe an hour. I don't know how long.

Another menacing cackle sounded suddenly and echoed in my ears. My eyes shot open, and I strained to see in the darkness. Nothing moved. The silence hummed.

My face suddenly felt hot, moist. It heated for several seconds, then cooled, then heated, then cooled. A foul smell surrounded me.

She was breathing on me.

I couldn't speak. All I could do was reach over and tug on Dylan's shoulder. He must have sensed an urgency in my touch because he sat upright.

"What's wrong?" he asked.

The breath continued to hit my face.

My mouth moved so little I may have passed as a ventriloquist. "Turn on the light," I whispered.

He reached across his body and turned the toggle on the bedside lamp. When the light filled the room, nothing was out of place.

I exhaled heavily and rubbed the sleep from my eyes.

"What's going on?" Dylan asked.

"Something's happening in this house," I said, unable to contain it any longer. "Earlier, there were two girls. One was in the hallway, lying on the floor, and there's another that followed me in here – or I followed her. I don't know. I heard her laughing." My tears pooled and trickled down my cheeks.

Dylan rubbed my back reassuringly. "Would it make you feel better if I looked through the house?"

To be honest, I wasn't sure whether that would make me feel better. The girls could obviously appear and disappear at will. Who's to say that they would just pop up in front of Dylan to verify what I had told him?

But not knowing what else to say, I only nodded.

Dylan got out of bed and rounded it to my side before reaching down to take my hand. "Come." He said.

I stayed close to him, clutching his hand as we moved along the hallway, in and out of each of the upstairs rooms, then down the stairs and around the first floor. There was nothing out of place. The doors were all locked. The windows were all closed. There were no girls. There was nothing.

I sheepishly followed him back to the bedroom. Embarrassed as I was, I was immensely thankful that he was there with me that night. I contemplated what I would have done had I been alone, but I couldn't fathom the situation.

The House on Valley Street

He tucked the comforter around my hips and moved to the other side of the bed before climbing in. He turned to face me and said, "It's not that I don't believe you."

I frowned, questioning his meaning.

"I know you think that there's something wrong with this house – some kind of a haunting or something."

I opened my mouth, but no explanation came out.

"I just don't know whether I believe in hauntings. I've never seen anything."

Rather than press the issue and carry on an uncomfortable conversation at four in the morning, I thanked him. "Thanks for checking for me."

"Anytime." He smiled and leaned in to kiss my forehead. The stubble on his chin scratched against the bridge of my nose.

I wrapped my arm around his shoulder and held him to me. He was close, and I didn't want him to move away.

His kisses trailed from my forehead to my temple, to my cheek, and to my lips. His kiss was soft, gentle.

My breathing gradually became heavier, and I lay flat on my back, tugging him over me. He swung his leg over my hips and straddled my body, kissing me more excitedly, passionately.

"Just a second," he said, grinning.

He reached for the bedside lamp when suddenly, the girl appeared, slack-jawed, standing still at the side of the bed.

Before either of us could scream, a piercing siren filled the air, and the girl disappeared. We both covered our ears.

"What the hell?" Dylan said. The smoke alarm was deafening.

I wrapped the comforter around me, and Dylan tugged his shirt off the dresser, shoving his arms into it as we moved down the steps.

"I don't see any smoke," I panted.

As soon as the words left my mouth, I saw light wisps of smoke billowing out of the bathroom and into the foyer. Flames cackled just beyond my line of sight.

Dylan pulled the front door open and ushered me out. "Go outside," he said.

"I need to get my recorder," I said, moving around him.

"I'll get it," Dylan called.

I marched past him into the kitchen. I tore my bag from the back of one of the chairs and frantically shook its contents onto the tabletop. A Chapstick rolled to the floor, and a nickel and two pennies spun and rolled across the table.

"Shit! It's not here!"

"Leave it! We're going." Dylan pulled me by the wrist to the front door. Just as he reached for the handle, I remembered where my recorder was.

"It's in the bathroom! Let go!" I writhed out of his grasp and pushed the bathroom door open. I'd taken the recorder out of the pocket of my jeans when I'd changed into pajamas the night before. It was on the vanity.

Dylan stood frozen, dumbfounded, for only a moment before lurching toward me again. "Sophia! What the hell are you doing?"

He didn't understand why I needed that recorder.

I didn't either, honestly. At least not entirely.

Maybe it was because it was a gift from Mom just before her stroke.

Maybe it was because it held some of my most intimate, most honest thoughts.

All I knew was that I needed it.

Smoke was rising to the ceiling, and it was thick enough that the light fixture was now only a glowing orb behind the darkness.

I fumbled blindly through the smoke, feeling for my recorder. As soon as it touched my hand, I clutched it and fell to the floor, drinking in the cleaner air that hung low in the room. I turned on my hands and knees and crawled toward the door.

Bare feet stood on the linoleum in front of me.

"I got it. Let's go," I said.

Dylan didn't answer.

"Dylan, get down here. There's less smoke. Come on!"

He still didn't answer.

"Dylan?"

"Yeah?" Dylan called from the foyer. "I'm holding the door open. Trying to let some of the smoke out. We need to get out of here, Sophia. Christ."

My heart sank. Dylan wasn't standing in front of me.

The smoke was now so thick that I couldn't see the body attached to the knotted feet. The tips of its toes were all that came into focus. They held a bluish hue, and the toenails were overgrown and jagged.

I stood and ran from the room as quickly as I could. My feet slapped against the floor as I struggled to hold myself upright. My back ached, and my lungs burned.

"Come on!" Dylan said, guiding me through the door.

The clean air slapped me with a ferocity as shocking as the smoke inside. I coughed several times, ushering the smoke out of my body.

Flames poured from beneath the roof of the garage. Large flakes of ash danced through the dark sky and glided to the ground, glowing amber, then orange, then gray.

Sirens sounded in the distance. I stumbled to the curb across the street and turned back to the house. The fire had only just begun to reach the house, but the garage would likely be beyond hope by the time help arrived.

"Cripes almighty! Are you alright, darlin'?" Gene came tromping around the house as fast as his rickety joints would allow, shielding his face from the radiating heat. "I saw the smoke and I called for the authorities. What happened?" He was breathing heavily.

"Gene! Oh, thank you. Thank you." Tears welled in my eyes as I shivered on the curb. "I don't know what happened. The garage. It spread to the house." My words came out in gasps. "We were sleeping and the alarm --"

"We?" Gene asked, tightening his bath robe around his shoulders. "Is someone still in the house?" His tone was full of alarm, and he spun in his loafer slippers to face the siding that melted like a wax candle.

"No, it's –

I spun to the left, then the right. Dylan was gone.

"I meant 'I.' I was sleeping. I'm sorry. I'm just so shocked," I said, discreetly scanning the shadows around the house. *Where is he?*

"You just rest that head," Gene said. "That fire will be out soon," he said, sitting beside me. "You're alright, darlin'." He rested one wrinkled palm at the top of my back and patted me lightly.

I was too distracted by Dylan's sudden disappearance to feel assured by Gene's touch. I knew he wasn't in the house.

"Thank you, Gene, really. But please, go back inside. It's cold out here. I'll be fine."

"Nonsense."

"Really. Please. I just need a minute to think." I felt utterly horrible, dirty, ungrateful for pushing Gene away the way that I had, like a child complaining about a handmade birthday gift. But I couldn't hold myself together much longer, and I didn't want to lose my mind while Gene was beside me.

The firetruck was rounding the corner at the end of the block. Its lights glowed red against our faces.

"Suit yourself," he said, standing. "I'm happy you're safe." He shuffled away and disappeared behind the house.

Where is he? I thought again as the firetruck came to a squeaking stop.

Suddenly, an arc of water came into focus, accompanied by the sounds of gushes and spurts of water rushing through a hose. Dylan rounded the garage, tugging hard on the green garden hose, aiming it at the heart of the blue and orange flames dancing about the shingles on the roof.

Relief flooded over me, and unable to contain myself, I burst into tears.

CHAPTER 18

"They don't know yet," I told Lucee. "Could have been some kids. It could have been electrical. You'd think that a week would be long enough, but they're still investigating." Even though she couldn't see me through the phone, I curled my fingers into mock quotation marks around the word "investigating." These things always took longer than they should.

A part of me thought that perhaps the fire had cleansed the home of whatever spirits lay inside. But deep down, I knew something else had awoken.

"At least no one was hurt," she said. "It's so crazy, though."

"I know." I sat on the patio behind the house, watching a squirrel make off with a piece of stale bread I had thrown in the grass that morning. My phone was wedged between my shoulder and my ear.

"It's nice that Dylan was there with you," she said. "I mean, for support and stuff."

"I know."

"You're not saying much."

It was true. I was focused on trying to understand who would start my garage on fire. That wasn't something that kids I knew did for fun or for pranks or even on accident. That didn't just happen in the middle of a neighborhood. And I didn't trust the investigators to be thorough enough. I had a suspicion that they would land on a reasonable explanation and go with it without proper depth into their investigation. I could figure it out before they did.

"I'm just preoccupied," I said, suddenly conscious of my poor posture. I sat upright.

"How's your mom? Did you tell her?"

"No. And I don't plan on it. She would freak out." The squirrel had returned for a second piece of bread.

"You know what she'd say, right?" She asked, knowing the answer.

"She'd want me to leave here."

"Exactly."

"Which is another reason why I'm not going to tell her. Everything will be fine." I sounded more convinced than I was. "I need to finish this novel. And things are getting interesting with Dylan. I'm just not ready to go."

"How's that going, by the way?"

"It's fine. I've been doing some research, and I've got a couple of chapters done—

"Not that. Dylan. How's it going with him?"

Despite what I had been through, mention of Dylan forced a slight smile. "Great. He's a really good guy. He was a little upset the night of the fire, though. I went back for my recorder."

Lucee paused. "I heard that."

"Heard what?"

"That smile in your voice. You really like him, don't you?"

I spoke without hesitation. "I do."

"And he was there during the … fire?"

"Yeah."

"What time did you say you made it out of the house?" She was seemingly pasting clues together.

"About 4."

"So either he was staying the night or you guys were prepping for a morning shift milking cows on the family farm."

"You caught me." I chuckled lightly. Something blue caught my eye near the shed in the back corner of the yard.

"You dirty ho!"

"Again. Caught me." I smiled and kicked at a late-season dandelion on my way to the shed.

"How was it? Was he good?" Her voice rose like a child told she could open a Christmas present a day early.

"You are way too excited right now." I blushed.

She sighed heavily into the phone. "Are you going to give me any details or not?"

I stooped to pick up a pale blue handkerchief, grasping it by a corner as though it certainly held a flesh-eating bacteria. I assumed it was Gene's. After all, he had been working near there when he trimmed that tree the other day.

"Well," I said, grinning despite the handkerchief, "it – he – was great. We went out for dinner and came back here, and, well, you know."

"Was it awkward?"

"Not at all."

"Aw, you're meant to be."

"Don't get ahead of yourself." I opened the screen door and plucked a crumpled grocery bag from the drawer under the oven. Tucking the blue linen inside the bag, I said, "I can't wait to see him again, though. But things are weird with the fire and everything. I feel awkward about just sweeping it under the rug and moving on with our relationship. Doesn't that sound weird?"

"Not really. I think it's better if you move on. Why stop everything to worry about this?" she waited. "I mean, everyone is safe. Nobody got hurt. I say move on."

"Maybe you're right." I hung the bag from the back of a chair and sat at the kitchen table. It was nice to talk to Lucee; she had a way of putting things in a better perspective for me when I was at risk of losing myself in my own head.

My back was to the wall. Although nothing had happened after the fire, I didn't feel comfortable turning my back to any open space in the house. In fact, I hadn't spent much time there since. I'd kept myself busy with errands while the repairmen patched the bathroom wall. Thankfully, that's as far as the fire had spread in the house. The bathroom mirror and vanity were destroyed, but the toilet and the shower still worked. The room still smelled like smoke, though, so I did my best to avoid it.

"You're damn right, I'm right," she laughed. "I've got to go. I need to be to work in an hour."

After we'd hung up and I'd decided I'd pressed my luck long enough inside the house, I moved outside to examine the garage for the third time in the past half hour. The walls were charred, and there was a gaping hole in its roof. Luckily, there wasn't much inside at the time of the fire. And I was lucky enough that I had decided to park on the street that night.

I drug my hand along the blackened wall, my fingertips turning black in the ash.

The boxes I had moved there were destroyed. What wasn't burned had been drenched by the firefighters.

A thought occurred to me then.

Was it possible that the hat I had found in the basement was somehow connected to the spirits in the house? It was a man's hat, but all of the apparitions or ghosts or whatever you'd call them had been female. Did that matter, though? Maybe the hat belonged to a father or a grandfather, and maybe a young girl cherished it as a memory of her loved one.

Or maybe I was reaching.

Professor Tochek had said that the way the tribal members had lain loved ones to rest was to burn something that belonged to them, something they loved. Since everyone in town seemed convinced that this home was built on sacred lands, then perhaps it wasn't too far of a stretch to believe the spirits belonged to members of the Patsuket tribe.

I suddenly tore the soggy flaps back from the cardboard box and rustled through its wet, smoke-stained contents until I found what was left of the hat. Its brim curled upward, black around the edges, and it was warped, such that it would no longer fit on any semi-round skull.

Moments later, I was rustling through drawers in the kitchen, searching for the matches Lucee and I had used on the cleanse. Various receipts and coins flipped about the inside of the drawer until I found the small, white package.

Matches and hat in hand, I moved to the center of the backyard, hoping that passersby would not see me and contact the authorities claiming arson.

I knelt in the grass and ripped a match across the bottom of my sneaker. The flame flickered in my trembling fingers, but when I held it to the edge of the hat's brim, it wouldn't spread. I spun the hat and tried the other side.

Nothing.

The leather was still soaked from the firemen's hoses. I dabbed the flame into the dirt and resorted to Plan B.

Beside the shed, at the base of the tree Gene had trimmed, were several crisp, dead branches that he'd left behind. I gathered them and propped them into a teepee-like structure, tucking a handful of dead leaves below it. If I were going to burn the hat, I needed a bigger fire, something more substantial than a little match. I knelt beside the pile, adjusting and tweaking it like a hairstylist admiring his work, and when I was convinced that there were sufficient chances for the flame to spread, I snapped another match across the bottom of my sneaker.

I crawled around the pile, touching the match to the leaves at various points. More than once, the flame caught, then died out almost immediately.

I dropped the match in the center of the pile and ripped yet another across my shoe.

But again, the flame caught, grew, then faded and died.

The wind blew, and an ember glowed orange close to the ground.

I scurried forward and crouched low, my face brushing the grass, and I blew lightly into the embers, watching them glow and grow. Smoke curled upward and drifted away, fading like a ship on a far-off horizon.

When the embers grew to flames, I turned the hat upside-down so as not to smother the flame, and I placed it into the fire. It crackled softly like puffed cereal soaking in milk until its edges began to darken and curl.

I monitored the flame, adding dead leaves and blowing periodically until the hat was nothing but a charred heap. And in that moment, when I stared at the hat, I felt sorry. I felt sorry for the hat. Sorry that its life had come to this. Japanese mythology says that household items that have served their purpose for at least a century are rewarded by being brought to life. Umbrellas hop about on one foot. Brooms reach this way and that with new arms.

This hat would never come to life. This hat represented the end of life.

What a shame.

As the flame died out, I watched the house from my spot in the grass. I was waiting for a green mist to float from each window or a burst of light to radiate from the home's center, officially marking the home's cleansing. But nothing happened.

The House on Valley Street

Nothing visible, anyway.

I didn't see anything different, but the house *felt* different, even from out in the grass. It didn't look as menacing. It felt like a home, not a tomb. For the first time since I'd moved in, I truly saw it as a typical house.

The House on Valley Street

CHAPTER 19

As I moved through the house later that afternoon, I felt as though a weight were absent from my shoulders. The rooms were lighter. The walls were brighter. The sun shone stronger through the windows.

There was a knock on the front door.

"Special delivery," Dylan said when I opened the door. He held a bouquet of white roses and a large red candle. "I thought the candle might help the smell in the bathroom," he said, stepping inside. "Not all fire is bad." He winked and kissed my cheek. "And the flowers are because girls like flowers. Girls like flowers, right?"

I hugged him tightly, and we stood that way for some time.

When we parted, I listened to the echo of our heels tapping the floor and admired the home's new air. For the first time, it was nothing more than lumber and drywall. Nothing ominous. Nothing alive.

Now, I was ready to finish my novel.

"Feels different, doesn't it?" Dylan asked.

"It does." I inhaled deeply and looked up the stairs. It wasn't long ago that a young girl – or the apparition of one – came pounding down those steps. I could still hear the saliva gurgling in her throat. But now, the stairs were cleaner, less menacing. They were innocent bystanders.

"Do you finally believe in all this?" His shoulders felt so strong under my palms.

"I'm just glad it's over, whatever *it* was."

I took the flowers and the candle from him, sniffing each deeply. The flowers were magnificent and fresh. The candle smelled like cinnamon and brown sugar. I placed it on the side table beside my car keys.

"Are you hungry?' I asked, leading him to the kitchen. I pulled a tall glass from the cabinet, filled it with water, and stuffed the roses into it before placing the bouquet at the center of the table.

"What's this?" he asked, holding the plastic bag I had hung from the back of his chair.

"Oh!" I crossed the room and took hold of the bag. "That's Gene's."

"Eugene? The neighbor guy?"

I nodded.

"Why do you have it?" Dylan's smile faded.

I hesitated, then said, "It's his handkerchief. I found it outside. Gene came over and cut down some branches in the backyard, and I think he dropped it. I'll just go drop it off." I owed him an apology, anyway. I hadn't spoken to him since the night of the fire. I made for the door, but Dylan gripped my wrist.

"I don't think you should go over there, Soph," he said. "You don't want to be in a house alone with an old man. You can't trust him."

"You can't be serious."

Dylan said nothing and didn't release his grip.

"You're serious?"

He nodded. "I'll take it," he said. He took the bag and left, leaving me awe-struck in the middle of the kitchen. The screen door swung closed behind him.

What the hell was that? I briefly hoped I hadn't just endured the first sign of a crazy boyfriend. I'd really hoped not.

I opened the screen door and stepped out onto the porch, watching Dylan tromp through the yard to Gene's back door. He knocked and waited, glancing over his shoulder once toward me.

Nothing happened.

He knocked again and waited.

Nothing.

After a moment, he turned to come back, the white grocery bag hanging from his hooked pinky finger. It slapped the side of his leg as he walked, spinning and swinging back and forth.

"He wasn't there," he said, moving around me to bring the bag inside.

"Give it to me," I asked, reaching. "I'll just hang it on his door."

Dylan frowned and pulled the bag away.

"What's your deal?" I asked. "Why don't you like this guy?"

"Who said I didn't like him?"

"It's pretty obvious." I tugged the bag from his grasp and traipsed across the lawn. "He's an old man," I called behind me. "I don't get it."

Spider webs clung to the door jamb, and box elder bugs swarmed a nearby window. Tiny beetles congregated in a sea of orange along the door's glass. I knocked for good measure.

Just as Dylan had said, there was no reply.

The bag had twisted around two of my fingers on the walk over, cutting off my circulation. The tips of those fingers were purple when I managed to free them from the bag's handles. I opened the screen door to drape the bag over the inside door's handle. As soon as I opened the door, though, I nearly doubled over.

The House on Valley Street

A horrendous odor surged outward from the home, reeking of roadkill and rot. A horrible thought seized me. I tried to count the days since I'd last seen Gene. *Oh, no, I thought.*

It wasn't uncommon for older people to pass away in their homes and not be found for days, sometimes weeks, especially for those who didn't receive frequent visitors. The sound of the beetles buzzing and colliding with the home's vinyl siding was the only noise accompanying my now-ragged breathing. Dylan was staring, arms crossed over his chest.

With calculation, I reached forward and turned the door handle. The door was heavy, sticky with the late autumn humidity. I nudged it with my shoulder, and it gave.

"What are you doing?" Dylan called, and he stomped across the yard. "Sophia!"

I ignored him and stepped over the aluminum threshold.

The home was dark and silent. I pulled my blouse over my nose to block out the ever-present scent that I was sure signaled death.

"You shouldn't be here," Dylan said from the doorway.

"Don't you smell that?" Brushing off his warning, I moved further into the home. The floor was coated in a layer of dust that would rival that found in an untouched wine cellar or the catacombs of ancient Italy.

"You shouldn't be here." Dylan grabbed hold of my upper arm. His fingers were gripping me tightly enough to leave white spots that lingered on my bicep after I'd pulled free from him.

"We need to make sure he's okay. Don't you smell that smell?"

"You don't understand," he said.

But at the moment, I didn't care what Dylan had to say. My conscience told me that something could be wrong, and who else was around to help? No one. I moved through a narrow corridor, following the smell, listening for any sign of life in the home. But there was nothing but silence, except for the swishing of my sneakers against the hall's worn, brown carpet. Anticipation and tension pulled my shoulders to my ears. The smell was growing stronger, and it intermingled with the peppery scent of old people.

At the end of the hallway were two rooms. My heart lifted at the realization that the smell could be wafting from week-old deli wrapping left to fester in a corner of the kitchen. The sound of flies buzzing seemed to reverberate off the walls of the narrow hall.

The kitchen was small. It was filthy, covered in dust and cobwebs, but there were no dishes in the sink, no food on the counters, no trash cans to be seen. Everything was in its place, but it looked as though it hadn't been touched in years. An old milk crate lined with empty bottles was tucked neatly against the far wall. Dull yellow roosters bordered the ceiling.

"Dylan?" I called. "You should see this. It looks like nobody's been in here in ages."

He didn't answer.

"Dylan?"

Still nothing.

The smell had grown stronger, but I couldn't locate the source. I flipped a light switch, as though that would somehow boost my olfactory sense.

A single red hand towel hung from what I assumed was the oven, though I'd never seen anything like it before – at least not outside of a hipster, in-with-the-old magazine. It offered three doors, one on the left and two stacked on top of the each other on the right. Each door was made of ornately decorated brass, and the whole appliance stood on four clawed feet. I touched the knitted hand towel, and as it swung like a pendulum along the brass bar that ran the length of the oven, dust wafted from it.

I surveyed the room. There were two more strange appliances behind me. Both stood on the same brass claw feet. The larger of the two again offered three doors; the smaller had only one.

Curiosity had gotten the better of me, and I tiptoed to the larger one. I gripped the handle of one of the smaller doors and tugged.

The House on Valley Street

The door opened with a thud, and icy air shot toward me and enveloped me in a cloud of mist. When it had cleared, I saw that the compartment was empty. I checked the lower compartment, and it, too, was empty.

The handle to the third, larger compartment on the right side of the appliance was loose; it jiggled slightly under my touch, as though this side received the most frequent use. I lifted the handle, and the latch popped, allowing the door to swing free. Another gust of icy air puffed from the ice box, enough to take my breath away.

At the bottom of the freezer were four skinned rodents stacked on top each other, heads and tails removed. They must have been squirrels. A chill, having nothing to do with the cold, ran down my spine.

The smaller of the two appliances was a refrigerator that hummed with electricity. I tugged on a lever to open it, but the door stuck. I jerked it harder, sliding the entire machine several inches across the floor until the door finally popped open.

It was empty.

For only a moment, I seemed to catch a waft of the stench from my right. I followed the scent to the only other room off the hall. The door was open only a crack, and no light escaped the cavernous space.

I waited a moment, hoping to hear something in the room that would give me hope that what I would see on the other side of the door wasn't Gene's lifeless body, left to rot on the floor after a heart attack or some kind of hemorrhage or God knows what else. The only sound was coming from the flies.

The door creaked menacingly against my trembling fingertips. My breath hitched. I could almost see the bed.

"You shouldn't be here," Dylan appeared beside me again. He reached for the bedroom door's handle and held it still against my force.

Beneath a furrowed brow, his eyes shone with an emotion I couldn't quite place. It wasn't fear. It wasn't anxiety. The straight line of his mouth and his hard stare told me he was *angry*.

"What's going on?" I asked him, not lowering my hand from the door. "What's in there?"

He said nothing. In a fleeting moment, I pushed his arm aside and forced the door open.

The smell penetrated my eyes, my nose, my mouth. I doubled over, wrenching, coughing hard, eyes watering. Even in the dark, I could see bare feet at the end of the bed. Unmoving, bare feet.

Flies buzzed incessantly, circling the body and for only moments, pausing to land on its scalp, the corners of its closed eyes, and the tips of its toenails, browned and curled with age. The smell was unlike anything I had experienced before. It was as if I had stumbled upon an open graveyard for the summer's collection of roadkill, full to the brim of rotting flesh, clumps of fur, and crawling maggots.

I held my shirt tightly over my nose and mouth. The woman's body lay still on top of the duvet. Beneath a white slip, her sternum lay sunken into her chest, still. Thin, withered arms lay close to her sides, and wispy, gray hair curled around her reedy face, some attached, some lying in clumps that had fallen away from her scalp. Her lips were parted slightly, the skin around her mouth sinking further inside itself.

"You shouldn't be here."

Dylan stood firmly at the foot of the bed, apparently unaffected by the sight of this woman.

My heart thudded in my throat. "Dylan? What's going on?"

"We need to leave." Even in the dim light of the bedroom, I could see that his face held no expression.

"We need to call the police!" Forcing my voice to steady, I stepped backward. My mind was racing.

Why isn't Dylan reacting?

Who is this woman?

Am I safe with him?

Dylan stepped toward me.

"Leave now." His eyes were hard, unblinking.

I refused to believe that this was the Dylan I knew, the man who laughed with me over hot chocolate, the man who shielded his eyes from my pajama-clad body, the man who I shared my body with.

"I—

I opened my mouth, unsure of what would come out, but Dylan caught me before I could speak. He wrapped his arm across my mouth, holding me from behind. He pushed me into the hallway and into the kitchen. With his foot, he pushed aside a braided floor mat in the kitchen. He ducked and tugged hard on an iron ring in the floor, lifting a door and revealing nothing but dank darkness below. His breath held steady as he shoved me down through the opening.

"Not a word," he said, cold and hard. He squared his shoulders and closed the door, leaving me in the blackness.

I landed with a thud. A new smell of dirt and mold wafted all around me. My ears strained to pick up any sound above me, but for what felt like an eternity, there was nothing. Minutes passed.

Then, I heard the screen door creak open and swing closed again, followed by the shuffle of footsteps across the worn carpeting.

Gene.

He moved about the house very quietly. His steps moved into what I knew was the bedroom. A clanking sound echoed through the home's foundation before he left the bedroom and moved to the kitchen.

The trapdoor over my head sunk beneath his weight, and my breath halted. My arms swung wildly around me, searching for something – anything, but all I felt was cold, damp walls surrounding me. There was nowhere to go. I had nothing to defend myself. Instead, I sat as close as I could to one wall, clutching my knees to my chest. My only hope was that when he opened the door, I could stay hidden in the shadows.

The metal handle clinked beneath Gene's arthritic fingers, and as he fumbled, I gave a final push toward wrapping my mind around what I had seen just minutes earlier.

Suddenly, soft, warm fingers were seemingly birthed from the dirt beneath me. They crept up my thighs, then around my hips.

I froze.

And then they pulled.

I don't know how far I fell, but I landed with a jolt that reverberated up my spine, resonating in my skull. When I could move again, I scrambled to my feet and slammed my head on a low dirt ceiling. The hands tugged me along a dirt tunnel some fifty paces.

His hand was across my mouth before I understood what was happening. My fingers clawed at his, digging for air.

"Shh," Dylan spat in my ear, dragging me through a cold tunnel that smelled like mud.

After several minutes of his stifled groans while dragging my writhing body, he stopped. The space around us was still black, but the wall I now leaned on was no longer made of dirt. It was hard and rough – it felt like plywood.

My mind raced.

What does he know?

Is he going to hurt me?

Will anyone ever find me here, or will my body end up like that woman's in the bedroom, left to decompose, stowed away here?

He released me and took a half-step back, breathing heavily. "I told you you shouldn't be here," he said. "Why didn't you listen to me?" He stood close enough that I felt the warmth of his breath brush my face. His voice was stern and ragged, like a father whose son had fallen out of a tree he was told to never climb.

"Get away from me!" My voice shook, and the tips of my fingers still tingled from my futile attempt at prying his hand away from my mouth. I shoved his chest with every ounce of strength I had.

His body moved, but only minimally.

My knees buckled. My head swam, and I let it fall against the plywood sheet behind me. I sank to the ground. "I want out," I whispered, tears building in my eyes. "Let me out of here." I wrapped my arms around my knees, holding them to my chest, and my body rocked.

"No."

I rubbed my palms into my eyes and gritted my teeth. "Let me out. Now." The tone in my voice startled me. Despite the flutter in my stomach and the sweat accumulating at the small of my back, my words were strong.

"I can't." I sensed him closer to me again. He placed a hand on one of my knees.

"Don't touch me!" I growled, kicking blindly, hoping one foot would catch him in the jaw.

"You…can't…yell," he said through clenched teeth.

"I'll scream," I threatened, though I knew it would be pointless. The only person who might hear me would be Gene, the man who knowingly housed a rotting body, positioned like a decomposing Sleeping Beauty, tucked neatly on a queen-sized mattress in his home. For all I knew, he slept next to her – it.

Dylan's hot breath hit my face again. "Listen to me. I'm trying to keep you safe."

"Safe?! Look at me! Does this look safe?"

"You don't know what he's capable of," he said, his voice softening slightly.

"He's not the one who brought me here." I dug my fingernails into the dirt at my sides.

"I brought you here to keep you from *him*," he said. "You should never have been in his house. I shouldn't have let you in. It's my fault. He's dangerous."

"You haven't mentioned the elephant in his bedroom."

"It's his wife."

"His wife?"

"His wife. Her name is Estelle. She died years ago, many, many years ago."

Something in Dylan's tone made me ask, "How many years?"

"Several hundred."

I scoffed. "You're an asshole, you know that? You've dragged me through some underground tunnel, you won't let me out, and now you're lying to me? I can't fucking believe I ever let you touch me."

He stopped, and though I still couldn't see him, I sensed a shift, like his shoulders drooped.

Dylan spoke, his voice low. He faced away from me. "I tried to keep you away from here as long as I could. I didn't think you'd come into his home. Neither of us should be here."

"You've already *kidnapped* me," I spat, eyes burning. "What's a little trespassing?" My eyes flickered about in the blackness, waiting to pick up on any traces of movement, any specks of light, but there was nothing.

"Trespassing?" he scoffed. A hot gust of his breath hit my face. "You think I'm concerned with the law? This is so much bigger than our legal system, Sophia. The police couldn't help either of us if they tried."

"Either of us?" My voice rose. "I'm the only one who needs help!"

He stepped closer so that I could feel his body heat across my entire front. He spoke quietly through clenched teeth. "Shh! You don't understand." And just as soon as his aggression had come on, it faded. He sighed heavily. "Do you have any idea who he is?"

"He, who? Gene? I *thought* he was a little old neighbor guy, but I guess I wrong there." I cocked my head violently with each syllable I spoke. "Maybe 'mad scientist' better fits the bill? Amateur taxidermist? You tell me."

The air around me cooled again when Dylan stepped away. The change was so sudden that I shivered. I inhaled deeply, resolving to conserve my energy.

"Did he kill her?" I asked in a low tone.

Dylan paused. I couldn't tell what exactly he was thinking, but his tone seemed to shift again. "No."

"Why does he keep her? I mean, why not bury her? I don't understand."

"He wants to bring her back."

"Bring her back? This is real life. He can't just wait for a lightning storm to pump life into her like some Frankenstein monster. And why are we down here? Where are we?" The dirt walls around us felt like they were closing in. I wanted out. The conversation was too outrageous for anything to sink in, especially when I felt like I was sinking myself.

The House on Valley Street

"We're in your basement – at least we're very close to it."

I hadn't thought the plywood door I'd been leaning against would possibly lead into my basement.

"What? How did you – Oh, my God. You're working with him, aren't you?" My hair was beginning to stick to my forehead, despite the cool, dank air. "Are you going to kill me and stash my body somewhere to watch me rot, too?"

Another rush of warm air brushed past my cheek, and I realized that Dylan was reaching for me.

I pressed my back into the plywood as hard as I could, but I couldn't get further from him.

"Don't touch me!" I pressed both palms forward and shoved, toppling forward from my knees. My chin hit the ground first, hard, and when I ran my tongue across my front teeth, I tasted blood.

Dylan's fingertips lightly brushed my back. I writhed under his touch.

"Sophia," he said, "I'm not going to hurt you." His hands continued moving until he found each of my shoulders and hoisted me up. "I'll explain everything to you, but you have to trust me." We stood face-to-face in the blackness, our breaths the only sound. "Do you?"

"Do I what?"

"Do you trust me?"

"Not yet." I turned away and ripped at the plywood. As it pulled away from the wall, a new smell filled the area: mildew and moldy basement.

The House on Valley Street

CHAPTER 20

Dylan sat at the kitchen table, lightly fingering the pages of the book he'd given me. I stood in front of the sink and leaned against the counter, watching him. I hadn't turned my back to him since we left the tunnel.

"Look," he said, "what I'm about to tell you is going to sound insane."

I waited, but when he didn't continue, I said, "More insane than everything I've seen today? Go for it."

He clasped his hands in his lap and leaned his head over his knees. His jeans were stained with dirt from the tunnel, and his hair was unusually disheveled. One side of the collar on his black polo was tucked under.

"That woman is the old man's wife."

"You already said that."

He ignored me and continued. "She was murdered," he said, "a long time ago – a very long time ago -- by my ancestors – members of my tribe. The old man invaded our lands and killed our people, burning their homes to the ground, but not before he befriended the people. He tricked my great-great-great-grandfather, Achak, into thinking he was a friend. Achak taught him the ways of our people. Then one night, Eugene and his men took Achak's wife, Gaho, and their eight-year-old daughter, Lomasi, while Achak was away on a hunt. When he returned and discovered their home was destroyed, he went after Eugene. But he and his men were still off torturing Gaho and Lomasi when Achak reached Eugene's camp." He swallowed loudly. "Achak crept through it and found Estelle, Eugene's wife, alone. But his business wasn't with Estelle, so he prepared to leave the camp to find his family. Before he got far, he heard the screams of his wife and daughter and the whoops and cheers of the men who were hurting them. That's when he went after Estelle. He strangled her, no doubt fueled by the cries of his family."

A sob rose in my throat, but I choked it down. My trembling fingers fumbled with my sweaty hair before tucking it behind one ear. I didn't know which was crazier: his story or my believing his story.

"Still with me?" Dylan asked.

I nodded. "It's just so sad." I shivered and crossed my arms over my chest. "Why did he never bury her? And what happened to Achak?"

"After he killed Estelle, Achak asked the gods of the skies to keep Eugene alive so that he may never be reunited with Estelle's spirit as revenge for taking Achak's family from him. As a result, Eugene was immortalized. He watched his loved ones die generation after generation, and he hasn't spoken with his wife since the day he killed Gaho and Lomasi. After Achak prayed, he killed himself."

"How did he do that?" I couldn't think of an ancient weapon efficient enough for one to commit suicide with.

"He threw himself off a cliff," he said, leaning back in his chair and resting his head against the wall. "His body was eventually recovered and buried beside his wife and daughter."

"I still don't understand. How are you involved?"

"Achak taught Eugene the ways of our people. Eugene knew our death practices, and he knew that my ancestors would never fully rest in peace if the ceremony wasn't completed in its entirety."

"The fire…" I thought aloud, recalling my conversation with Professor Tochek.

"You know about the ceremony?" Dylan furrowed his brow and lightly chewed his lower lip. His eyes held an emotion I hadn't seen in him before. I couldn't place it – pain, maybe. I wanted to comfort him, to stroke his back and console him, but I couldn't bring myself to touch him. I didn't know whether I could trust him anymore – not after the way he looked at me in Gene's house. Not after the way he touched me. The way he spoke to me.

Besides, there was too much I still didn't understand.

"I did some research not too long ago," I said, staring at the graying laces of my Converse. "The mouths get stuffed with ashes. Something special to the dead gets burned to release the spirit."

"And do you know what happens to the spirits if they're not released?"

"I can only assume it's like some kind of purgatory."

"Something like that," Dylan said, dropping his head to one shoulder as if telling me his family's history was exhausting. "The spirits can't move on, and they have no body to inhabit. So they wander the land near the resting places of their bodies. They can only move so far from their bodies. It's like there's an invisible tether holding them. Eugene knew that. He rushed back to my ancestors' home and took something, something that held enough memory and love and meaning, something that held a part of their spirits."

"What was it?"

"We don't know." He ran a hand through his unkempt hair. "But that's how I'm involved." He shrugged. "My ancestors are in a perpetual state of unrest because of a murderous traitor. He has something of theirs, and I need to find it."

"There are other houses on the block, though," I said, looking through the window above the sink. "Why the tunnel? Why this house?"

"My ancestors are buried on this property," he said matter-of-factly. "Eugene owns the property and rents it out. He bought this house to keep an eye on them, to be sure that they never move on."

"That's not right. I rented this house from a guy in Georgia."

"Did you ever meet him?"

I paused, then shook my head.

"What's the name?" Dylan asked.

I squinted, as though my eyes could search out the name from deep within my memory. I reached to the top of the refrigerator and rustled some papers until I found the right one. "E&H Properties," I read from the rental agreement.

"Eugene Hexton."

Oh, my God. How did I not notice that?

He sighed. At the look of bewilderment on my face, he said, "You didn't have a reason to suspect anything, Sophia. There's no reason for you to have noticed that. As for the tunnel, I needed a way to access his house to search it regularly. I've been coming here and working in the tunnel for years, right up until you moved in."

My heart sank. My mouth went dry. "So you used me to get into the house."

"Not at all. I told you – I've been coming here long before I knew you." He stood and slowly moved across the kitchen to me. "I really like you, Sophia. Everything that's happened between us was entirely real." He gripped my upper arms gently. "Everything."

I pulled away.

His arms fell to his sides, and his lips parted. He hesitated. "Please don't be afraid of me. I'll never hurt you."

"Never? Who are we kidding? I hardly know you," I said, more aggressively than I had intended. "The way you spoke to me, the way you dragged me earlier – And if it weren't for the things I've seen in this house and on that man's bed, I wouldn't believe a word you've told me."

"Everything you've been seeing here, the things you've heard – it's all real. It's my ancestors. They're asking for help."

I envisioned the little girl curled on the floor of the hallway upstairs, moaning, and I shuddered. "What about the girl on the stairs? What about Molly Danielson? She's not part of some ancient tribe."

"Eugene killed her, Sophia. She wandered into his house one day and found Estelle. Regardless of her disability, he couldn't let her spread his secret."

"If you knew that, why didn't you call the police? Why didn't you do something?"

"I had no proof. I couldn't tell them that an undead man abducted a little girl. And I'm absolutely sure that he started the fire," he added. "You're making him nervous, and he wants you to leave."

"My God." My vision wavered for a moment, and a sudden rush of nausea came over me. "Why didn't you tell me you knew about all of this? Why did you let me believe I was crazy? And why the hell did you let me stay in this house by myself for all of this time, Dylan?!"

"Would you have believed me?" He squared his shoulders. "I've been trying to protect you," he murmured. "There's something about our relationship that's," he paused, "different. You're important to me." He leaned against the counter beside me. "I didn't know of any other way. And as for today, I was angry. I was. I was baffled at your willingness to march into danger the way you did, but I was still trying to protect you. I needed you to get out of there, to get to safety, immediately."

I opened my mouth to respond, but my phone vibrated on the table and interrupted me.

It was a text from Lucee:

Still on for tonight? Meeting me at 6, right?

Shit.

I'd completely forgotten about the dinner plans I'd made with her.

"You should go," I said to Dylan, but when I turned around, he was already gone. I spun around again, half expecting him to reappear, but he didn't. My head swiveled like a satellite dish. A single tap drew my attention to the foyer. Dylan was crouched on the lowest step, his head barely visible from the other side of the banister. He held one finger to his lips, as if to say, "Shh."

A moment later, there was a light rap on the back door.

My heart leapt into my throat, and my stomach dropped. Gene stood just on the other side of the screen door. He'd surely already seen me; I couldn't ignore his knock.

Think, think, think, I told myself.

He smiled innocently and gave a tiny wave, clutching his handkerchief.

I had no choice.

I opened the door.

He can't know I've been in his house, can he?

"Howdy," he said when I stepped outside and joined him on the patio. He tipped his straw hat.

"Hi, Gene. How are you?" I gave a most convincing smile in the face of a killer who was housing a centuries-old corpse in his bedroom.

"Just fine, darlin'. Say, I just saw my hankie hanging from the back door. Figured you were probably the one that put it there. Thought I'd come by and thank you for returning it."

I couldn't help but study his features. White stubble grew from his chin, and deep-set wrinkles framed his gray eyes. He wore a plaid shirt and pale blue cotton pants with his cowboy boots. They weren't just worn in, not just old – they were hundreds of years old. They may have been on his feet when he killed Dylan's ancestors.

"I found it in the yard back by the shed. I figured you must have dropped it when you were trimming that tree the other day."

He nodded, glancing over my shoulder into the house. I sidestepped in front of the door.

"I really appreciate your help with all of the yard work," I stammered. "I'll be sure to have some lemonade ready for you when you mow again Sunday night."

"Well, now that you mention it," he said, scratching under his hat and around his thin, graying hairline, "lemonade sounds pretty darn good." He nodded toward the kitchen and smiled a smile that his eyes weren't a part of.

"Shoot. I'm all out," I said, nonchalantly brushing sweat from my brow. "I was just getting ready to head to the grocery store, though."

He eyed my dirt-covered jeans and sweat-dampened hair.

"After a shower, of course," I added. "I've been pulling weeds up front."

He paused a moment and said, "Rain check, then." He turned toward his house. "Thanks again for returning my hankie. Wife stitched it for me years ago." The corner of his mouth turned up into a sad smile that faded almost as soon as it had appeared. "And darlin'?" he asked as he began to limp away. "I'll take care of tending the land. I don't mind the weeds one bit. They keep me busy."

Moments later, he disappeared into his back door, the screen door swinging shut hard behind him. I thought for a moment that the smell of rotten flesh had come wafting from the open door, but it disappeared so quickly that I wrote it off as my imagination – and a very strong memory of the way that smell had first struck me just hours earlier.

"Dylan?" I called from the foyer. An immediate eerie sensation came over me, and my ears tensed, straining for any sounds behind me, in front of me – anywhere. Though I had recently learned of the identities of the spirits in this house, my uneasiness had returned.

Just a few hours ago, I had thought that the house was ... better, cured, in a way, but now, all of my anxiety had returned. Perhaps I'd felt differently about the situation since I knew the story, but the spirits were still strangers, unfamiliar and potentially dangerous. They just wore nametags now. "Dylan?"

He was not in the living room, nor the bathroom. I gripped the banister and padded up the steps. Just before I rounded the corner into the bedroom, my phone vibrated again in my pocket, sending a jolt of panic up my spine. It was another text from Lucee:

Yes? No? Maybe?

When I looked up from my phone, Dylan was sitting on the bed.

"He knows we're together, you know," I said, wincing when I said "together." Could we still be? After I'd seen that look in his eyes, that absence of emotion, I wasn't sure. "He's seen you here before, remember? Why did you hide?"

"I think he's starting to suspect that I've been in his house. He just can't figure out how. If he thinks I was in there, I don't want him to think you were with me. I don't need him coming after another person I care about."

My heart swelled, but I dismissed it. "Another?"

"He's been threatening our family for years, since my grandmother became a medicine woman."

At my furrowed brow, he explained. "Modern medicine people probably aren't what you think of. There aren't rain dances or anything. Modern practices are similar to voodoo – healing, cursing, all of it."

My blank expression told him I still didn't understand.

"Eugene's been threatening my grandmother, saying that he'll kill her and my brothers and I if she doesn't release the curse and let him reunite with his wife in death. Until he gets what he wants, he'll make sure the souls of my ancestors never rest, either. Everyone is in a sort of stalemate." He sighed heavily and ran his palm over the dark stubble along his chin. "I can't let her get hurt."

My gut clenched, and I yearned to throw my arms around him. But before I could sort my feelings, my phone rang.

I bit my lip and answered.

"Were you planning on texting me back in this lifetime?" Lucee asked.

"Sorry," I murmured when I'd walked into the hallway. "I've been…" I wasn't sure how to put it, so I said, "busy."

"Busy with who? Your tall, dark, and studly boyfriend?" She giggled, oblivious to the hush in my tone.

"Actually, I'm with him right now. Can I take a raincheck on dinner tonight?"

"What?! No way. You can't blow me off for a guy. We haven't seen each other enough lately, and I was totally looking forward to it. I even got my nails done."

"It's not like that," I said. "Dylan and I –

It was as though something in her mind clicked, and she suddenly heard the confusion, the shock, and the wear in my voice.

"What happened?" she asked.

"I can't really—

"Is he there with you right now? Did he touch you, Soph? These bastard men think they can do whatever they want to women. I swear to God; if he touched you, I'll kill him."

"Lucee, it's fine. He didn't." *But he sort of did, didn't he?*

"Then what is it?"

I couldn't bring myself to tell her what I'd learned. She'd believed everything I'd ever told her about the house, but this was too much. Besides, something told me that keeping her in the dark was one way of keeping her safe.

"Nothing."

"Good, then. I'll see you soon."

Before I could argue, she made a kissing sound into the phone and added, "I've got to go. I'm picking up my check at the bar." And she hung up.

I stood there a moment, wringing my hands. Dylan was waiting for me in the bedroom. The truth was that he had touched me, but he didn't hurt me. He was only trying to keep me safe, but the severity in his point-blank stare when he pushed me into the crawlspace in Eugene's kitchen was scorched into my mind. He'd flipped a switch, just like that. I wasn't afraid of him, not for my safety, at least. I was afraid of his dedication, his commitment to defeating Eugene. I was afraid that if it came down to it, he would abandon me for the sake of his long-dead relatives. Then again, he would also be saving his grandmother.

I shouldn't expect him to choose me over his own family, should I?

Logically, I understood why he'd behaved the way he had. He didn't hurt me physically, but my ego was bruised. I kept picturing my mom talking to me when I was small, telling me to never put up with a man who lays his hands on me. She'd told me stories of a boyfriend from her teen years who'd wrapped his grease-stained hands around her throat and pinned her to a wall over something trivial – I couldn't remember what it was. I felt compelled to address the situation with Dylan, even though I wasn't sure why. Maybe it was a need to prove that I could protect myself. But more likely, I think I was uncomfortable at having discovered a completely different side of him so abruptly.

I found Dylan sitting on the edge of the bed, lightly fingering a folded piece of paper.

"What's that?" I sat beside him.

He looked up as if startled out of a daydream. "It's a letter." He folded it again and slipped it into his pocket. "From Jackie."

"Your brother?"

He nodded.

"Is he – is he okay?"

He nodded again. "He's fine," he said. "Just checking in."

He laced his fingers together and rested his hands in his lap. His head hung.

After a minute of silence, I said, "Now what?"

"Now what, us? Or now what with the little old neighbor man?"

I rubbed my eyes hard and brushed my hair away from my face. "I'm sorry I've been so hurtful and angry, but I was shocked, Dylan. I'd never seen that look in your eyes or heard that tone in your voice before." I fumbled over a jumbled onslaught of emotions transformed into seemingly incoherent sentences. I just couldn't properly explain the way I was feeling. "The way you pushed me – I get it. I understand that you were trying to keep me safe. I believe that. But to be honest," I sighed, "it scared me. That's all."

"I didn't mean to scare you," he said. "I just couldn't imagine him taking you from me." He lowered his eyes to the floor and after a pause, said, "I know we haven't known each other long, but there's something about you that's different, something about the way I feel when I'm with you.

"And it sounds strange," he continued quickly, "since I never knew them and their deaths were so long ago, but it's like I can still feel the pain from my ancestors' deaths, too. And now that he's been threatening my grandmother—well, I just realized when we were in his house that he was close to taking you, too."

Before I had time to second-guess myself, I'd crossed the room and straddled Dylan's lap. I hugged him tightly, my face on his shoulder.

The House on Valley Street

"I'm sorry," he said.

I drew back and kissed him softly, his fingertips brushing my thighs. Our kiss began slowly, our noses brushing, our breaths mingling. In only moments, my pulse quickened as his mouth opened slightly wider, allowing his tongue to explore mine.

The shock, the repulsion, the pain, and the fear that I'd felt in the hours leading to our kiss melted away, transforming into a rush of desire. My inhibitions faded, and I found myself yearning for him. His hands ran from my shoulders, down my spine, and to my hips, where they rested, gently encouraging my body to rock to and fro in time. He kissed me with a strength, a fervor that sent heat rising through my chest, spreading across my face. I was breathless.

He fell backward and in one fluid movement, pulled me on top of him. Parts of my body I had never considered had suddenly come into my consciousness.

Between gasps, I whispered, "You have to go."

He froze, frowning, and said, "What?" The hurt suddenly returned to his dark eyes.

I smiled, pecking him on the lips several times. "Lucee's going to be here soon. I have to get ready for dinner."

The tension in his body melted away, and he reached for the hem of my shirt, tugging it up my midsection. "I can help you change," he said playfully.

I lifted my arms and allowed him to pull my shirt over my head. Standing at the foot of the bed, my back toward him, I peeked over my shoulder, my tousled hair falling delicately down my back.

He cleared his throat lightly.

In an exhilarating moment of inhibition, I daintily lowered the strap of my black and nude floral bra. Touching it as though it were made of thin glass, I guided it along my shoulder until it hung limp against my arm.

Dylan cleared his throat again, this time louder. When I turned to look at him, I caught a glimpse of a figure standing in the doorway.

"Lucee!" I shouted, scrambling to find my shirt on the ground and cover my bare skin.

Dylan swung his legs onto the floor and rubbed his chin. A boyish grin spread across his face. The Dylan I'd fallen for was back.

"If this is what you wanted to do instead of getting dinner, you should have told me," Lucee said, leaning casually against the doorframe. "I knocked, but you must not have heard me. I guess you were too busy." She raised her eyebrows and smirked. "I'll wait downstairs while you two finish up. Nice to meet you, Dylan," she added. She tossed her hair over her shoulder and left.

When the click-swish-click of Lucee's stilettos on the stairs stopped, I covered my face with both hands, as though my palms were ice packs that could cool the heat raging through my cheeks. "Oh, my God."

Dylan chuckled. "Just when things were getting good." He stood close enough that I was able to lean my forehead against his chest.

"I'm sorry," I said.

"Me, too."

"You really do have to go now."

"I know." He kissed the top of my head lightly and said, "I'll stop by later."

When I'd regained my composure, I followed Dylan down the stairs and gave him a quick kiss on the cheek at the front door before he left. When the low hum of his car's engine faded and it disappeared around the end of the block, I mustered the courage to look Lucee in the eyes.

She grinned.

I flushed and headed back up the stairs to change.

Lucee tromped into the bedroom behind me and sat on the bed, drilling me for details while I sifted through clothes.

"Is he a good kisser? He's not sloppy, is he? Lots of slobber? Oh! Does he cuddle after? I never cuddle after. Too much body heat. I don't need to lie in a puddle of sweaty man smell." She continued this way while I slipped into a short, black dress and strappy sandals.

Though my body was going through the motions, my mind was too preoccupied. Eugene, a killer, was a hundred yards from my door. I tried not to, but I imagined what he was doing with his wife – or *to* her.

The House on Valley Street

CHAPTER 21

After dinner with Lucee, I felt a sort of renewal, a light and airy feeling that I hadn't felt for some time. Being with her made me feel carefree, rejuvenated. We'd laughed from our corner booth at the restaurant, making up conversations for strangers seated across the room, whose lips we tried to read, with no luck. She'd flirted with our waiter, complimenting his sneakers, a pair of yellow Jordans that he'd probably paid an ungodly amount of tips for. And he'd flirted right back, periodically using his "sexy Spanish," as Lucee called it, referring to her as "Chiquita," and winking from time to time.

We'd gorged ourselves on chips and salsa and that white queso dip that costs an extra two dollars but is always worth it. By the time our fajita platters had arrived, we'd barely had any room left. Our margaritas had just filled in the cracks.

Maybe the margaritas were the cause of my sudden hunger that night. Lucee had dropped me off at home half an hour earlier, and I'd been sitting on my bed, paging through the book that Dylan had given me. I left the television on in the room, just for background noise. My stomach grumbled, and at first, I didn't know whether my stomach was yearning for more or whether it was angry at me for what I'd given it at dinner. After a few minutes of gurgling, I decided it was the former.

It was almost 9:30. I didn't know when Dylan planned to come back, but I had hoped it wouldn't be much longer before he did.

Just as I descended the last step, a car with an obnoxiously loud, thumping bass crawled past the front of the house. Its underside glowed a light blue. "That can't be legal," I whispered, pulling the blinds apart to watch the car pass.

In the kitchen, I tugged open the refrigerator and scanned its contents. Milk, onions, cheese, a tube of cinnamon roll dough, leftover soup from the day before. Nothing appetizing in the least.

I searched the freezer, too. Frozen pizza, popsicles, ice cubes. Nada.

Back in the fridge again, I rummaged the shelves, pushing things aside, as though touching them might arouse some inkling of desire. I moved from the top shelf down, feeling my hopes sink each time I moved lower.

The cooling system kicked on when I'd left the door open long enough to alter the fridge's temperature. I grunted and opened the crisper drawer. I'd heard once that if you're hungry a lot, it's possible that you're actually just thirsty, and you're just confusing your body's signals. I shrugged and reached inside the drawer for a can of Coke. The cans were buried under two bags of salad mix and a bundle of just-past-their-prime-but-not-old-enough-to-justify-throwing-away oranges. As I struggled, my hair fell into my face, and several strands managed to get into my mouth.

With one hand still digging through the drawer, I reached to my lips, fighting to pull the strand free before gagging. I tossed the bulk of my hair over my shoulder, and it swung to and fro as I finally freed a can from the drawer.

As I stood, my hair continued to swing, this time with a swish. It continued to swing (*swish, swish, swish),* after I'd stood upright, still facing the refrigerator. The swish became a sort of flick, a strong flick, like a cat toying with a dangling piece of yarn. I was immobile. My face was inches from the refrigerator. My hair continued to whip on its own.

I had three choices: I could stand in my spot and endure the touch, I could run a hand through my hair and hope to find something incredibly benign like a piece of tape stuck in there, or I could turn and face whatever stood, undoubtedly hunched and trembling with temptation, behind me.

The House on Valley Street

My fingers twitched as I briefly imagined what I might feel if I reached blindly. A rush of heat grazed my ear, and my hair was suddenly being gathered at the nape of my neck and divided into sections. A moment later, I felt it being plaited into a loose braid.

"Stop!" The word exploded from my gut before I'd considered the consequences. My hair fell limp, and the heat was gone from my neck. I strained my eyes left and right, hoping that my peripheral vision could tell me whether the danger had passed. The small hairs on my forearms still stood on end.

Slowly, I turned around, the cold air from the still-open refrigerator washing over my backside. My breath trembled.

The car with the loud bass passed by again.

Nothing was out of the ordinary behind me. The dishes lay where I'd left them. The green checkered cloths hung neatly on the towel bar in front of the sink. In the darkness, everything was in its place.

Without turning my back again, I reached backward and pulled the refrigerator door closed. Then I tiptoed across the now-chilled linoleum, Coke still in hand, and rounded the corner into the living room, brushing my fingers of my free hand through my hair to ensure that all traces of the braid were gone.

Just as my bare feet crossed the threshold, a glowing figure emerged from the dark bathroom at the base of the stairwell. It slowly edged out of the bathroom, its moving staggered and jerking. It was a feminine figure, outlined in a bright, white light, as though it stood just in front of a spotlight. Had it been close enough, I would have stood eye-to-eye with it, but there were no features or details within the glowing outline – only darkness.

I found myself running. With nowhere to go and no time to consider it, I ran directly into – and through – the figure. I felt like I'd plunged myself into an icy lake mid-winter, but I didn't stop. I gripped the banister for extra speed and balance and hauled myself up the stairs as quickly as my legs could carry me.

On the bed, I pressed my back against the headboard, waiting, straining to hear any unusual sounds from downstairs. I'd flipped the light switch on when I'd run in, and the television was still on from earlier. Pat Sajak was inviting a contestant to spin the prize wheel on a rerun of Wheel of Fortune.

A low creak sounded at the back of the house, beginning slowly, a quiet growl growing to a piercing shriek.

The sound carried through the kitchen and into the living room. Creaks followed, slow, steady, and deliberate. My fingers gripped the sheets at my sides. My knuckles went white.

I counted the groans the steps made.

One, two...

I considered running, but where would I go?

Five, six...

I held my breath.

Nine, ten...

I was beginning to feel the room spin around me. I opened my eyes wide to orient myself and inhaled deeply for fear of losing consciousness.

A shadow danced across the hallway. Seeing no viable alternative, I squeezed my eyes shut once more. At least if I passed out, I wouldn't see it coming.

I balled the comforter and bit into it, hoping, praying, that when I opened my eyes, it would be over and whatever that thing was would be gone.

The steps continued into the bedroom and around to the far side of the bed, dragging and slapping unnaturally against the stiff carpet. The mattress sank beneath an invisible weight, tipping me into its crater like a car that edges too closely along a sinkhole. Something gripped the comforter and tugged – not a steady, firm force, but in a rapid, jerking movement, just as my hair had been whipped earlier.

A thought occurred to me then: if it had worked before, it could work again.

"Stop!" I shouted again, feigning strength. *Please, please please,* I mouthed.

I sat breathless and silently counted to three. A violent, panicked *thud, thud, thud* sounded on the stairwell, gaining speed and volume.

Before I had time to prepare myself for whatever careened up the stairs, Dylan rounded the corner and nearly leapt toward me, firmly, yet gently, pulling the blankets away from my chilled body.

"Are you okay?" he asked, winded. "What happened?"

Before I could answer, he said, "I heard you scream. I thought it was Eugene. I didn't know what was happening."

I wrapped my arms around his shoulders and buried my face in his neck. I willed myself to sob, letting go of my fear and my panic, but nothing came. His warm, broad hands caressed my back, and I clung to his sweet, woodsy scent.

"I'm sorry," he said. "I'm sorry this is happening to you." He voice was low, quiet. A hint of pain danced just below the surface.

I clung to him more tightly. "We need to do something," I said finally.

"I know. I'm trying."

My eyes darted about the room, from the doorway to the spot on the mattress that had sunken beneath an invisible body, and back again. My mind reeled. I kept replaying everything that had happened: Gene, Dylan's ancestors, the body, the maggots, my hair. My thoughts spun until I succumbed to what I can only assume was shock, and I fell asleep.

The House on Valley Street

CHAPTER 22

I awoke with a start, realizing that I was alone in the bed. My heart lurched.

As the room slowly came into focus, I was able to see Dylan standing at the closet, quietly pulling my clothes from their hangers and dropping them into my duffel bag. He wore the same loose jeans and black henley from the night before.

"What are you doing?" I suddenly became aware of how unattractive I likely was in that moment – particularly, my breath. I smoothed my hair and tucked it behind my ears. My joints were sore, as though I'd run a marathon the night before.

"I'm getting you out of here." He continued to drop articles of clothing into the bag.

"Where am I going to go? I'm not ready to go back home. I came here for a reason." My novel flashed into my consciousness, but I dismissed it, knowing full well that it hadn't been at the forefront of my priority list for quite some time now. There were other reasons I didn't want to leave. For one thing, I couldn't leave Dylan in this situation. I wanted to help.

"You're going to stay with me." When he'd emptied the closet, he moved to the dresser, gathering the three necklaces and a ring my mom had given me that, all together, lay in a golden heap. She had worn the ring for as long as I could remember, but after the stroke, her fingers tightened into a perpetual claw. The ring dug into her skin. I'd asked her why she didn't simply wear it on the other hand, but she'd only shrugged and insisted that I take it, if I wanted it.

"Don't you live with your grandmother?"

He glanced over his shoulder in my direction but didn't turn around far enough to face me. "No."

"I thought you said you lived with her after your brothers took off." The vertigo I felt as I sat up sent memories of the invisible force on the mattress racing through my mind. I shivered.

"I did." He moved to the edge of the bed and pulled me to my feet. "But I don't anymore."

Is he being deliberately cryptic? I thought.

"I spend a lot of time with her, but I have an apartment, too," he said.

My expression must have tipped him off to my puzzlement.

"I didn't invite you to my apartment because you hadn't seen enough of this house yet," he said. He spoke like a little boy who had to explain to his mother why he hadn't yet finished his nightly chores.

"What's that got to do with you and your apartment?"

"I –"

"And what do you mean I hadn't seen enough? Things have been happening in this house since I moved in."

He paused, thinking through his words carefully. He still held both my hands firmly. After a moment, he said, "I didn't want you to think I was…" He waited again. "…taking advantage of you."

Seriously?

"I didn't want to be that guy who swooped in and took the damsel in distress back to his place, you know? I wanted to keep my distance and step in when the time was right."

A jumble of emotions passed through my gut, then my chest, then my head, where they loitered, teasing me like an unsolved crossword puzzle. I frowned. He knew all this time that the house was haunted, and "haunted" didn't even seem to cover it. He knew that I was terrified, but he sat back in the shadows in an effort to keep himself from looking like a pervert?

He gingerly released my hands and studied my face. The subtle crease in his brow revealed a genuine concern, along with compassion, anxiety, and fear all at once.

"Why?" I asked.

"Why?"

"Why are you so concerned with how people perceive you?"

He sighed softly and licked his lips. He opened his mouth, thought better of it, and closed it again. His expression suddenly hardened.

"And what about me?" I asked, ignoring the shift. "Am I just supposed to go where you tell me to when you tell me like a puppy dog?" My voice had risen an octave.

Just as soon as it had gone, a boyish grin returned to his face. "Sophia?" He knelt to one knee and theatrically clutched my left hand an inch from his nose. "Would you like to see my apartment? Stay awhile?"

"This isn't over," I said. "Let's go. But only because I want to – not because you say." I fought a grin.

Twenty minutes later, we were in Dylan's car on the way to his mysterious apartment. The backseat held my duffle bag and two grocery bags. One was full of my books, and the other was overflowing with Oreos, hot chocolate mix, and all of the perishable food my kitchen had held: bread, bologna, and oranges. I'd considered bringing some Cokes, but I couldn't bring myself to reach into that drawer again.

"How far is the apartment from the store?" I asked, feeling as though a weight had been lifted from my shoulders the moment we had stepped out of the house.

"Not far. Short commute." He winked. His window was cracked, allowing the chill wind to whip his hair. A car commercial played quietly on the radio, muffled by the hum of the wind. A salesman did a poor impression of Abraham Lincoln and swore that his deals were the best around and that he couldn't tell a lie.

I closed my eyes and inhaled deeply. It was as though I could smell the holidays on the horizon. Thanksgiving was coming soon enough. A twinge of guilt settled in my gut when I realized that I hadn't yet made plans with my parents. I briefly imagined them sitting alone at their small, square dining table, Mom waiting with tears in her eyes, arm limp at her side, as Dad cut her food into bite-sized pieces. I had no choice but to push the thought aside. It wasn't healthy to think that way. I willed my thoughts to vanish entirely, to simply melt away, leaving nothing but blissful calm. Despite the cool air swimming through the car, the sun felt warm on my face.

"Shit!" Dylan boomed.

My seatbelt pulled taut across my chest, barely keeping my face from smashing into the dashboard. Dylan was still swearing under his breath as a young motorcyclist came around the front of the car on Dylan's side. He wore reflective sunglasses and no helmet. His blonde hair was buzzed close to his head. He gunned the bike with a tinny whine.

"Did you see that?" Dylan asked. "What a dick."

I rubbed my neck. "Probably just bought that thing," I mumbled. "He's already about to crash it."

There were very few cars on the roads. Even the parking lots were largely empty. I imagined that most families were curled up at home, enjoying blankets and meals cooked in Crock Pots on the first truly chilly day of the season.

We sat in silence until Dylan parked in front of the book store.

"What are we doing?" I asked, merely curious.

He smiled and stood from the car. He opened the back door and reached in for my bags. "You wanted to see where I live, right?"

"You live in the store?" I asked, standing and following him to the door.

He struggled to balance my bags in one arm so that he could slide the key into the lock on the store's front door. "I can do that," I said, swiping the stretchy key ring from his outstretched hand. On the ring were his car key, the front door key, and two others, plus a tiny, leather-bound book.

I slid the right key into the lock, and it clicked several times. When I turned the handle, it wouldn't budge. I withdrew the key, flipped it upside-down, and tried again. Nothing.

The House on Valley Street

"Am I not smart enough to play with this toy?" I asked.

Dylan only chuckled while I focused intensely on jiggling the lock. Maybe it was finicky, and I needed to come at it from just the right angle...

"You just need to read the instructions a little more closely," he said. He nodded toward the battered, maroon door that stood just feet from the entrance to the bookstore.

"There are two doors for the store?" I asked.

"Nope."

With a light scoff, I quickly jabbed the key into the dated bronze handle on the maroon door and pushed it open. "Funny. How long were you going to let me struggle before telling me I had the wrong door?"

"Who says I was going to tell you?" He adjusted my bags under his arm and stood back, letting me walk in first.

I led the way up the steep, gray, carpeted steps. Old cigarette smoke clung to the steps and to the wood paneling on the walls. The stairwell was dimly lit by a single lightbulb dangling some six feet over our heads, well out of reach. I briefly considered how challenging it must be to change the lightbulb, since the process would require that a ladder be placed on the stairs.

At the top of the steps were two doors, one to the left and one to the right. This time, I waited for instruction.

"The one on the left," Dylan said. "And it's the round key."

"What's through that door?" I pointed across the hall.

"Storage space for the store."

I selected the only key on the ring with a round base and opened the door to Dylan's apartment.

I nearly gasped.

The space was absolutely immaculate. A small foyer bathed in natural light invited us in. A mahogany hat tree stood just inside the door. Our steps echoed against some sort of ceramic tile. The amount of whiteness in the space was shocking and beautiful. Everything was spotless.

"Should I take my shoes off?" I asked, suddenly intimidated.

Dylan scoffed and dropped my bags near the hall tree. "No. What's a floor for if you can't walk on it? Go ahead and look around if you want."

Mouth agape, I moved into the galley kitchen and caressed the white marble countertop. It was so smooth that I wasn't convinced I was even touching it.

A deep farmhouse sink overlooked the living space, lit by a full wall of floor-to-ceiling windows that opened to the narrow Reef River that passed behind the store.

A sleek, white couch and matching chair left the room feeling welcoming, open, and airy. It was by no means overcrowded.

A massive canvas coated in sporadic streaks and dabs of black and red paint decorated the wall adjacent to the windows.

I eyed a stack of aged novels sitting on a small glass table beside the couch.

"What do you think?" Dylan asked, tucking the bag of oranges into his stainless, side-by-side refrigerator.

"This is…" At a loss for those writerly adjectives I'd wished I'd mastered, I said, "amazing. How did you afford this?"

"I put a lot of work into it," he said, leaning casually against the pristine, shining countertop. "It was pretty rough when I bought it."

"Bought? I thought you were renting."

"I was, but the old woman who used to own this place gave me an offer I couldn't refuse."

I sat softly on the overstuffed chair in the corner of the room. "You own the whole building?"

"That I do."

"Impressive."

"Like I said, I got a good deal. Finish the tour?" He helped me to my feet and led me down a short hallway lined with black and white photographs of safari animals.

"This is interesting," I said, pausing to admire them.

"My mom took those," he said without stopping. "She was into photography back in the day – before she went rogue."

I found those in a box of her old stuff when I was younger. Bathroom's right here." He waited for me to catch up.

The bathroom was just as immaculate as the rest of the space. Natural stone tiles lined the floor. A masculine, black vanity stood in contrast against a gleaming, white bathtub.

"Wow," I breathed.

"There's a spare bedroom next door, and this," he said, turning around, "is my bedroom." He opened a door across the hall from the bathroom and waited for me to enter first. In the middle of the room was a large, sleek bed topped in fresh, white linens. A single nightstand stood beside the bed. The far wall was lined with bookshelves that reached from one wall to the other. A woodsy smell drifted from the bed, and I felt a brief desire to bury my face into the pillows and inhale his scent.

"Have you even slept here yet? Everything looks so perfect." I padded across the new carpeting, conscious of how dirty my shoes probably were, and I fingered the spines of books that looked like they may have been ancient. There were hundreds of books. Some bore aged, tattered bindings. Others looked like they'd never been touched. There were gray books, black books, lemon-yellow books, and sky-blue books.

"Just a few times," he said. "I call these my inventory overflow." He joined me beside the bookshelves and pulled a contemporary novel down.

"Not enough room in the store?" I felt a rush of intimacy. Being in his bedroom, inhaling his scent, moving into and around his space all struck me and warmed me. I focused closely on his body and the way he moved so gracefully, returning his novel to the shelf and lightly fingering the others nearby. His arms were strong and steady, his movements smooth.

I couldn't help myself.

I reached for his hand.

He turned to me and answered softly, "I'm just not ready to let go – of the books."

Sweet breath brushed against my face as his lips parted and he tilted my chin toward them. His lips were soft and eager but inviting, not aggressive. I took the invitation.

Blood pounded in my ears, and heat flowed from my fingertips to my toes. We kissed slowly at first. My breath wobbled on its way out, and my fingers tangled themselves in his hair.

He broke our kiss and trailed his lips across my cheek and jawline, then down my neck. All at once, we nearly lunged at each other. Hands groped. Breath mingled. He ran his hands down my back and around my behind and lifted me off the ground, pressing my spine against the book shelves. I wrapped my legs around his waist eagerly and pulled him in, holding him tightly.

He broke away again and nodded toward the bed, breathing only slightly harder than normal, waiting for my permission to move.

I said nothing but nodded. In an instant, Dylan had carried me to the bed and placed me down gently before climbing over the top of me. I kicked off my pumps, and he reached up my dress, grabbed hold of the waistband of my tights, and tugged them down my legs. I pulled his henley over his broad shoulders, fingers splayed wide.

We continued this way, undressing each other one garment at a time, until all that separated us was my bra and panties and his blue-and-white checkered boxers.

We switched roles then, turning out attention to our own clothing. I reached behind my back and unclasped my bra, one hook at a time, and when it dangled loose at my back, I held the cups against my breasts, savoring the moment. I particularly admired Dylan's expression while I waited to expose myself to him.

His eyes trailed my trembling body, and he whispered, "You're so beautiful."

Before he could touch me, a panicked knock pounded on the front door.

"What the hell?" he murmured, staring into my eyes for one frozen moment. "I thought I locked the outside door. Don't move, okay?" He pecked me lightly on my forehead and pulled on his jeans before padding barefoot out of the room, leaving me shivering with anticipation.

"What are you doing here?" Dylan demanded.

There was a muffled reply that I couldn't make out. I suddenly felt very uncomfortable and pulled the sheets up to my chin.

"Where is she?"

Another muffled reply.

A moment later, Dylan appeared in the doorway, eyes wide, lips parted.

"We have to go," he said, more breathless than he'd been at the peak of our intimacy.

"Go?" I sat up straight and re-hooked the clasps of my bra. "Who's here? What's going on?"

"My brother's here. It's my grandma, Sophie. Eugene's got her."

CHAPTER 23

I'd never gotten dressed so quickly in my life. And I'd never seen such focus and determination as Dylan showed, racing down the stairs with me and leaping into his car, pausing only a moment when we saw the motorcycle his younger brother, Jack, had parked beside it.

"Where are we going?" I asked, clutching my seatbelt.

"I don't know." He said it with such matter-of-fact finality that I thought he may have transformed into a different person altogether. "But her house is this way."

Jack took a sharp left into a gravel driveway surrounded by tall evergreens when we were several miles out of town. The backend of his motorcycle swung out, and he fishtailed several times. Dylan hit the brakes hard before we turned in. He spoke suddenly. "I knew this would happen," he said, almost more to himself than to me. "I should never have gone into that house." He gripped the steering wheel with both hands.

Despite the narrow driveway, we must have been going 30 miles per hour, which feels entirely different when one isn't on a public road.

The car screeched to a halt at the end of the half-mile driveway. A tiny farmhouse that used to be white before years of the Midwest's scorching summers and blinding blizzards had taken their toll stood in front of us.

Twirling vines climbed up the home's façade. A porch wrapped from one side of the house to the other. No fencing or chicken wire covered the crawlspace below the porch, leaving an open invitation to neighborhood raccoons. The steps leading up the porch slanted heavily to one side.

Beside the steps was a hand-painted sign staked into the dirt. Four wooden panels crossed the spike, each decorated with a scripted name:

The Sloans

Iris

Elliot

Dylan

Jack

The names had been painted in a canary yellow that had faded from what must have been years in the sun and snow. Tiny chips of paint fell away from the letters. Seemingly untouched was a vibrant, deep blue iris, painted beside Grandma Iris's name. The flower was so exquisitely detailed, from the veins in each petal to the stigma, painted in the same canary yellow.

Dylan tore out of the vehicle and around the side of the house. "Stay here," he said before he disappeared.

"Wait!" I called after him. "Don't just run in there! What are you going to do?" I ran after him, past the painted sign, but by the time I rounded the corner, the only clue that he had been there was a swinging side door.

I didn't have time to think.

What's the plan?

Are we just diving into Gene's arms?

We were fish taking the bait, rabbits diving into snares. Danger was on the horizon, and we were heading in.

I waited a split second before tugging the door open. Eyes squeezed shut, I strained and listened, pressing my ear to the door. No sound came from inside the house – not a single note.

Despite the risk, I couldn't stand there knowing that Dylan could be in danger. Moreover, it was late in the afternoon, and the sun was beginning to set, ushering in an icy breeze. I wasn't interested in waiting outside in the dark.

I slowly pulled the side door open, its torn screen flapping, and stepped in.

The smell of apples and cinnamon rushed forward. I tripped over a small rise in the flooring and caught myself on the wall-papered doorway.

To my left was a tiny kitchen, furnished with pea green appliances. A handful of cat figurines lined the windowsill over the sink. One of the cats was a Siamese with a head that bobbed up and down again and again.

A small dining room was on my right. In the middle of the room was a red Formica table, stacked high with ceramic bowls and a mound of long, black feathers and twine and short twigs and autumn leaves and cracked egg shells. Boxes of mason jars, large and small, lined one wall of the room.

A soft hum of voices sounded from down a narrow hall at the far side of the dining area. I tiptoed across the floor and reached for the wall at the other side of the room, as though it were some sort of anchor, a safe zone.

Light poured from an open door that I imagined led to a bedroom. Low voices continued from inside. I rounded the corner inch by inch until I could see inside. A thin, elderly woman stood in the corner, face blank, eyes open wide, entirely frozen in place. Jack stood beside her, one grease-stained hand on her back, stabilizing her in case she swayed. But I doubted that she would. She was like a breathing statue.

The House on Valley Street

Dylan knelt in front of her, clutching her left hand to his cheek.

"He has her soul," Jack said, caressing her back lightly. He rubbed his free hand on his torn jeans. "Her body is here, but her soul is gone."

"How?" The word escaped my lips before I realized how inappropriate my curiosity was in that moment, but neither Jack nor Dylan reacted. I couldn't retract the question.

Jack shook his head. "We don't know. But this kind of magic takes years to master. I've only heard of it being done once before, and that was in an ancient legend of our tribe.

"I need you to stay here with Jack," Dylan said suddenly. He stood and gripped my shoulders with the sort of severity in his expression that I'd seen when we were in Gene's house. "I have to find him."

"Find him?" My voice was weak, infantile compared to Dylan's.

"He has to be close," Jack said. "His magic can't travel very far. Even experienced tribe members need to maintain a certain distance from the victim's body. Sometimes it's a few hundred feet; sometimes it's a mile. It all depends on his power."

"Please. Stay with Jack," Dylan said. He and Jack made eye contact and seemed to share an unspoken word. Then he nodded and left.

I stood there, unsure of my next move. How could I help if I did nothing but wait?

Jack shrugged a thick, leather jacket with built-in shoulder and elbow padding off his shoulders and draped it beside him on the room's twin-size bed. He sat close to the edge, ready to pounce if his grandmother swayed, though the likelihood of her moving at all was slim if not altogether impossible.

Dylan's grandmother remained frozen in her stance, like a sleepwalker. Her arms hung limp at her sides. Her thin, bare legs were slightly bent beneath a knee-length wool dress. Pieces of her graying, stringy hair dangled in front of her unblinking eyes. She breathed heavily between thin, pale lips but did nothing more. She merely stood.

"What's going on?" I asked Jack. "What can I do?"

He waited a moment, seemingly weighing his options, deliberating. Then, he said, "Dylan cares about you. I can tell that he does. He doesn't want you to get hurt."

He paused a moment, and when I said nothing, he asked, "Do you have a lighter?"

"I saw a book of matches in the dining room." I turned to get them without asking what they were for. I pocketed one book and gathered two more for Jack. When I got back, Jack was standing in front of the window. He'd just opened it, and cold air was flooding the room, blowing Grandma Iris's hair into her damp lips, where pieces stuck. Jack was tying a piece of twine into a knot on the windowsill. He left a tail at the end and dangled it outside.

"What are you doing?"

"How much has Dylan told you? About our kind?"

"Your *kind*? You mean your tribe?" I placed the matches into Jack's open palm. "He hasn't said much, but he told me about the history between your ancestors and Gene -- Eugene." I thought it best not to tell him that I knew quite a lot about his family, particularly his own falling out with his brothers.

"I'm a pathfinder. Did he tell you that?" He reached into each pocket of his fitted, black jeans, then began rummaging through old batteries and loose change in a small drawer in the bedside table.

"He hasn't said too much about you." *A pathfinder?*

After finding what he was looking for, Jack placed a single, slender candle in the center of the sill.

"He didn't tell you that I left? He never mentioned me?"

"He may have mentioned you in passing."

Jack gave me a *Yeah, right* kind of look and continued. "I'm sure he told you that I left. And it's true. I did. And I wish I hadn't. I left him in a shitty situation, but while I was gone, I learned some things. I spent time with other members of our tribe." He continued to work as he spoke, tearing matches from the booklet and placing them in a neat row on the sill. "There were things that I always wanted to learn, but our grandmother didn't want to teach me. Too dangerous, she said. But I found someone who would teach me.

"I've become what we call a pathfinder. My soul can leave my body and travel to the spirit world—sort of like another dimension." He ignored my puzzlement and continued. "I originally did this because I wanted to contact our parents. I thought I could get closure – for Dylan, too. But the more I learned, the more I came to understand that this isn't something to take lightly. I can't just suit up and head out on a Sunday afternoon to have a chat with my asshole father. Finding takes a tremendous amount of energy and concentration. And our grandmother was right – it is dangerous."

"How does it work?" I sat carefully on the bed, where I traced the top quilt's oval stitching with the tip of my index finger. There was something inherently intimate about what Jack was doing. I was uncomfortable watching him.

"It's a little like meditation," he said. "With enough focus, I can separate my consciousness and my physical body. My consciousness -- my spirit -- can enter the other world."

"The other world?"

"The spirit world. Like I said, it's essentially a parallel dimension. Everything looks the same; time passes in the same way. I can even see my own body. It's like a one-way mirror. Spirits can see us, but we can't usually see them. There are exceptions, of course. For me, when I'm in the spirit world, I can't communicate with the living."

"How far can you go?"

"I don't know yet." He turned toward me and leaned against the floral-papered wall beside the window. The sun had set, and blackness was swallowing everything outside. He dragged his left hand across his right cheek as though checking for stubble. "I haven't pressed my boundaries. But when I find the end of the line, I'll hit an invisible wall. I won't be able to go any further."

"Is that what makes this dangerous?"

"Not quite. The longer my spirit is away from my body, the harder it is to reunite the two. My spirit could get lost."

"Didn't you say that everything looks the same? Can't you see your body and just go back to it?"

"It does. In the beginning. But as time passes, the spiritual connection to the body – a memory, so to speak – fades. When that link breaks, the spirit is left to wander, separate forever. That's what these things are for. They're like my breadcrumb trail."

In the window sill were a lit candle, two loose, unlit matches, and the knotted twine.

"The candle lights my path in case I can't see. The twine is essentially an extended metaphor – an invitation to enter, not unlike the Rapunzel fairytale. I can use the twine to guide me."

"Don't you need a bigger rope? That must be only two inches long."

"It will grow."

"Grow?"

"This window will act as a portal; it will be affected by my magic. And that'll include everything on the sill. The candle's flame will grow. Its beam will be like a lighthouse beacon. The twine will lengthen into a rope." He tucked his grandmother's hair behind her ear. "I'm sorry that I can't answer more of your questions, but I need to begin now. I'm going to find her spirit. Dylan should not be left to fight this battle alone."

I nodded and stood clumsily. "I- I'll wait in the hall."

"When I'm gone," he added, "I'll need for you to light this." He produced a sprig of lavender from the breast pocket of his leather jacket. "Light it and put it in the window. Its scent will help to guide my spirit – and my grandmother's -- home."

I took the lavender and one of the loose matches and turned to leave. Before I closed the door, I called in, "What's the second match for?"

"Backup," he answered from his seated position on the floor in the middle of the room. He crossed his legs, back to me, and I closed the door.

I was immediately face-to-face with a photograph of Dylan and Jack as children, dressed in matching green button-down shirts and khaki pants. They were standing with their backs touching, their arms crossed, both grinning animatedly.

I leaned against the wall below the picture and slid to the floor.

My mind spun.

How will I know when Jack's gone?

Is Dylan safe?

What is Gene doing to Dylan's grandmother?

A stuttering hum, not unlike a cough, escaped from behind the bedroom's closed door. Jack's voice hitched and cut, then sounded steadily and repeated. It began loudly and gradually grew quieter. His volume grew once more, little by little, as he repeated some sort of incantation in the tribe's language. His voice became so loud that he was booming. But it soon quieted. He continued this way, chanting and moaning in a sort of roller coaster of sound.

How does Dylan think he can help find her soul without entering the spirit world?

Does Dylan even know there is a spirit world?

Does Dylan know his brother is a pathfinder?

After what felt like an hour, Jack's voice did not ascend from one of its many rollercoaster plunges. At that point, I knew he was gone.

When I opened the door, I met Jack's back. His body still sat cross-legged on the floor, eyes closed, stoic. His grandmother remained unmoving.

I couldn't force myself to look at either for more than a moment. Being near them made the hairs on the back of my neck stand up. It was like looking into a casket at a funeral or traipsing through a wax museum after hours. Jack breathed slowly, evenly, and Grandma Iris still huffed in and out. It was as though they were sleeping with their eyes open.

I lit the lavender and placed it on the sill, the lit end dangling just over the edge, and resumed my seated position in the hall.

Then it occurred to me.

If Gene had to maintain a certain distance from Dylan's grandmother's body, then there was no way that he was home. That was too far away.

His house was empty.

My house was empty.

I could find it. I could find whatever belonged to Dylan's ancestors. I could release their spirits. But I needed to hurry.

CHAPTER 24

Before I could convince myself to stay, I was in Dylan's car, turning the key that he'd left in the ignition. I tore out of the driveway and onto the county road, forcing the gas pedal down hard. I had no idea how much time I had left. For all I knew, Jack could have found his grandmother's spirit by now, and he could be reuniting her with her body already.

Minutes passed as I drove in silence. I pulled up to the familiar, gray two-story minutes later, breathing heavily with anticipation and anxiety.

Inside, the house was quiet. Frighteningly so. Something felt wrong. Goose bumps covered my forearms.

A light scratching sound came from the kitchen, as though someone were tapping her fingernails against a tabletop impatiently.

I don't know why I did it, but I rushed into the kitchen. Any other day, I would have run from the sound, but this day, I nearly lunged for it.

Just before I crossed the threshold into the kitchen, a long stick of the white chalk Lucee had left hit the floor and shattered. Pieces were still spinning, and dust was still rolling upward from them when I read the message on the chalkboard.

In small, jagged, capital letters was a single word:

BRICKS.

Bricks?

There were no bricks in the house. I hadn't seen any in Gene's house, either.

I vaguely remembered seeing white, painted bricks when I first moved in, but I couldn't recall where.

Was it in the basement?

The garage?

And in that moment, I was struck by the sudden realization that the bricks were in the one place I never went, the one place that Gene monopolized: the backyard. They were in the shed, piled along one wall. I'd only caught a glimpse of them as Gene stored his lawn mower.

I tore through the screen door and ran to the shed. A padlock still held the door closed. Beside the shed was a pile of unused landscaping rocks. Already shivering, partly from anxiety and partly from the cold night air, I lifted one of the rocks and bashed it into the lock, but nothing happened apart from a small spark. I tried again. The force sent a shock up my arm and through my shoulder. It seemed to reverberate in my skull.

A large branch lay at the base of the Chinese elm in the corner of the lot. I drug it frantically, grunting, panting, and heaving, to the front of the shed. I needed to hurry. Every crackling leaf sent adrenaline coursing through my veins. Gene could return at any moment.

With all the power I had, I lifted the limb to my hip and ran toward the shed. With a crash, the limb barreled through the aged wall and tore a hole large enough for my arm to reach through. I dropped the limb with another grunt and began tearing away at the shed's splintered wall with my hands, piece by piece. Despite the cold, a layer of sweat was forming on my forehead. Pieces of my hair were sticking to my face. My breath came in white puffs of steam.

As the hole grew, a patch in the floor of the far corner came into focus. White bricks lay on the dirt, partially covered by pea gravel and weeds.

When the hole was big enough, I dove through and began clawing at the bricks.

Faster.

Faster.

Faster.

At first, I ignored the clanking sound coming from outside the door, partially masked by my heavy breathing.

But it gradually became too loud to ignore.

I froze, heart thudding in my chest and my ears.

The streetlamp in front of the house cast just enough light to touch the interior of the shed. In that moment, something moved across the door behind me, breaking the light and casting a long shadow on the far wall.

I turned from my knelt position to find Estelle standing behind me.

Gene's wife stood in the grass, head tilted to one side, mouth hanging unhinged. Her wrinkled, paper-thin skin was the same sallow, gray, rotten tone it had been when I'd seen her on the bed. Maggots crawled through her forearms. Her knees were bulbous knots on broomstick, sickly legs. Her eyelids had begun to decompose, revealing black cavities in her skull.

With no words, she lunged.

I fumbled for the bricks as the decaying woman groped about my feet and ankles. I swung my arms wildly, catching a brick with my left hand. The fingernail on my small finger tore away from the skin. It throbbed angrily, and blood trickled down my finger.

Still kicking wildly at the woman, I gripped one brick, and with a breathy grunt, I tore it from the dirt and hurled it at the woman's skull. It connected, and she let out a shrill, spotty cry with lungs that hadn't breathed for centuries.

I sunk my fingers into the divot the brick had lain in and thrust about, searching for anything that may have been buried.

There was nothing. Nothing but dirt.

The woman was now on her knees, crawling up my legs, the skin above her brow dangling over her eye socket. Even through my tights, her skin was too soft, too loose. Bits of her skin peeled away from her knees as she crawled. The scent radiating off her putrid body was overpowering. I choked back bile.

I clawed frantically at the pile of bricks now, ignoring the ache in my finger. Bricks tumbled while the woman's bony knuckles brushed the hem of my dress. I drew back a heel and sent my stiletto into her skull. It punctured the fragile bone like a toothpick in a boiled egg. She grunted and lunged for me, seemingly unaffected. Olive green mucus coated my heel.

I lost control and heaved, vomiting bile into a heap inches from my face. My vision was blurred by my tears. That moment of vulnerability was all the woman needed. She gripped my hair and pulled, thrusting her other hand into my face, gouging at my eyes. Her thumb shot into my mouth, where the nail caught against my front teeth. It separated from the skin and tumbled to the back of my throat, sending me into a fit of coughing and vomiting once more.

Suddenly, the woman was drug from me, groaning as more of her skin tore away against the rough dirt.

I wiped my mouth with both hands, tears streaming down my cheeks. I pressed my palms into my eyes, and for only a moment, I could make out Gaho, Dylan's ancestor, standing beside Estelle. Nearly glowing in the light, Gaho raised one delicate palm toward the elm beside the shed. A branch trailed down from the top of the tree, answering Gaho's call. It wove gracefully around Estelle's fragile midsection, pinning her rail-thin arms to her sides.

Another thin branch swooped down below Estelle's feet, pushing them out from under her with such force that one of her ankles snapped. She tumbled backward to the grass, her thin foot swinging.

Gaho lowered her hand and smiled gratefully toward me. In awe, I watched as she turned her back to me and knelt, arms open wide. Lomasi, her daughter, peered cautiously around the corner of the house, her face barely lit by the streetlight. When she saw her mother, Lomasi came bounding forward. Achak, the girl's father, was not with her. I imagined him wrestling with Eugene's magic somewhere in the spirit world.

While Estelle was restrained, I had no way of knowing how far Gene was and when he would return. Though I felt the need to process what I'd just witnessed, there was no time.

I thrust my hands into the dirt where the bricks had stood and dug.

Dirt packed in below my fingernails, and bits of gravel tore at my knuckles. Something smooth suddenly grazed the back of one hand, and I gasped slightly, still breathing heavily. My fingers fumbled over the silky stones, seemingly of their own accord, and pulled.

In my hands was a centuries-old necklace made of river rocks and bound together with brittle twine. Centered on the necklace among the tiny rocks were three large stones, each slightly larger than the one that came before it.

I was rubbing the dirt from the largest stone when my hair began to whip back and forth against my shoulder blades, sending a shiver careening down my spine. I turned slowly, clutching the necklace in my lap.

Lomasi stood frozen, her delicate fingers still laced in my hair.

I leapt to my feet and backed away. My heel sunk in the mud, moistened by my vomit, and I twisted my ankle and fell backward, thudding against the shed's back wall.

When Lomasi caught sight of the necklace, she immediately snatched it from my grip. The young girl, wearing a dress made of brown fur, sat cross-legged in the middle of the shed and lightly fingered each of the stones. She moved so slowly, deliberately, as she studied each piece.

"Was that yours?" I asked, my throat still burning with stomach acid.

Lomasi stood abruptly and ran from the shed, necklace in hand.

"Wait!" I called. I kicked my shoes off and limped into the yard, where Lomasi stood beside her kneeling mother, who was still standing guard over Estelle's body. Lomasi lifted the necklace to Gaho's face. The mother and daughter embraced tightly, and tiny tears trickled down the young girl's cheeks. Gaho smiled with wisdom and stood. Her matching fur dress hung stiffly at her knees while she padded gracefully toward me, barefooted. She took my hand gently, sending a burst of ice shooting up my arm, and placed the necklace on my palm with a nod.

"I don't understand," I mustered. "Isn't this what you need? I thought this would fix everything."

Gaho stood silent, stoic. Her eyes were wide and friendly. She nodded again.

I suddenly remembered Professor Tochek's instructions. In order for the spirits to be lain to rest, I needed to burn the necklace and …

My heart sunk.

…and bury a bit of the ashes with each family member's body. But I didn't have the bodies.

"Can you tell me…" I hesitated. I wasn't sure how Gaho would react. I wasn't sure how to ask the question. "Can you tell me where your body is?" I shivered at my own question. For a moment, anguish rose from my gut for the sake of this family. The poor child.

Gaho only smiled and gave a single nod. She padded lightly past me and into the shed once more, her black hair hanging like silk, cascading down her back. She pointed a delicate finger toward the hole in the ground where her family's necklace had been buried.

"Here?" I asked.

She nodded again.

I fell to my knees and resumed digging by hand. The dirt was light and sandy, and it gave way easily.

Suddenly, I couldn't believe my stupidity. How would I exhume three bodies by hand? I needed a tool, something to help me dig. Centuries' worth of dirt presumably covered them, far too deep to reach without a shovel or a hoe or something.

Above us, in the shed's loft, was a pile of garden tools. I stood on my tiptoes, grabbed hold of a wooden handle, and pulled.

A plastic rake came tumbling toward my head. It thudded to the ground.

I gripped another handle and tugged with a grunt.

A pitch fork plummeted downward.

I tried once more, stretching on my tiptoes, reaching for another tool. I pulled, and a small shovel fell to the dirt.

Gaho and Lomasi stood in the shed's doorway and watched calmly as I propelled the shovel's blade into the ground.

I tore into the earth like a maniac, gouging it and tossing the piles aside. Despite the cold, sweat trickled down my spine, and my hair stuck to the back of my neck. A plume of white mist billowed from my mouth with each heavy exhale.

When the pile of excavated dirt had grown substantially, Gaho lightly touched my arm, leaving an icy sensation again. With a sad smile, she nodded toward the hole, as if to tell me that I'd dug far enough.

Dropping the shovel, I fell to my knees again and reached gingerly into the hole, afraid of what I might touch. I moved slowly, touching the dirt cautiously like a toddler playing in a sandbox for the first time.

I pressed deeper into the soil, and my fingers caught, entwined in stringy hair. With a gasp, I immediately withdrew my hand and looked to Gaho. For what, I'm not sure. Perhaps approval. Or maybe confirmation.

Lomasi knelt beside me and peered into the black hole. When she stood again, she was running her fingers through her own hair.

"I'm so sorry," I said to her, unsure of what else to say. At the street, an obnoxiously loud engine sputtered.

Gaho stepped forward and took Lomasi's hand, pulling her gently from the hole.

The House on Valley Street

I withdrew the pack of matches from my dress and stumbled out of the shed and into the moonlight. I tore the grass away from the earth to clear a space for the fire and limped to the base of the elm. Matches held between my teeth, I hastily gathered dead twigs. I reached for leaves, too, but they were too small and wouldn't provide enough kindling for a fire.

In Gene's yard was a tall maple tree whose leaves had fallen in a sea of red and gold at its base. Heart thudding, I trotted to the tree and stooped, scooping leaves into my arms, one eye on the house.

The house was quiet, lifeless, and still. I'd just turned to add the leaves to the kindling when I realized that my body was casting a long shadow in front of me. A light was coming from Gene's house.

Without turning back, I ran as quickly as I could and dropped the leaves into the pile. I knelt and with trembling fingers, built a conical structure out of the twigs and stuffed it with the dead leaves. I spat the matches to the ground and tore one free, dragging it forcefully against the back of the book. When the flame glowed orange, I held it shakily at the base of the cone.

Just as Gene's back door tore open, the fire caught, igniting the leaves.

I'm not going to make it.

Footsteps bounded through the dead leaves.

I have to finish!

I was digging again, praying that Achak's and Gaho's bodies were buried beside their daughter's.

Please!

Gene slammed into the side of the shed.

"Sophia!"

But that wasn't Gene's voice.

"Dylan?" I called, breathless.

"Sophia! What are you doing here? Are you okay? I thought you were going to stay with Jack." He stepped over Estelle's body as though it were nothing but a heap of clothing and threw himself at me, holding me tightly, like he thought he'd never see me again. "What happened? Are you okay?" he repeated.

"Please, Dylan. I'll explain later. You have to help me before Gene comes back. We have to uncover Achak and Gaho. I already found Lomasi."

"What? Why?"

"I found it, Dylan. It's a necklace."

Eyes wide, he immediately fell to his knees and began scooping soil from the hole without another word.

Outside, I adjusted the twigs, encouraging the slow-growing flames. I pulled the necklace over my head and placed it gently in a spiral in the center of the fire. I spun, searching for Lomasi and Gaho, but they had disappeared when I'd entered Gene's yard.

"They're here!" Dylan called. "All three of them are here."

"I need their mouths open," I shouted. "Can you do that?"

Dylan shuffled and grunted lowly before replying, "Done."

I lowered my head to the ground beside the fire and blew lightly, stoking the flames. "Come on," I whispered. "Burn faster."

The heat had broken the twine in several places, leaving tails that curled upward and glowed orange at the tips.

"Sophie, we can't wait much longer," Dylan called from inside the shed.

He was right. I stood and pulled my scarf from around my neck, tossing it on the fire. Still barefoot, I stomped on it, stepping quickly, slapping my foot like a rabbit.

A light switched on in Gene's house.

"Are you ready?" I asked.

The screen door tore open, and he threw himself through it. "Get away from there!" Gene shouted, hobbling across the lawn.

"Ready," Dylan said. "Hurry, Sophia!"

"I'll kill you!" Gene bellowed, running as quickly as his centuries-old body would take him.

I dug into the ashes, still glowing, and scooped as many of the stones as I could, ignoring the searing pain. I blew on my hands as I limped into the shed. Dylan had lit a flashlight and was aiming it into the hole.

"Estelle! My Estelle!" Gene was still screaming, just steps from the shed.

For the first time, I was staring at the bodies of Achak, Lomasi, and Gaho – the skulls, specifically. All that Dylan had uncovered were the skulls; the rest of their corpses lay beneath the shed's wall, their feet below the elm tree.

"Sophia! Do it!" Dylan stood in the doorway, guarding me from Gene, who regarded Dylan with a ferocity, an evil I'd never seen before. His tired, old eyes seared through him and to me. He lurched forward.

With a pang of sadness, I dropped a handful of ashes and stones into the gaping mouths of each skull as evenly and as quickly as possible.

Despite his age, Gene wrestled with Dylan. Dylan jabbed Gene in the throat, and when he recovered, he threw an uppercut at his jaw.

Estelle groaned in the grass. Her voice revitalized Gene, who took two giant steps backward, steadied himself, and lurched forward once more.

"It's done!" I shouted. "I don't understand!"

"You have to –

Gene caught him off balance and knocked him to the ground.

"—bury them again! Throw the dirt back in!"

The House on Valley Street

I sunk my hands into the dirt and thrust it into the holes, covering the corpses as best I could. My knees burned through my torn tights. Bits of gravel had dug into my kneecaps. My ankle ached.

In a moment, in a flicker of light, it was done.

Gene was gone. Dylan was still lying on his back, hands shielding his face. He rolled onto his stomach and onto his knees. "Sophia? Are you alright?"

"I'm fine," I said, working to steady my breathing. "Where did he go?"

Dylan stood and edged his way to the doorway, peering outside like a police officer surveying a scene. "Estelle's gone, too," he said.

He took my hand and guided me into the moonlight. "Can you walk?" he asked, studying my gait.

"I'll be fine."

"How did you do that? How did you know where to look?"

"I got a clue," I said. "I think it was Jack."

"What?"

I brushed the excess ashes from my hands and pressed my palms together, still feeling the pain from the embers.

"Let's go. I'll explain on the way to –

The ancestors caught me off guard. The three of them stood hand-in-hand, just outside of the shed. All three smiled.

"Thank you," Achak spoke, his voice low. Long black hair fell over his shoulders. "You've relit our paths. You've shown us the way back."

"Thank you," Gaho spoke softly.

Lomasi smiled wide. Her front tooth was missing.

After a moment of comforting silence, Molly Danielson, a bright-eyed, blond-haired, eleven-year-old, emerged from behind the shed. Her gait was smooth, her smile broad. She didn't speak, but her grin communicated what she couldn't.

It was like being shrouded in light, in warmth, in life. One by one, the ancestors and Molly passed by us and into the shed. First Lomasi, then Gaho and Achak, smiled once more and lowered themselves to a seated position over their graves. Like an ice cube in a pot of boiling water, they sank into the earth and rejoined their bodies. Molly followed suit and lay beside the family's graves. While I hadn't found her body, I knew it lay there, and she knew, too. She melted into the earth and disappeared, leaving the two of us huddled in the dark.

"What just happened?" I whispered.

"They rejoined their bodies," Dylan said, "in death."

"Where are Eugene and Estelle?" I asked, suddenly spinning, frantically searching for her.

"They're gone, Sophie." Dylan smiled. "That means my grandmother released them. The curse is over."

CHAPTER 25

Dylan draped one arm over my shoulder where we stood in the driveway. "Thank you," he said. "I wish I could be angry that you didn't stay with Jack, but I can't."

I smiled. "I didn't know you were a motorcycle man," I said, eyeing the bike he'd arrived on.

"I had to take Jake's bike since you took my car. Remember that guy we almost hit on the way to my apartment earlier? That was my brother."

I laughed lightly. "I know that. About Jack," I started, "how do you know he's okay?"

"I just know."

"What's going to happen to Gene?"

"Nothing. He's gone."

"What about your grandmother?"

"She's the only person who could have released Estelle. If Estelle is gone, then she must be okay."

"I'd really feel better if we went over there to talk things through," I said.

"Absolutely," Dylan agreed. "We need to go. I need to check on her. I know she's alive, but she could be hurting."

I pulled away to get into the passenger side of the car, but Dylan tugged at my wrist. "There's just one more thing," he said. He kissed my forehead. "I love you, Sophia."

A grin spread wide across my face, and a warmth rose from my belly up through my chest. I hugged him tightly, nuzzling him.

We stood that way, holding each other in the driveway, melting into each other as the day's events sunk in.

When he released me, he said, "I mean it, Sophia. Thank you."

"We should go," I said softly. I looked down at my clothing. My dress was stained with mud and vomit. My shoes were still somewhere in the backyard, and my tights were torn, exposing several of my toes. "I should probably shower," I said.

"Can you wait until we get back to my place?"

For the sake of Dylan's grandmother's wellbeing, I agreed. "All of my clothes are at your house anyway, aren't they?"

He only smiled and got behind the wheel.

"What about the motorcycle?" I asked.

"We'll take care of it later."

The ride out of town was silent, a blissful sort of silence. Dylan reached across the center console, offering his hand. We laced our fingers together and sat in peace, the radio off, the windows rolled all the way up.

When we reached Grandma Iris's house, he put the car in park, turned the key to OFF, and turned toward me. "I can't thank you enough, Sophia."

I smiled tiredly. "I didn't do it by myself, you know."

He nodded, and after a moment, asked, "Are you ready?"

"Ready?"

"This is sort of a big step." He tried to wink, but his eye was beginning to swell closed from one of Gene's blows.

I raised an eyebrow.

"You're meeting my family."

"Your sense of humor never ceases to amaze me," I said, standing from the car with a grunt.

Just before we walked in, I grabbed hold of Dylan's wrist and said, "Just one more thing before we go in."

He waited.

"I love you, too," I whispered.

He beamed brightly and led me into the house.

In the bedroom, Grandma Iris was resting on the bed, her chest rising and falling comfortably beneath the comforter. Jack sat at her side.

The House on Valley Street

"You got my message, then?" Jack asked.

"I did," I said, recalling the piece of rolling chalk. "I didn't know you could travel that far."

"Neither did I. You look like hell, by the way," he said with a weak smile. "We have a shower here, you know."

"I imagine you'd look about the same if you swallowed a dead lady's fingernail."

He grimaced.

"How's she doing?" I nodded toward the bed.

"Recovering well. She's just tired."

Dylan gently brushed the hair away from his grandmother's face.

"There's just one thing we need to do still," Jack said. "We need to sweep the houses – both yours and Eugene's. We have to clear the air. Normally, I would need help from Grandma Iris."

"She won't be able to perform that kind of magic for weeks after what she's been through," Dylan said.

"But I can do it," Jack said. "I can do it tonight. I just need a little help."

"You can do that now?" Dylan asked, baffled. "But I thought—"

"I learned while I was gone," Jack explained. He pushed up his sleeves and clapped his hands together. "Are you ready for this?"

"What do you need?" I asked.

"Do you still have those matches?"

I nodded.

"Light 'em."

The House on Valley Street

CHAPTER 26

It took a while. It took writing, rewriting, and editing – a lot of editing -- but it was finished. My 300-plus page novel was complete. It was finally ready for its readers. It was finally ready to be shared.

Dylan and I sat in unashamed, beautiful silence for the entire drive from the house on Valley Street to home, my parents' home. We'd spent the past several weeks together in his apartment. I hadn't been in the Valley Street house except to gather the rest of my things that morning. When I'd done so, the home was finally nothing but a home, a lockbox of childhood memories, a construction project.

I finally spoke as we pulled into the winding, gravel driveway.

"Thank you," I said, lightly squeezing his hand. His skin felt smooth and warm beneath mine. He was so strong, so powerful, and all mine.

"For what?" He glanced at me as he cranked the wheel and navigated the curves.

"For helping me with all of this. And for coming with."

"For helping *you*?"

"You have no idea."

"I think *you* have no idea, Sophie. You have no idea what you've done for me and my family. My brother and I talk again. I'm not worrying about my grandmother anymore. I can focus on the store. And I have you by my side all the way." He kissed my hand lightly. "But since you insist, you're welcome." He squeezed my knee affectionately before putting the car in park and pulling the key from the ignition. "Ready?"

"I think so. It's been awhile since I've seen Mom, though." I absentmindedly wrung my hands in my lap. "I hope she looks better than the last time I saw her. I mean, healthier. I hope she's made progress."

"It's going to take a lot of work, and it's going to be a long recovery. You know that."

"I know. But it still hurts to see her that way."

"I know it does," he said, leaning back in his seat. "You just have to have confidence. Don't look so much at the downside. At least she's alive."

I nodded, unbuckled my seatbelt, and gathered my tightly bound manila envelope, holding it close to my chest as I stood from the car and walked around it toward the driver's side where Dylan stood. The snow crunched beneath my boots, and my breath gathered in a fog in front of my face. I could smell the gray smoke rising from the home's fireplace and swirling above its roof.

As we entered the garage, Dylan slipped his hand into mine. The excited barks and whines of my parents' Labradors echoed through the space.

Just outside the door, I squeezed Dylan's hand tightly and grinned. "I hope she likes it," I said.

"I hope she likes *me*," he answered.

And I opened the door.

ABOUT THE AUTHOR

Siara Schwartzlow has always had a love for scary stories that make her peek over her shoulder at night. An English teacher in Wisconsin, she enjoys reading, painting, sewing, and spending time with her family and friends.

The House on Valley Street

Made in the USA
Columbia, SC
10 April 2018